This literary novel is a
philosophical and metaphysical
novel written in the
Visionary Fiction genre...
...in case you were wondering.

"Linn offers wise nuggets of truth that are easily digested and assimilated without one even realizing it. I am amazed at the way she has crafted a delightful novel that offers such profound message of truth and hope, while still being a light-hearted and fun story. It reads like a summer novel but unlike those quick, throw-away stories, the wisdom she offers stay long after I finished the novel. I believe the insights she offers are the truths that were within me all along but that I had forgotten."

—Kimberly G. - CT

"I loved reading Linn's novel. It was imaginative and unusual. Linn has a great sense of humor and 'observation' of the world."

—Ingrid S. - Guilford, CT

"<u>Dreamtidings of a disgruntled starbeing</u> by Linn Aspen is a beautiful and spiritual story that spans the Universe. It incorporates the basic truths of love and forgiveness into the adventures of a young girl who unknowingly is a spirit from another world. How she reacts to adversity within her earth family and learns to forgive makes an inspiring story for young and old alike."

—Judy K. - Middlefield, CT

the DREAMTIDINGS of a disgruntled starbeing

Life with a psychopathic brother

LINN ASPEN

CHICKADEE VISION
PUBLISHING

St. Johnsbury, Vermont

Chickadee Vision Publishing
P.O. Box 4
East St. Johnsbury, Vermont 05838
www.chickadeevision.com

Photo credits:
cover photo 'baby' courtesy of Picsea on Unsplash
cover photo 'Earth' courtesy of Vimal S on Unsplash
Tidings photo courtesy of Jeremy Morris on Unsplash

First published by Chickadee Vision Publishing in 2023.

ISBN 979-8-9874107-0-7 (pbk.) — ISBN 979-8-9874107-1-4 (ebook)
ISBN 979-8-9874107-2-1 (hdbk.)

For anyone who wishes to be informed of Trigger Warnings, please visit:
https://booktriggerwarnings.com

OUT BEYOND IDEAS

Out beyond ideas of wrongdoing and
rightdoing, there is a field.
I'll meet you there.

When the soul lies down in that grass,
the world is too full to talk about.
Ideas, language, even the phrase
each other
doesn't make any sense.

—RUMI

PROLOGUE

22,236 MILES FROM EARTH
— In a Geosynchronous Orbit —
As Per: Kalanna Boon

«Kalanna, dear.» Gompsie, in his scaled down, travel-easy, dragonesk form, looks frail and jagged; his poofy hair tousled, his plumed tail-feathers twitching. He takes his glasses off and taps them against the leathery surface of his desk. «My dear child, it is as we feared. The Thubans have influenced Dwinn.»

«No!» Kalanna feels her legs give way. «This is all my fault!» Buxtin, their devoted bioship, quickly produces a hover chair to catch her.

«Surely not.»

«But it is! If his father hadn't been a Thuban, he never would have trusted them.»

«There, there.» Narrowing his prominent brows, her grandfather looks at his glasses and stops tapping them, the silence just as unnerving as the thumps. «Rativett and Ortet are down there. They're middle-lived and should be able to help.»

«They're middle-aged and for all that time they've never visited us in their dreamstate. Probably they have no idea who they are, so how could they be of any help?» Kalanna straightens, taking the hover chair by surprise. «I will incarnate. I'll go through the

Arcturian Gate and won't forget who I am and then, in my dream-state, I will come here and visit you and together we'll change the outcome. That can't be too hard.»

«Not hard?» A tiny breath of fire escapes her grandfather's lips. «It would be quite hard, my dear. Most notably, and despite going through the Arcturian Gate, you won't know that he is your son, nor that you came to save him. Furthermore, should you, against all odds, succeed, you can't just swish back here. You have to live out your Earthly life, staying down there for what might be a hundred years!» He puts his spectacles on, then takes them off and begins to bend them straight. With a longing look, he places them to the side. «Besides, you'll need at least thirty of those Earth-years to prepare. By then he'll be too old for you to influence.»

«Three. I'll prep for three years and incarnate as his sister.»

«His sister! And end up with the same mother as him; a coldhearted one who's the reason the Thubans were so interested in his incarnation to begin with? The kind who's perfect for spawning psychopaths.» Gompsie picks up his glasses. «Besides, Naarlet would never agree.»

«Who says I'm asking Naarlet?»

1

PLANET EARTH
— Terra Firma —
44.5956° N, 75.1691° W
Friday, February 12, 7:48 p.m. EST
As Per: Klara Tippins

Klara hummed as she gazed up at the darkened sky while snowflakes—large as fairy slippers—landed on her forehead, her nose, her cheeks. The flakes melted, as flakes do, and icy water ran from her cheeks down her neck and she stopped humming.

"Fi-ickle snots," she shuddered, glaring at the sky. "Why today of all days? It's my birthday and your clouds are hiding my stars—my home!"

From over in the big oak, she felt the barred owl stare at her with his black penetrating eyes, twisting his head this way and that, snorting and sighing at her unseemly brashness towards his sky. Though it was too dark in the nun's old garden for her to see him properly, she knew he was there— glaring.

"Love you too, Owl!" Her breath floated up in a cloud of

mist. It'd gotten cold. And late. Why hadn't her dad, Mr. Tippins, brought down her telescope already? Sure, now with the snow falling, it could be argued a telescope was of little use. Still, weren't they wondering where she was, Klara being the birthday girl and all? If she had a cellphone she'd call them, but Mother wouldn't let her. Imagine, thirteen years on this planet and still no phone!

Peering up at her family's apartment, Klara double-wrapped her scarf to keep melted snow from dripping down her neck. Being an old, refurbished convent, the windows were tall and narrow with wrought-iron framing. Pointlessly, she waved with her mitted hand, hoping against hope, that someone might wave back. But nothing. Of course. Just brightly lit, creepy windows.

Of the three buildings surrounding the courtyard, theirs was the middle one, giving them a superior view of the valley of Pennington. In Pennington people shopped in boutiques and sat with friends at cafes drinking coffee and never once considered living high on a hill in some old nunnery. Mother, of course, didn't mind living far away from everyone and everything because, 'gee whiz, Klara, we don't have to look up at anybody!'

The hat on her head began to slide. Reflexively, she grabbed hold and balanced it to its sweet spot. Stretched and wonky, this required both skill and patience, though Klara had had plenty of practice. It was the only hat she had and the source of much ridicule at school. Having once been

Mother's hat, not only was it large, it also reeked of hairspray and was frighteningly beige.

As it slid once more, she let it go. It landed in the snow with a silent *poof* and Klara stared at if for a moment, then she bent down and, humming sweetly, smoothed it over with her mitten, covering it completely.

Loud thumps from the main door interrupted her artistry.

Mr. Tippins?

Probably. Probably it was Mr. Tippins trying to open the massive church door to finally come see her.

2

Arched and made of solid oak, the massive door was a beast to open. Particularly if you didn't know the precise angle to use on the pull rings and where to pound the door. Even then it was a chore, especially in cold weather, which, this close to Canada, was pretty much always.

Loud grunts began to accompany the thuds; loud enough to reverberate through the door. Klara glanced at the buried hat. Would Mr. Tippins notice it missing? Would he mind? Things were always up in space with him, his mind ambling when, all of a sudden, his ship would land and he'd baffle everyone with his presence.

Picking it up, the hat was so well coated with snow it was no longer beige. Muttering, she whacked it against her legs, blew on it, brushed it, whacked it again—still the snow clung. Resigned, she pulled it over her head, feeling her brain go numb with cold. Why? Why, oh why, of all the planets in the universe did she have to find herself on the most obnoxious one?

Over at the door Mr. Tippins labored a crack open—no more. Klara was on her way to help him when an assertive "Jesus Christ!" came from the other side—clearly *not* from Mr. Tippins.

"He'd be the man to call on," Klara called back. "I do believe it's his door."

"My dear goodness!" a distinctly female voice exclaimed. "I was unaware of somebody being there. I very much apologize." There was a roundness and a bounce to the woman's speech, making it sound kind and welcoming. "How do I—"

With a sudden generosity, the door released and the woman stumbled out, almost knocking Klara over. As she grabbed Klara's shoulder a pleasant warmth radiated from the woman's hand, and she was tall. Not only tall, but beautiful in a way that transformed everything around her.

"Dear child, what must you think? Using his name in… what is it you say… unnecessarily, and then running you over like… like one of those things that runs things over… a…"

"… a car?" Klara ventured.

"No, not a car… a steamroller." The woman removed her hand. "They say a lot of first impressions. All I can hope is that none of it is true."

"It's fine," Klara managed. She wanted to say more, but hearing an adult apologize was disorienting.

"My name is Rani Ghaiwal." The woman held out an ungloved hand and Klara quickly took it.

"Klara Tippins."

"It is a pleasure running into you, Klara Tippins," she smiled. "I am a brand-new resident and only earlier today moved into my apartment. Up there." She pointed to the windows of Klara's apartment.

Klara was astounded. "That's where I live!"

"You are pulling my leg! I am on the second floor."

"Then we live right above you!" Klara drew in a sharp breath. "Just so you know, I'm the quiet one. Any loud music is my brother's doing."

"You have a brother? How very special. Is he older or younger?"

"Both."

"Both?"

"He was born three years before me so he should be older, but I don't think he is."

"All the same he looks out for you?"

"Not exactly. Though, in his defense, it can't be easy having a sibling like me."

"And what kind of sibling are you?"

"The better one."

Owl whistled sharply and Rani spun around. "There is an owl here?"

"Uh-huh. One that's quite annoyed with me." Repositioning Mother's hat, snow predictably dribbled under her collar. "Showed up last week and hasn't let me out of its sight, even follows me to school. The big white tufts over its eyes making it easy to recognize."

"I must meet this owl." Cautiously, Rani walked towards the tree. "Though I seem to remember a drop-off…?"

"There is one up ahead, but the property is fenced in, so no worries."

"And one gate?"

"Two gates: one to the west and one to the east. The western gate you've probably met. It opens to the parking lot, is well-shoveled and tells you good morning when you go by—even when it's not morning."

Rani smiled. "And what of the other gate, is it also polite?"

"Hardly. The eastern gate leads to the woods: to goblins and trolls. It's rather maladjusted from what I gather, though I've never walked through it. That's strictly forbidden."

"Do you like living here?" Rani reached out and righted the hat on Klara's head.

"I…" Klara faltered. "I'm sure the nuns liked it. Most of them. Most were content."

"You knew them?"

"No, but the walls hold their thoughts—especially the stone walls. Some of the woodwork too, in particular the benches, the ones that used to be in the chapel." Klara bit her lip. She had surely said too much. She glanced at Rani, but Rani looked no more perturbed than if Klara had commented on the weather. "So, Rani," she quickly moved on, "why did *you* move here?"

"The Big Apple became exhausting after a while, at least

for me. I need solitude and when I don't have it, it becomes like a thirst. A few long years back, I bought a cottage in Pinebrook, made plans to live there in my retirement with nothing but birds and the occasional wind for company. Then, when I was indeed retired, I realized the cottage would not hold all my books—"

"You have a lot of books?" Klara interrupted.

"I do. I love books."

Klara nodded enthusiastically. "Me too."

"So I decided to keep the cottage but look for an apartment also. Imagine my joy when I found Mountain Manor with ceilings tall enough for nine-foot bookcases! To live in an old, refurbished abbey is to me like living in a novel; dark mahogany millwork, old Victorian fireplaces... my goodness. I have stayed in many old apartments, both in Mumbai and then in Brooklyn, but nothing like this."

Wanting to contribute, Klara searched her mind. "I like the chimney pipes," she decided.

"Chimney pipes?"

"The tubes that stick up from the roof. Have you seen them?"

"I'm afraid I was so adrenalized by everything inside this chateau, that when the realtor took me outside, it was all a blur." Rani looked up at the roof. Though there was nothing to see but night, she kept looking.

Pressing one hand to the top of her head, Klara peered up and pointed. "I think the lacy edges make the pipes look like

Victorian bloomers; as if some ungodly women came to snoop on the nuns and got stuck with their unmentionables sticking up."

"Unmentionables?"

"Sure. Probably they'd hoped for a scandal only to find the nuns just sitting there, day after day, staring at nothing. After a while, the women got bored stiff and passed out."

"The garden is *that* stodgy?"

"Rigid benches, prissy roses, sullen statues—nothing's more stodgy than that. Sit in this garden too long and you'll turn to stone."

"Turn to stone…?" Rani wasn't gazing at the roof anymore; she was staring at Klara, a concerned look on her face. Sneepers, now she'd worried the woman.

Klara pivoted on her heals, slamming her toes together to warm her feet. Think happy. Happy, happy, happy… "I like how snow brings everything together; the way mansions and junk yards look equally pretty and how it removes hedges so everything belongs. Also, the light… winter lights don't scream at you the way summer lights do; they hold you. I like that too."

"You have a most unusual mind, Klara Tippins. May I ask how old you are?"

"Thirteen. My birthday is today."

Rani slapped her thigh. "My star, now I get it! This morning a book kept jumping out of my bookcase driving me nutty. Now I see that it does not want to be with me—it wants to be yours! Wait here and I will fetch it for you."

With joint effort they managed the door open, then Rani ran up to her apartment while Klara sat down on the stairs to wait, her mind running loops inside her heart. Could a grownup be a friend? Surely Rani must think her silly. And why would she give Klara a book? Would it be ill-mannered to accept it? To not accept it?

Not a moment too soon, Rani returned. Brimming with excitement and slightly out of breath, she held the book out to Klara. "It is part of Vedas called Upanishads. Old Hindu philosophy. Very wise. Happy Birthday, Klara."

On the cover was a painting of a large tree with people sitting underneath. They all sat on mats, except for an old man who sat on a pillow. The book was not heavy. It was not large. But holding it… "This book is enormous!" Klara clutched it to her chest. "It fills my bones!"

"The word 'Upanishad' is Sanskrit and means 'come close and I will tell you something,' which is to say the wisdom was passed orally from generation to generation and for a very long time. Nobody knows how long. This is why you will find many things in this book, Klara. My guru, for example, used to reference it when speaking of kindness. 'We are all of one heart, Miss Ghaiwal,' he would say. 'Being kind allows you to see the part of yourself that others carry, so be kind in all matters; kind in ways that cost you little and in ways that take all your strength.' Then he would remind me of his favorite passage from the Isha Upanishad: Those who know themselves to be all beings, hate no one. Some gurus say very little. He was not one of those gurus, and though I liked his words very much, they were not particularly easy to follow."

"My grandpa Gompsie says things like that. He tells me to see with my heart and seek fairness, not justice. 'Fairness looks for middle ground,' he says, 'Justice does not. When you look to be fair you flow with the workings of the Universe: When you demand justice you close doors. Justice is rigid—the Universe is not.' He says stuff like that. Not wanting me to close doors and all."

"You have a very wise grandfather."

"Yes… though he might not be my grandfather. We meet on his spacecraft while I dream so it's hard to tell, him being all transparent and flimsy and stuff."

"I see…" Rani rubbed her chin. "I too have dreams where I am told things. With time I have learned to listen and I find that, when I do, magic happens. Like moving to Pennington and running into you!"

"You think so? You think meeting me is magic?"

"Absolutely! So now, why don't you tell me more of your magical thoughts as we walk up to our apartments?"

3

Klara was getting warm in her jacket as she stood in the Tippins' entryway trying to grasp her family's indifference to her arrival; her brother's music booming so loud it rattled her teeth.

Mother was in the galley kitchen doing dishes —as always. She did not look up. Klara peeked into the living room where Mr. Tippins sat by the fireplace reading his paper, a wool blanket over his knees. He also did not look up. Drake?— Klara gave the rooms a quick scan—was probably in his room.

She placed the Upanishads on the wooden floor and unzipped her jacket. "Hello!"

Putting the paper down, Mr. Tippins removed his pipe from his mouth. "There you are," he said, blithely stating the obvious. "Where did you go?"

"Where did *I* go? *You* were supposed to bring my telescope."

"Oh that." Mr. Tippins put his pipe back, leaving it to dangle from the corner of his mouth. "Drake and I tried it out on the balcony. Surprisingly decent quality. I would have called you, but mom told me you don't have a cellphone."

"Mother doesn't think I need one as I don't have any friends."

"Oh…"

"More pressingly—apart from the telescope being decent—it's MINE!" Mr. Tippins ducked behind his paper. "So where is it!"

"Klara!" Mother shouted. "No need to shout. Your brother is borrowing it, is all." She gave Klara a wry smile. "Now, be a whale. Don't be shellfish."

"I'm not selfish!" Klara felt herself getting hot. "Besides, Drake never borrows—Drake takes, takes, TAKES!" She hurled Mother's hat at the floor. It landed with a timid *thop*. Glaring at it, Klara stomped her foot.

"What did I tell you!" Mother slammed a spatula into the kitchen sink, then stared appalled at her apron and quickly wiped off the soapsuds.

"NOT FAIR!" Klara bellowed.

"Klara?" Mr. Tippins dropped his newspaper. "Klara, don't make your mother upset."

"NOT FAIR!" Klara bellowed even louder. "I was to… I was to see my home!" Tearing off her jacket, an arm got stuck in the sleeve. She growled, then viciously pummeled the unassuming apparel to the ground. The boots came off easy. One sailed quite beautifully into Mr. Tippins' office, the other crashed into the wall, barely missing the kitchen doorway.

"Klara Josefina Tippins!" This time a plate got hurled into

the sink, splashing worse than the spatula. Mother leaped back. "Look what you made me do!"

Leaving the scattered boots and the crumpled jacket on the floor, Klara picked up her book and, rounding a corner, marched down the hallway towards her room. With head held high, she stomped past Drake's room. "Curse on you," she hissed. "A curse on all of you," she added as she passed Mother and Mr. Tippins' bedroom. Then she stalked into her room and slammed the door—WHAM!

Dark.
Very, very dark.
Now she'd done it.

Like most rooms, Klara's room had a light switch by the door (for situations such as these). Most unfortunately her switch did not connect to anything, as the lamp had been removed when her uncle rigged her teapot gondola across the ceiling. At that time, they'd also painted the walls and the ceiling a blue color—the darkest of dark blue color.

Of course, a sane person would simply open the door and let light in from the hallway (and technically she could do that), however, this wasn't just any closed door; this was a Slammed Door and slammed doors warrant a certain regard.

And so, sliding her socked feet along the floor, she made her way to her bedside table, zigzagging past the piles of books neatly stacked on the floor and making sure she did not accidentally trample her Japanese teahouse. Made from a huge cardboard box years ago, it was getting rickety and she'd never forgive herself if she ruined it.

As Klara pulled the cord on her bedside lamp, the room flooded with light. So much light she almost knocked over her twin-bell alarm clock, Frau Rudenclunk. Exhausted, she tumbled onto her bed. No wonder she didn't like birthdays. And how screwed up was that? Who doesn't like birthdays? Old people—like thirty-year-olds!

Gazing at the rigged gondola-teapot dangling overhead, she waved to the starbeings inside: two dollhouse dolls and a tiny dragon—all found at a garage sale; all members of the Galactic Support Team, traveling from Headquarters to Earth in a space shuttle. The space shuttle being the aforementioned teapot; their 'headquarters,' an old chandelier that hung in the ceiling by her bed; and 'Earth,' a globe her grandma Nelly gave her, now standing on a dresser.

Even though she'd only paid fifty cents for the wooden dolls (a grandmother and a child) it was clear they were high-end. What with hair of real wool, clothes with handstitched hems, even bendable arms and legs and all.

She'd removed the apron and fluffed up the grandmother's hair. It felt right, even if the doll still looked more like a grandmother than the legendary space captain Gompsie Writtum.

The child wore denims and a knitted sweater and had Klara's light-brown eyes and wild mousy-brown hair.

Without being sure why, she'd named her Kalanna Boon.

The dragon, Dwinn, was her favorite. Though he was mostly red, his frills, spikes, and wings had tips of gold. The wings did not move; nothing moved—he was that small.

Three tiny dolls; more dear to her than her own family. With a sigh, Klara changed into her nightgown. Then she slipped the Upanishads under her pillow, crawled into bed, and pulled the covers to her chin. "Goodnight, starbeings," she said. "Goodnight, Earth-globe, goodnight moon… oh, and goodnight telescope, sorry I lost you to Drake. Someone should have told you I *always* lose."

She turned the lamp off, closed her eyes and had almost fallen asleep when, through the wall, she heard Mother mention Klara's name in the kitchen…

4

The convent had been built with thick, dense walls. All the same, the wall between Klara's room and the kitchen was new construction and paper thin.

"That's ridiculous!" Mother huffed. "I would never have agreed. Who ever heard of a thirteen-year-old with a telescope!"

Mr. Tippins murmured something unintelligible in reply.

"I don't care that it was free! I don't care that your cousin wanted it off his hands. I would not have agreed!"

"… … …"

"You thought I'd be pleased? Well there's the problem then—YOU THINKING. I'm the one to be out there in the frigging cold, putting the darn thing together—ME! Then stand there like some idiot looking at—stars? Did you think of that?"

"…"

"I'll tell you what *I* think. I think we should let our dear Drake keep the telescope." Klara pulled the cover over her head.

"You can't give it to Drake!" Even through the covers, Mr. Tippins' voice was audible.

"Why not?"

"Because we gave it to Klara."

"Well then, Bruce." Somehow, Mother's sharp voice managed to purr and Klara held her breath. "We'll have Klara give it to Drake. You know there'll be no peace until he has it."

"You're asking too much."

"TOO MUCH?" Mother snarled. "ME, asking too much? As if you took the telescope for Klara's sake. Please, you took it because YOU wanted it. Admit it. Not for a second did you think of how I'd suffer. You… you're so selfish it's sickening."

A loud slam, then the scraping of a chair.

"Go ahead!" Mother shouted. "Leave—it's what you always do."

Tossing off the covers, Klara stared into the dark room. Mr. Tippins got angry… who would have thought *that* could ever happen.

As her eyes were slow to adjust, the darkness remained dark—dark and kind. With nothing to orient herself with, she could be anywhere she wanted. Perhaps this bed was in a bedroom in Paris, that would be nice. While listening to the final quiet of the day she'd struggle to fall asleep, eagerly awaiting the next day's adventures with friends—there would, of course, be friends.

When she was little, she'd lay staring at the ceiling holding her breath. The day would have been cruel and she'd hope to leave the way Grandma Nelly had left. One minute, Granny was with her, the next minute the breathing had stopped and she'd been gone—just like that.

Klara had been four. A scrawny four-year-old with an uncanny ability to hold her breath.

5

PLANET EARTH
— Terra Firma —
44.5956° N, 75.1691° W
Saturday, February 13, 7:13 a.m. EST
As Per: Klara Tippins

Waking up, Klara lazily stretched to where her warm feet touched the cool parts of the comforter. It felt delightful, yet something else—her mind paused—a fluffy expansiveness of her being and a scent of... basil? Had she made a visit to Buxtin?

A knock on the door and Mr. Tippins' head poked in. He was unshaven and his gray stubble, along with his smudged glasses, made him look almost endearing. "Can we talk?"

Sitting up, Klara anxiously crossed her fingers as his long jerky legs bumbled their way around her teahouse. A near miss and she squeezed her eyes shut.

"About the telescope," he said, slowly sinking down to sit at the edge of her bed. "Don't you think you're too young for something like that. Something... that advanced?"

Klara opened her eyes. "Hard to say as I barely touched it,

but… no… no I don't think so."

"Your mom says so and you know how she is." Mr. Tippins unsuccessfully righted his glasses.

Klara knew how Mother was, of course she did. She knew how obstinate Mother was but also how jealous she got when Klara spent time with Mr. Tippins. Yet here he was. And why? Because Mother was desperate for him to do her dirty work, that's why. Well—Klara smiled wryly as she pulled the Upanishads out from under her pillow—she and Mr. Tippins would have themselves a nice long bonding then.

"I met a person yesterday," she began. "Her name is Rani Ghaiwal. I mentioned my sky family and she has one too! She's Hindu."

"I see."

"She gave me this." Klara held up the book.

"Did she?"

"She gave it to me for my birthday and I told her all about my home planet."

"You don't say." Looking out the window, Mr. Tippins bent his neck, making crunching noises.

"I told her I'm a Draconian starseed. A starseed is someone from a different star system, you see, who's been seeded here on Earth." Klara glanced at her father who made no acknowledgement. "I told her I'm from Otim Dorum which orbits the Aldibain star in the Draco constellation. Draco is latin for Dragon, Otim means 'connecting love' and Dorum means 'planet,' though some call it Oopsie Daisy after we allowed reptilians from Thuban to rule us. Thuban or Alpha Draconis, is another star in our constellation which, by the way, used to be the North Star."

"The North Star?" Mr. Tippins unexpectedly lit up. "That was 4,600 years ago, if I'm not mistaken."

Klara looked keenly at her father. "So, anyway, we thought they'd make good leaders and help us evolve. And certainly we evolved, but not by them being good leaders. They sought chaos and mayhem like an unquenching thirst and were ruthless in their domination. Many, many generations suffered as it took a long time for us to bring our hearts together and focus back on our... our humanity, though we weren't exactly humans, more like dragons. And I know what you're thinking: Creatures from a constellation don't necessarily look like the constellation. I mean, what if beings from the Lyra constellation looked like harps!" Klara burst out laughing. Mr. Tippins did not interrupt. "Probably humans named the constellation Draco because we visited Earth from there a long time ago and people took notice. We were, as you might guess, the dragons that people talk about; some with long bodies, some with wings, some indeed breathing fire. The dragon society hosts many varieties and not all of us are nice like us, that goes for individuals as well as societies."

"Uh-hum."

"Our kind, those from Otim Dorum, have visited Earth since before the cretaceous period, some ninety million years ago. Earth is such a pretty place and soon others came. They came from Orion, Sirius and the Pleiades. Some of them thought dinosaurs would be a good idea while others weren't so sure. In the end the dinosaurs got to be a little much. I guess that happens sometimes, huh?"

"What?"

"You have a good idea, but it doesn't work out."

"Sure." Mr. Tippins did not sound sure.

"I bet, with a proper telescope, one could see our star Aldibain from here."

"I suppose." Mr. Tippins monotonously tapped the tip of his elbows with his long bony fingers, his brows furrowed.

"We're not full dragons anymore," Klara pushed on, encouraged by his silence. "At least not those who travel through the cosmos. No fire-breathing allowed, that's for sure, too much of a hazard, and the wings have pretty much disappeared from lack of use. All that said, my grandpa does have that long snake-like body and a funny way of sitting down on his coiled tail. I visit him sometimes on our spacecraft, Buxtin. It's a bioship and quite sentient. Miss Rani found this interesting. She told me—"

"Your grandparents are dead, Klara, you know that."

Klara's heart gave a tug. She put the book aside, then stared out the window along with Mr. Tippins. A while they stared, the two of them, watching the pale morning light pussyfooting its way through the oak's many branches. Somewhere in there, Owl sat cocking his head.

"Your mom is planning a birthday party for you. She called her brother and—"

"Mother called Uncle—No way!" Klara whacked her pillow in excitement. "For years Mother has refused to talk to him. All she ever talks about is how she won't talk to him. He gave her an earful when he installed the dryer, didn't he, about Drake stuffing the cat in there?"

"You remember?"

"Of course!" Klara pointed to her Japanese teahouse. "That's what the dryer came in."

Mr. Tippins cleared his throat but said nothing.

"I can't believe Uncle Otto is coming to celebrate my birthday," Klara sighed.

"They haven't called back yet, so don't get excited."

"They? Who are 'they'?"

"Your Aunt Frida from Florida may also come, but not from Florida, she's divorced. She and her son Pontus live with Otto now."

"The ex was a Mohawk, right? And her son has long black hair and a proud nose?"

The back of Mr. Tippins' neck flushed. "Pontus' dad is Mohawk, but I have no idea about the nose. Don't stereotype, Klara."

"Okay." Pensively, Klara listened as Mother banged pots in the kitchen sink. "She hasn't called yet, has she?"

"What?"

"You made a deal with Mother to throw me a party if I

gave up the telescope. She hasn't called yet, has she?"

"I don't… Getting hungry for breakfast, Klara?"

"No."

"Me too." He gave her knee a couple awkward pats, then stood up and left.

With Mr. Tippins gone, Klara pulled off her blanket, grabbed her book and went out into the hallway. Nothing was easy with Mother. Klara shook her head. What had it been like for Drake? Had Mother left him alone as a toddler the way she'd take off when Klara was little? Had she locked herself in the bathroom while he screamed? Klara had had Grandma Nelly—he hadn't.

In the hallway, the walls were lined with pictures of Drake; large photos taken at a studio and smaller snapshots to commemorate all his accomplishments, like walking and hitting at bat at little league. Klara thought of how Mother constantly bragged that Drake always had such a glint in his eyes, even as an infant. Yet, as Klara examined her brother's young face, all she saw was a terrified child.

With a sigh, she walked into Mr. Tippins' office where Mr. Tippins sat poised behind his desk staring out a window, absently clutching his briefcase. She cleared her throat. "That notwithstanding," she said, surprised at how composed she sounded, "I think Drake should have the telescope."

It was possible Mr. Tippins was taken aback. He could also be proud, or relieved—it was hard to tell. "Y-yes?" He stuttered.

"Seems like a piece of him goes missing when something doesn't belong to him. That must be hard."

"Hard?"

"For sure. Besides, I'll never be as lost as he is."

Mr. Tippins righted his glasses and blinked a few times. "That's mighty big hearted of you," he finally said. "Well then, I'll make sure to get you a party." Clenching his hands tightly over his chest, he smiled broadly. And though his smile never reached his eyes, the glasses stayed put, making him look almost composed.

Was it true? Might people come to her birthday? If so, that called for a celebration.

Klara eyed the welcome mat by the front door; a nautical ropy thing that might glide quite well on Mother's polished floors. If she sprinted and landed just right on the mat, how far might she glide? She glanced back at Mr. Tippins. Fortunately, he was still staring out his window searching for some horizon.

She grabbed on tight to her book.

One—Two—Three... *Go!*

Holy potatoes, she almost reached the living room fireplace! With no one around, she ran one loop around the coffee table. "Hello Mr. Tippins' pipe." Bigger loop. "Hello outdoor balcony. Hello plants on windowsill. Primrose Number One, Primrose Number Two, Primrose Oops-not-looking-so-good." Another loop.

She was on her fourth loop, when—

"Klara Tippins!" With hands on hips, Mother stood in the doorway, a fur hat on her head. "Stop running like that, like… like some crazy person. Did you wash your hands?"

"Hands?" Klara pondered the foolishness of washing perfectly clean hands, and the strangeness of Mother's hat. "Why is there a hat on your head?"

Mother's face instantly burst with pride. "Your dad picked it up for me in Saint Petersburg. It's made of Russian sable fur and was to be an anniversary gift, but I couldn't wait." She pivoted her head this way and that, showing it off from all its various angles. "When we go to the Ice Festival today, I want people to see it. It's a little tight so I'm stretching it out."

"The Ice Festival is *today!*" One of Klara's favorite events, the Ice Festival was an occasion for people to make ice sculptures with chainsaws, then light them and walk around with snow creaking under their shoes drinking piping-hot cider saying, 'Isn't this amazing?' How did she ever forget?

"There will only be you and me this year so I'll have you all to myself."

"Not… dad?"

"No, dear, he's busy."

"What about Drake and his latest girlfriend… Chrystal?"

"Drake refuses. Doesn't want people to know you're related to him," Mother chuckled. "We'll go once the company leaves." Turning, she walked into the kitchen.

"Fuddeldum to him," Klara muttered as she left for the

bathroom to tend to her 'dirty' hands. As she passed the kitchen, she noticed Drake sitting at the table. She shot him an angry stare, but as always, he did not notice. However, a new, and very large gadget was on the counter. The size of a storage box, it boasted buttons and levers in all directions. "Whoa!"

Mother looked pleased. "You like it? It's a Gaggia espresso coffee machine."

"Who drinks coffee?"

"Our guests of course! Your dad picked it up at the Malpensa airport in Milan. It's very expensive and sure to impress them." Mother adjusted her hat. "People won't like you unless you keep a pristine home. Remember that; always keep a pristine home."

"People like you because you clean?"

"Klara Tippins. Go. Wash. Hands."

"Advice magnifico, mamma!"

"And don't forget to put the mat back!"

Klara was just about to wink at her mother, when the Gaggia machine shot a data-beam at her, hitting her right temple.

"Mother, that thing is broken."

"But we just… how would you know!"

"It told me!"

"Hands! Now!"

6

Heading down the hallway to the bathroom, Klara noticed Drake's door standing ajar. Perhaps she should check on the telescope?

Peering inside, she got the weird sensation she always got around Drake's stuff. Like gunpowder. Like wet gunpowder getting stuck to the roof of her mouth. It only happened with him and sometimes with graveyards. All the same, there was the matter of the telescope. She set her jaw—gunpowder or not—she was going in.

One step in and she had nowhere to set her next foot. Wall to wall the floor was littered with crumpled papers, unfinished schoolwork, clothes (including undies and socks), dirty plates, empty pizza boxes and milk cartons—How unfair!

And the walls too were cluttered! Unorganized shelves took up some space, but mostly the wall was covered with old Halloween costumes, thumbtacked like bizarre mementos. She spotted Count Dracula, the Grim Reaper, a red devil costume, a vampire. And there on a shelf, nearly hidden among candy wrappers and dry pizza crusts, lay her telescope.

"Sorry," she whispered and blew it a kiss. Then she snuck out the door and walked to the bathroom, all the while massaging the roof of her mouth with her tongue.

As anticipated, the bathroom was a bleach endurance test. In fact, the stench was so noisome it caused Klara's eyes to water. Giving the Upanishads an encouraging pat on the back, she placed it on the floor and, standing on it for added height, looked in the mirror. Was there a glint in *her* eyes? She could not tell. What did it mean to have a glint? Would her life be different if Mother thought she had one?

An earsplitting *pfsssssssssss!* came suddenly from the kitchen, followed by—"DAMN IT! SHIT! SHIT! SHIT!"

Distracted, Klara splashed water on her nightgown. A lot of water. She hastily apologized to the gown, wiped her hands on its hem, picked up the Upanishads, and ran to the kitchen.

For the most part the kitchen was still a kitchen, even if, tantamount to an apocalyptic event, it was splendidly covered with froth. Froth was all over the cabinet doors, it dripped from the ceiling and dribbled, in long disjointed streams, from Mother's fur hat down Mother's face.

Clasping both hands over her mouth, Klara prayed she expressed dismay—not glee. She raised her eyebrows for added effect, but Mother was not looking, Mother was scrubbing foam off the coffee maker with the vigor of trying to resuscitate it.

Drake, meanwhile, was in his glory sprinkling the world with his nonsense while chowing down his usual bowl of *Cocoa Puffs.* With his hair buzzed short on the sides, it was only his curly bang that glowed in the morning light, his perfect cowlick making him look both boyish and classy. Klara couldn't see it, but people found him charming, outrageous, and so, so entertaining. Even Mother and Mr. Tippins hung on his every word. Like, how could there be a bowl of slimy cold oatmeal waiting for her when she'd repeatedly told Mother she hated the stuff? 'I don't like oatmeal—Sure you do—No I don't—Drake says you do—Drake doesn't know—Of course he does'—BLAH!

"You have to wipe with bleach-free deterrent," he informed, slurping the last of his cereal, "or it'll stain purple."

"Bleach-free *deterrent?*" Klara grinned. "Got any Drake-deterrent?"

"Not now, Klara." Mother grimly yanked the coffee maker's cord out of the socket and, holding the frothy contraption at arm's length, she exited the kitchen, leaving only a slight acrid smell behind.

One look at Klara's gown and Drake tossed his head back in mock laughter. "Hey, space cadet, did the faucet attack you?" Slapping his thighs like their uncle Otto, he shook his head. "Such a dimswitch, can't even wash her hands!" Leaving his dirty dishes on the table, he sashayed past her out the kitchen.

"Tilligumm to you, you snotfrat," Klara grumbled as she

watched him leave. "At least I'm not the kind of dimwit that can't tell their words apart." Putting the Upanishads on a chair, she sat on it and reluctantly began jabbing the oatmeal with her spoon.

She was busy turning it into a moon carter when Mother reentered the kitchen, grabbed Drake's abandoned dishes and put them in the sink. "Done yet?" Mother snapped, her back to Klara.

Klara laid her spoon across the crater. "Done!" She slid off her chair and was just about to take her book when Mother snatched it.

"The Umpash? … where did you get this?"

"Rani gave it to me."

"What's a rani?"

"A Rani is a person who lives below people named Tippins."

"The apartment below us is empty Klara. You're not reading it, are you?"

"Define 'reading.'"

"You use it to reach things?"

"Sure."

Mother seemed relieved.

"And I keep it under my pillow." Klara sat back down. "It informs me while I sleep. For instance, did you know life happens *from* us, not *to* us?" Klara tapped her spoon against the crater. "Which explains a lot, don't you think?"

—thop, thop, thop—

With each thop Mother's face tightened, so did her grip on the book. "Talking nonsense is like lying and you should not lie to your mother. There is no Rani. You made her up and I will speak to your teacher about letting you borrow books like this. Now go put on your birthday dress."

"I have a birthday dress?"

"Smarty-pants. Keep this up and I'll tell your aunt and uncle not to come. Do you know how lucky you are to have a mother like me to make such a fuss about your birthday?" The book fumbled in Mother's hands and, taking a decisive hold, she slammed it onto the counter. "Get going!" she barked. "And put your dishes in the sink. I'm not some maid!"

Carrying her bowl, Klara walked to the trash where, with one spectacular *thop*, the oatmeal slid into the bin. Then, under Mother's watchful eyes, she heedfully placed the bowl and spoon in the sink. She thought to grab the book, but Mother's hand rested on it. All she could do was give it an apologetic nod.

Klara owned one dress and one dress only: a sleeveless thing made of flimsy yellow fabric. As soon as she put it on, she shivered. Rummaging through her dresser she found her pink unicorn sweater and pulled it on. Faded and stretched, it might not be the most elegant apparel, but boy was it warm. Just as Klara did a pirouette, Mother walked in.

"For god's sake, Klara, take that horrid thing off!"

"I'm cold."

"You're not cold. Take it off."

"Then I'll wear a pretend sweater and tell our guests all about it."

Klara and Mother locked eyes.

"Fine," Mother sputtered. "Wear it. But you're putting your hair in a ponytail." Twirling around, she strutted out the door, leaving a scuff mark on Klara's floor.

Annoyed, Klara dug her eraser out from her school bag, then slowly placed it back in its pencil case, zipping the case closed. Scuff marks be darned, she wasn't some maid.

7

The welcome mat was in the living room where she'd left it. Being too unwieldy to carry she kicked it all the way to the front door, thankfully without Mother spotting her. Once by the door she twiddled it, back and forth, until it was perfectly straight. Then, stepping back, she paused and with an outstretched toe crooked it ever so slightly—*Vive la résistance!*

Now it was time to get her book back. Looking in the kitchen, the only thing on the counter was their old blender. Had Mother stuffed the book into one of the cabinets?

No.

A drawer?

No.

The trash—No. Except the trash bag had recently been replaced. Klara's heart began to race.

Perhaps Mr. Tippins knew about the trash. But Mr. Tippins was not in his office… nor was his briefcase. Had he left for work? On a Saturday? On *her* Saturday? Surely not. Surely, he'd gone to pick up a surprise for her at the store.

Perhaps balloons. That was it. The briefcase came along out of habit. Briefcases do that… right?

– *ding–dong* –

Before Klara could get the front door, Mother burst out from the bathroom in a cloud of hairspray, her bleach-blonde hair in a tight bun. "I'll get that!" Spotting Klara, she frowned and spun her finger, making twirly curls.

Klara bit into her thumb. She'd promised Mother a ponytail. Shoot! Shoot! Shoot!

First to enter was Aunt Frida. She handed Mother a grocery bag with wrapped gifts. "Hi, Agnes. It's been a while. Still well, I hope. We're not early, are we?"

With her pink, pink angora, enormous hoop earrings, black leather pants, and super high heels, no one would accuse Aunt Frida of being related to Mother—except for the hairspray. Somehow, they both loved hairsprays, though Auntie used it to look wild; Mother to look prim. Also, Aunt Frida's hair was not a fake blonde but a natural chestnut color, and she chewed gum, which Mother would never do.

Then Pontus showed up and Klara's heart sank. This boy was NOT tall and proud with long silky hair that blew in its own wind, nor were hawks called to whistle at his arrival. In fact, Pontus' brown hair was short and gathered to a point at the top of his head making him to look like a surprised fledgling. The eyes were brown and large like a calf's, the front teeth those of a rabbit. There was no denying it—the guy was a petting zoo.

As he unzipped, a pink nose stuck out from his jacket, followed by two inquisitive eyes and a pair of enormous ears. Klara reached out and stroked the dog under its chin. "Welcome to the party, little one."

Pontus smiled. Though he was not what she'd expected, his eyes were kind, she'd give him that. He carefully brought the dog out from inside his jacket. It looked sweaty but content. "Her name is Luna."

"Luna." Klara clutched her heart. "What kind of dog is she?"

"Good question." Aunt Frida reached over and patted Luna's head. "The people at the shelter weren't sure but guessed her to be a mix between a Chinese crested and a wire-haired terrier."

"Either that," Klara sighed blissfully, "or a mix between an angel and a dandelion puff."

Auntie laughed. "Always the one with the colorful mind—I remember you."

Last to enter was Uncle. As soon as he saw Klara, he pulled her in for a hug.

"For goodness' sake," Mother reached in and tugged at her brother's long beard, "you still carry this rug around?"

"Should be obvious." Otto affectionately stroked the wiry mat. "Might be time you had your eyes checked."

Mother let out a *pff* as if blowing a bug off her lip. As she stepped away, Klara motioned for her uncle to move in close.

"The box is still in my room," she whispered.

"What box?"

"The big one that came with the dryer. Mother is itching to throw it out, but I don't think she dares. I think she's afraid of ending up in one of your sermons."

"I'm a Quaker," he whispered back. "We don't have sermons."

"You don't? Well, whatever you do, don't tell her. It's my only leverage."

Uncle squeezed her. "I won't."

Mother spun around. "Tell me what?"

"Klara says that, between us siblings, I'm the most handsome one."

"Don't listen to her. And for goodness' sake, everyone take off your coats, I'll get coffee brewing."

"Where's Bruce?" Aunt Frida asked. "Shouldn't we wait for the father of the birthday girl before we start?"

"Bruce had to work," Mother called from halfway into the kitchen. "Urgent business. I tell you, the research department would be nothing without him."

Giving Klara a sympathetic look, Pontus handed her Luna and Klara quickly buried her face in the wispy fur. "I thought for sure he'd be at the store," she murmured. Luna gave Klara's chin a lick and Klara gave Luna a squeeze. The little one squirmed. "Pontus, I think she wants to get down."

Holding Luna firmly, Pontus lowered her, her spindly legs spreading wide as they touched the well-polished floor.

Shrieking, Mother ran back to them.

"Don't let it pee on my floor!"

Looking terror stricken, Luna wrestled to coordinate her legs. When she finally got traction, she glared at Mother and scurried around the corner and down the hallway, her tiny claws pattering. Klara followed and so did Pontus. Before they caught her, however, the little one scurried into Klara's room.

"OMG, your walls are dark! And the ceiling too?!" Excitedly, Pontus whipped his head around. Stopping abruptly, he gawked at the Japanese teahouse. "And you got a space capsule!"

"I do?... I mean, yes, I do."

"That's lit. Where did you get the big box?"

"It came with a dryer. We needed a new one after Drake locked our cat in the old one."

"You have a cat?"

"We did." Klara hitched up the bed skirt and found Luna against the wall, her large ears pressed against her body. "She looks scared."

Pontus crouched down. "I'll get her out, then you can sit with her on the bed while I check out your space capsule. That will calm her. If you let her crawl under the covers, she'll love you forever."

"And how, exactly, will '*you* checking out the space capsule' calm her?"

"... it'll entertain her?"

"From under the covers?"

"Sure."

Klara held up a corner of her comforter while Pontus pulled Luna out. As soon as he placed her on the bed, Luna dove under the covers, a wee hump moving about in circles. "Can she breathe?"

"Probably." Pontus examined the teahouse. "Okay if I go inside?"

Klara nodded and crossed her fingers that Pontus would have the wherewithal to lift the box and not try to squeeze through the door.

Turned out, Pontus did not have such wherewithal, and Klara held her breath as he wiggled inside.

"This thingamajig here," his voice was muffled from inside the box, "is that the communication device?"

"Is it brown and pink and looks like the branch of a cherry blossoms?"

"Kind of does, yeah."

Klara peered up at the starbeings dangling in the teapot. They all seemed to nod. "... It could be. It could be a communication device."

"I'm coming out." The box moved. Then it moved some more. Clearly, it'd been easier for a Pontus to make it into a box than it was to come out. Klara bit her lip and, hoping not to offend him, lifted the box off of him. "Hey!" he laughed, "the space capsule took off without me!" Standing up, he pointed to the teapot gondola. "Is that an alien spacecraft?"

"It is. Though I suppose it wouldn't consider itself alien."

"And what's with the octopus lamp?"

She followed his gaze. "Oh, you mean the chandelier. I painted it same as the walls because it's not to be seen. The bowl-like shades are various factions of the Federation and their connections are invisible."

"What's a federation?"

"A group of groups."

"So what does this group of groups do?"

"They help Earth and other planets like it; planets where the inhabitants emit a lot of fear."

"That's why the clothesline brings the teapot to the globe?"

"Correct."

Pontus rubbed his chin. "How does that work?"

Klara's heart fluttered. She couldn't believe he'd asked. "Well…" she began. "The craft is not so much a spacecraft as a re-location-identification craft. A scientist named Ork Buxiter discovered that instead of *us* being a result of time and space, time and space are created from our consciousness. In fact, time and space are coordinate points for our fractal consciousnesses to orient themselves. And listen to this, these points can be programmed! While the craft creates a Zero Field, you simply enter the new points into the system and—voilá—there you are; you, the craft, your crew, anyone programmed to be within the new coordinates. You can move to anywhere in space and time—instantly! The trick, of course, is figuring out the new coordinates. One time—"

"I mean, how did you rig it?"

"Oh… with a clothesline and two pulleys. Uncle helped me."

"Schweet."

To demonstrate, Klara climbed up on her bedside table and began working the pulley system. On impulse, she unhooked the teapot and handed it to Pontus.

"What's with the dolls?"

"The dolls are some of the galactic entities who are part of the Federation. Would you like one?" Klara bit her tongue. Now what had she done!

"Really! I can have one? Anyone? I'd love the boy with the wild hair."

"The boy? You mean Kalanna. You'd like Kalanna Boon?"

"Could I… oh I'm sorry, it's your birthday, I shouldn't."

Klara swallowed. "No, it's okay." She did not meet Pontus' eyes. "She… he'll bring you luck." Giving Kalanna a quick kiss on the head, she handed her over.

"I could use some luck." Pontus' shoulders slumped.

"Things okay at Uncle's?"

"It's not that, no. I mean, we could all use some luck. Everything's gucci at Uncle's for sure. Me and mom have the second floor. I'm good with it. Mom had hoped to move into that little cottage past the knoll, but Galileo sold it. She's upset, but I'm glad. Mom doesn't do well with privacy. Some lady from New York bought it. Can you imagine? Living in the City and coming here—and no gun to her head!"

"The lady… is her name Rani?"

"Don't know her name."

"Is she tall with a profound presence?"

"A profound presence?" Pontus looked at her curiously. "Don't know. Never met her."

"Galileo—is that what you call Uncle?"

"With a beard like that, what else would you call him?"

Klara was about to ask another question when a holler came from the kitchen.

"KLARA! PONTUS! TO THE TABLE—PLEASE!"

"Yowsers!" Pontus checked on Luna under the covers. "I thought they'd have thick walls in a place like this."

"Not thick enough for Mother."

"What's on the other side? The kitchen?"

"We'd better go."

8

The kitchen table had been draped with a fine linen-cloth (inherited from Grandma Nelly) and set with their best tableware; gold-rimmed dessert plates accessorized with intricately folded linen napkins and silver forks perfectly angled. On a footed plate in the center, between a pair of crystal candlestick holders, posed a white-frosted cake tastefully decorated with trailing violets.

There were no balloons.

Everyone but her brother was seated at the table; Uncle Otto and Aunt Frida sat on the left, Mother to the right. Uncle wore denims and a black turtleneck. In the bright light of the kitchen Klara could see gray streaks in his beard. Had it been that long…

Pontus grabbed the chair next to Frida and she moved to make room for him. "Mom, the stuff Klara has is fire. You should see it."

"Fire, you say." Frida smiled. "Knowing what I know of Klara, I'm sure it is."

Klara hesitated. Clearly it was meant for her to sit next to

Mother as that's where all the gifts were, but Mother would never allow a dog at the table and Luna was half asleep and the floor was cold. Awkwardly Klara stood there holding Luna, hoping for something to happen.

"Lordi! Lordi!" Aunt Frida called out. "Look at Luna. Took weeks before she'd let me near, but you Klara—she's melting right into your arms!"

"Klara." Mother gave Luna a stern look. "No dogs at the—"

"You know," amicably Frida folded herself into the discussion (inasmuch as it was a discussion) "Klara reminds me of you, Agnes. Always so good with animals."

Mother blushed. "Hush now."

"No, really," Auntie insisted. "If it wasn't for Drake, I'd ask you guys to care for her when Pontus and I go to Canada tomorrow. His folks up there have big dogs and—"

Mother bristled. "What *about* our dear Drake?"

"Well," Frida cleared her throat, "the cat, for one thing."

"What cat?"

"The expired one."

"Drake was a baby then." Mother defiantly raised her coffee cup, her pinkie at attention.

"He was nine."

"All the same, a dog would be quite safe at our place."

"So you'll take her then?"

Mother's pinkie quivered. "I… Well, of course I will… I'll scratch my back and you'll scratch my back, that's how we've always done it." She carefully lowered her cup, nearly missing the saucer.

Holding Luna tight, Klara sat down. However did Auntie manage that? She'd have to take notes.

"Time for gifts!" Mother turned towards the kitchen doorway, clapping her hands.

No sooner, Drake showed up with Chrystal at his side. "Gifts for me?" he said, tapping the doorframe. Chrystal laughed and rolled her eyes. She was pretty. They had all been pretty. Pretty and strong willed, like he needed the challenge. With his arm draped around her shoulders, the two of them made their way to the table but did not sit down.

As Klara picked up the smallest gift, Aunt Frida reached over and touched it. "There wasn't time," she apologized. "We'd have given you grander things if we'd known we were coming."

"Of course, you knew." Mother indignantly propped up her coffee cup, still as full as when she'd filled it. "You're always welcome for the big events. You know that."

Auntie patted Klara's arm, her hoop earrings swaying. "Just know that we placed a lot of heart in them."

Drake laughed. "Any gift is better than no gift, eh?" He punched Klara's shoulder. "For her birthday *I* got a telescope." Again he laughed.

"Oh, Drake dear," Mother snickered, "the things you say." Amusedly, she looked around the table. "Brothers... we all know how brothers are, don't we?"

Uncle furrowed his brow.

"Well, no, not you, Otto. You were always a saint."

Klara picked up a flat rectangular package with a sweet aroma. It was from Auntie. She tore off the paper and found a bar of white chocolate! "Thank you, Auntie."

Mother cleared her throat. "Klara does not like white chocolate."

"I do too."

"Don't be silly, white chocolate is vile. I'd never let you taste it." Smiling politely at her sister, Mother snatched the bar from her daughter. "Thank you all the same."

The next package had the shape of a book and, indeed, it was an old Bible!

Otto leaned across the table. "I got it from my father, and he got it from his grandfather. I thought you should have it."

Made of black leather, the cover was soft from wear and the gold that'd been gilded had worn thin. No doubt this book had given its previous owners great comfort. As Klara handled it, she felt sure there'd been a box. A wooden box to keep it safe, with a latch that let out a delectable *click* when you closed it. "What happened to the box?" she asked.

Otto's fork slipped. "The Bible box?" He pensively picked up his fork. "My grandpa told me it fell in the river. He couldn't swim so he had to let it go."

Opening the book, Klara stuck her nose between the pages and inhaled. "Old books smell divine, don't you think, Uncle? Like maybe in their old age they remember the trees they used to be?"

"Maybe." Uncle squinted at her. "How do know these things? How did you know there was a box?"

"Nothing exists outside of consciousness and, as everything is consciousness, everything holds information." Klara closed the Bible. "It's just a matter of listening."

Mother tapped a spoon against her cup. "Listening, blistering, enough of that. Go on with the gifts."

The last gift was from Pontus and had clearly been unwieldy to wrap; the large bow in no way hiding the fact it was a flashlight. Nonetheless, Klara put on a puzzled look, turning it hither and thither, occasionally shaking it.

"Go ahead," Auntie giggled. "Open it."

As the paper fell away, Klara's breath caught. The vintage flashlight was gorgeous with not a scratch in its shiny chrome. But there was something else, something Klara couldn't quite put her finger on. Finding the switch, she slid it back and forth, but nothing happened. She looked at Pontus. "Does it work?"

"I wouldn't know." Pontus nudged his uncle. "Galileo here told me to give it to you, seeing as I didn't have a gift."

Klara handed Otto the flashlight. He unscrewed the tail cap and looked inside. "Had a weird dream last night about this flashlight. A skinny, tall, and very bright being—"

"With a big ball of hair?" Klara cut in.

Her uncle scratches his beard. "Yes, now that you mention it. Anyhow, the being told me to give you this flashlight. Not any flashlight—this one." After turning the batteries over, he put them back and screwed the tail cap on. The light was dim, but it worked. Switching it off, he handed it to Klara. "Funny how your mother called us later and invited us."

"It looks like a spaceship," Klara remarked. "Uncle, did you see a spaceship in your dream?"

"That is enough," Mother cut in. "No need to upset our guests."

Drake tossed Klara a metal barrette with a golden bow. It almost hit Luna's head. "Here," he said, "one more gift."

It was clear the barrette wasn't new. Moreover, it looked familiar. Klara turned it over in her hand. It couldn't be, could it? His previous girlfriend had a barrette just like this. Did she drop it and he found it in his room under… under a box of *Cracker Jacks*? Pinching it gingerly, she discreetly placed it on the table.

"You're welcome," Drake said sarcastically. Then his face brightened and he moved to stand behind her, grabbing strands of her frizzy hair. "Now that you have that pretty pin, you could do something about this… disaster."

She should be outraged. She knew she should be outraged; anyone would be. All the same, she felt pride. Pride that her brother had correctly used the word 'disaster'—three syllables and everything!

While Klara mused, Drake kept pulling out strands of her hair. "It's Medusa, everyone! A round of applause for Medusa!"

"Oh, Drake dear, the things you say…" Mother sniffed her coffee, took a reluctant sip, shuddered and quickly put the cup back down.

"Chryss! Chryss, check out my sister's hair!"

Chrystal looked mortified.

… she looked mortified? Klara straightened. "Hey, bro," she said, letting out a chuckle, "be gentle with it, would ya? I'm growing it to knit you a sweater." Looking pale, Drake let go of the hair. Klara turned and smiled sweetly at her brother. "It's for your birthday."

"Oh god." Doubling over, Chrystal clasped her mouth, coffee shooting out of her nose. "Drake. Oh god—your sister is hilarious!"

Drake turned crimson, making Chrystal laugh even harder. Even as he sternly escorted her out of the kitchen, they saw her wheeze with laughter whenever she looked at his face.

"You may think you always win, Drake," Klara called after him. "But life isn't a game, it's a dance—and you're a terrible dancer."

Around the table, coffee cups paused mid-transit.

Stiffly, Mother walked over to the stove. She held up the coffee pot. "More coffee anyone?"

Reflexively, the adults covered their cups.

"I can make more."

9

Pontus and Klara sat on Klara's bed. While Klara petted Luna, Pontus aimed the flashlight around the room, occasionally pausing to go back to a previous spot. "Does the beam make some things glow on their own, or is that a trick of the eye?"

"You mean, does it cause things to self-illuminate?"

"Yeah."

"I wouldn't doubt it. Things never act normal around me."

"Like brothers and such?"

"I was thinking of espresso machines, but yes, brothers too." Klara fondled Luna's ears. They felt like silk. "Chrystal left, you know."

"I heard the door."

"No, I mean they broke up."

Pontus put the flashlight down. "How do you know?"

"He didn't go with her."

"That doesn't mean they broke up."

"It does if you're Drake."

"But they held hands," Pontus insisted.

"That was before she laughed at him. If he thought he

could make her apologize he'd gone with her—but he didn't. Tomorrow he'll pretend she never existed."

"Are you saying a guy like him can't take a joke?"

"Yup. And though she doesn't exist, he'll punish *me* for making her impossible to control."

"That's not fair." Pontus picked up the flashlight but didn't turn it on.

"As the universe is neither fair nor unfair, the only fairness you find is the one you hold for yourself."

"That's deep."

"Came to me in a dream." Klara looked at his stubby nose. Her own nose was just as stubby, but on him it looked nice.

"I too have profound dreams." Pontus tapped the flashlight pensively. "Once I hit a home run and everyone cheered, but then the ball turned into a goose."

"Yeah, that stinks… How's school?" Too late she realized she'd sounded like a parent.

Pontus shrugged. "At first it was hard to fit in. You know, coming all the way from Florida and all."

"Sure."

"It's better now. What about you?"

"Me? I will never fit in. Like last week when I forgot we had a biology test. It was on biomes and, as I'm sitting at my desk thinking I'm gonna flunk, it occurs to me I could channel the answers from the animals themselves. Worked pretty well too. Except for the rhinos; rhinoceroses mumble and aren't very cooperative. Things like that. Like everyone's watching a play while I'm talking to the chairs." She glanced at him. He didn't look uneasy. In fact, there was something peaceful about him, about the way his eyebrows rested on his forehead.

"What about sports?" He gave her a sideways glance. "Do you like sports?"

"I love sports. Last spring I almost won the Regional 500-yard dash."

"That's lit!"

"Yeah… But then a girl came up behind. She looked so determined I figured her family must really take pride, so I let her pass."

"Didn't *you* want to win?"

"Winning would be a hassle." Klara twirled a strand of hair around her fingers. "There are more important things than winning."

"Not in a race!" Pontus tossed the flashlight aside. He didn't look peaceful anymore. "You can't say winning doesn't matter when you're in a race!"

"Why upset? It's all for the best, really." Hair got caught on a bitten nail. "If I won, Drake would never let it rest and my parents would be livid with me for setting him off."

"But Klara?" He was pleading now. She did not like this.

With her finger still caught in her hair, she tried posing her arm to make it look natural. "You don't know Drake the way we do, how his mind never lets go. On and on he'd persist it was a stupid race for stupid people and they only let me win because they pitied me… on and on and on."

Pontus looked puzzled and seemed about to ask a question when Mother's voice came pirouetting through the wall. "Drake dear, I thought you left with Chrystal?"

With her finger finally untangled, Klara crossed her arms and moved away from the wall.

"Drake, I'd like a word with you." Now Otto was talking. He sounded stern. "I didn't want to say anything in front of Klara, but the way you talk to her is not only offensive, it's harmful. This goes for you too, sis. You may think it's all tongue in cheek, but if it continues, Klara might suffer psychological trauma."

"Bah!" Mother's voice shook the wall. "That girl's not at risk of being damaged. *I'm* the one being damaged. Have you any idea what it's like living with her? She *never* follows instructions. Like her knitting—you think she uses patterns? NO! *She* has to do it *her* way. It's maddening."

"She creates her own patterns?" Frida asked.

"Yes!"

"Oh, that's terrible."

"Don't patronize me! She's a horrid child I tell you. Always out to make me look bad. You should see the poem she wrote—evil, pure evil!"

Otto chuckled. "An evil poem?"

"Yes! The teacher told her to write about herself and she writes a poem. Who in high school writes poems?"

"She's in high school?" Frida seemed taken aback. "But she just turned *thirteen*?"

"Thirteen or not, she wrote it to spite me. Here! Read it!" A drawer slammed. "And Drake dear, please leave some cake for your father."

Pontus pressed his ear to the wall. Klara braced herself.

"Macy's Cat." The words boomed into Klara's room as, apparently, Otto decided to use his 'ministerial' voice. "An evil poem by Klara Tippins,"

"That is not what it says," Mother corrected. "Don't add to it."

"A lost kitten in a retail store jumped from mannequin to mannequin, yearning for love. So many mannequins. So many arms. But no matter which embrace it chose, it found only hollowness."

"See!" shrieked Mother. "See what I mean? The only reason the teacher brought me in was to show me. I was mortified. Mortified I tell you!"

"You weren't concerned?" Frida sounded baffled.

"Of course, I'm concerned! That's what I'm telling you. She's evil!"

Hiding her face in a pillow, Klara began to hum. For a moment it drowned out their voices and she marveled at how well it worked. Then came Mother's outburst:

"GET OUT!" she bellowed. "How dare you tell me what to do! Get out you BASTARDS! All of you! NOW!"

A lot of shuffling ensued. Then quiet. Klara breathed hard into her pillow. Mother was wrong. She wasn't horrid. She couldn't be. What had Mr. Tippins said. He'd said she was…

oh, why couldn't she remember? Now Pontus and all of them would disappear and she'll never know and she'll never see them. Breathe in. Breathe out. Breathe…

Pontus placed a hand on her shoulder. "Klara? I'm… I'm afraid we're leaving—You, okay?" He removed his hand. "Please put the pillow down." A quick look at her and his eyes widened. "Okay…" Stretching his leg out in front of him, he fiddled a hankie out of his pocket and held it out to her. She nodded, grabbed it, and brazenly blew her nose, all the while wondering why he kept a hankie, and if she was supposed to give it back?

She was still pondering as Aunt Frida showed up in the doorway holding a large canvas bag. "We're going. It was great to… oh dear, you heard…"

"I'll be fine." Klara's voice was thick and not her own. "I'll be fine as long as I never, ever, ever, have another birthday." She tried to laugh but sounded more like a drowning hog.

"I am so sorry…" Aunt Frida held up her bag. "We brought some things for Luna." She put the bag down next to the teahouse and looked around. "It's a very dark room you have. Otto told me about it."

"What did I tell you?" Uncle stuck his head in and chuckled. He chuckled the way uncles chuckle when they want you to think nothing's wrong.

Klara forgave him.

"She heard…" Frida's voice broke off. "She heard everything. Oh, my dear, dear child." Sitting down next to

Klara, her aunt drew her close.

Pontus scooted off the bed and Uncle took his place, leaving Klara sandwiched between her aunt and uncle.

"Sometimes, Klara," her uncle gently leaned her head against his chest, "sometimes people talk about others when, really, they're talking about themselves. About how they see themselves deep down. Remember that, Klara, none of what your mother said is true."

Klara's neck cramped and she adjusted herself.

Auntie smiled. "Everything will be fine. You'll see."

Klara didn't believe her, but she forgave her too. "What happened to Mother?" she asked. "The way she flicks her hand when she walks, like she's shooing life away?"

"Oh, that…" Auntie looked over at her brother. "Otto, what do you think?"

"Well…" Otto stroked his beard. "I can't be in her mind, but I gather she doesn't like changes. She was ten when our dad died, I was twelve and Frida eight. A great shock to all of us but having been his favorite she took it the hardest. After that, she wouldn't let anything change. Not even herself. In fact, she told me so."

"She's still ten?"

"In some ways, yes, but not in every way. And I'm not convinced it was a conscious decision, despite of what she said. It's just one of the ways we cope. Life is a challenge, you know. She's doing her best, remember that."

"There's a lot about my family I have to remember."

Uncle gave her a crooked smile and got up. "We'll be in touch." He reached down and petted Luna, snoozing on Klara's pillow. "When you come see us, we'll set up my telescope."

Klara nodded and they all turned and left.

All but Pontus. Pontus paused in the doorway.

"Happy Birthday, Klara," he said.

With the midday sun shining directly into her eyes, Klara stretched out on her bed, taking long deep breaths as Mother clanked dishes in the kitchen. Mother… Klara pulled Luna close and shut her eyes. She ought to read the Bible. With any luck it'd tell her the do's and don'ts of birthdays, but Mother made her too angry and sad and emotionally drained and all she wanted was to be somewhere else… Paris maybe, in that flat she imagined before. And what did it look like? Oh, yes, worn wooden floors, high baseboards, super high ceiling, and funny windows that opened wide and locked with hooped levers. And outside? Outside all of France waited for her.

She rolled to her side and onto the flashlight. Moving it out from under her ribs, she gave it a kiss and suddenly imagined herself on Buxtin… how very odd.

10

Luna yapped furiously and Klara startled. Her mind only half awake, she strained to listen beyond the yapping. Was someone—galloping—down the hallway?

She listened harder—definitely galloping… oh no, not Drake!

Snatching the Bible and the flashlight, she shoved them under her bed, finding Luna already there taking cover.

She was reaching for the teapot when the door flew open and Drake burst in dressed in a samurai costume many years too small; the pants reaching mid-calf and the tummy showing. If it hadn't been Drake, it'd been funny

"Me Genghis Khan! Whoahahahahah!" Ripping the clothesline off the ceiling he grabbed the teapot and, turning it upside down, shook it vigorously. With the starbeings in his hand, he held up Grandpa Gompsie up by the hair.

"Noooo!"

Yanking on the head, Drake dashed out of her room. Without looking, Klara stormed after, trampling her teahouse.

Round and round the apartment they raced. The more

upset she got, the more excited he got, until… until, *oh god*—Gompsie's head came off!

Struck numb, Klara watched as Drake flaunted the decapitated head in front of her. Then, with great excitement, he ran for the kitchen, opened the lid to the blender and dropped it in: first the head, then the body.

The other members were added and while Klara pelted her brother, screaming herself hoarse, all he did was laugh.

The pitcher's lid was slammed on, a switch flipped, and Klara watched, stunned, as a hideous racket spun everything into a blazing inferno. The sound was nauseating, but even more nauseating was Drake; laughing and clapping his hands as he danced around the kitchen. In a rage, Klara jumped her brother, almost knocking him over.

"What on Earth are you doing!" Mother turned the blender off and grabbed Klara. "I tell you to ignore him. But do you listen!" In trying to wrestle free, Klara tore her sweater and landed hard on the floor. "And now your sweater is ruined—finally!" With her hair half undone, Mother turned and stormed out of the kitchen.

Rubbing her sore butt and still dizzy with the screeching sounds of the blender ringing in her ears, Klara got off the floor. And there Drake was, his face close to hers: jaw set, eyes cold—he wasn't laughing anymore.

"All things dear to you I will destroy," he spat. Closing her eyes, she turned away. When she looked back, his eyes waited for her with hatred so caustic it blazed her heart. Her knees buckled.

Klara was still on the floor when Mother grabbed her wrist. "Rani," Klara blurted. "I want to go see Miss Rani."

"Stop with the Rani thing! You're coming with me to the Ice Festival. I don't care how you're dressed."

"No."

Frowning, Mother tightened her grip.

In the doorway Klara jammed one foot against the threshold, the other against the doorframe. "NO!" she screamed—and peed herself.

"What is wrong with you!" Mother yanked Klara through the door. "I'm getting you in the shower—Now!"

The water from the showerhead was icy cold and Klara shivered, her skimpy dress clinging to her like eel skin.
"Why make such a fuss?" Mother fumed, turning the water off. "Running around screaming about some dolls—*tchah!* You're too old for dolls."

"T-too old for d-dolls but t-too young f-for tele-s-scopes?" Klara stuttered.

"Hey, watch it. You have no idea how lucky you are to be with a family as tolerant as ours. Any other family would have sent you off to an institution a long time ago."

Klara hugged herself, her teeth clattering.

"Now look at you," Mother ranted. "You're all wet. How are you going to go outside all wet?"

"I'm n-not g-going."

"Well, I'm not leaving you alone with our dear Drake. Who knows what you'd do to him."

"I t-told you-u, I wa-hant to see Miss Ra-ani."

– ding – dong –

"Hold on, sweetie, someone's at the door." Dropping the towel she'd been holding, Mother swooped out of the bathroom.

"Sweetie pateetie patatoe tamatoe to you too," Klara grumbled as she stepped out of the shower and plucked the towel off the floor.

Wrapped in terry cloth and with hair dripping, she snuck out to the hallway and, together with Luna, quietly tiptoed towards the entryway. Peering around the corner they found Mother in front of a mirror, aggressively primping her hair.

– ding – dong –

"Coming!" Adjusting her pearls Mother cocked her head, smiled amicably at her reflection, then strutted to the front door—her hand flicking like crazy. With a grand gesture she flung the door open and both Luna's and Klara's heart warmed as a scent of comfort gushed in; a welcomed blend of something sweet, brewed, and hearty.

"And a good morning to you, Madam." Standing in the doorway, Rani was grace and gumption swirled into one. Placed next to Mother it was clear she was not tall; she had only seemed tall—and still did.

"We're not interested in anything you're selling." Mother began closing the door.

"So sorry for the confusion, Mrs. Tippins. I am your new neighbor, Rani Ghaiwal." Rani held out a hand.

Mother looked at the hand. "Rani?" she croaked. "You said your name was Rani?"

"Yes, and still it is, I believe." Chuckling, Rani withdrew her hand. "Yesterday I met your daughter, Klara, and my goodness, Mrs. Tippins, what a special one she is."

"Yes, yes," Mother adjusted her necklace, "all my children make me proud."

"Of course," Rani concurred. "I have met many children in my life, and what a blessing, they are *all* so special. Sadly, with retirement it had to end. I do not miss the long hours, I will tell you that, but I do miss the children very much."

"You're a nanny?" Mother's voice brightened. "How fortunate. I have an urgent errand just now but hate to leave my little angel." Mother chortled nervously. "I… it's my dooth." She clasped her cheek. "I need to dee a dentith."

"Sorry to hear that, Mrs. Tippins, about your tooth. Regrettably, I never worked as a nanny. My work with children has been as a pediatric surgeon. All the same, if you need to see a dentist, as you say, I would be more than happy to spend time with Klara."

Even from behind, Mother looked stupefied and Klara inched closer.

"Klara," Rani called out. "How very good to see you."

Klara was about to reply when Drake's door flung open and Drake appeared, his outgrown samurai costume newly accessorized with a pair of plaid slippers.

"And your son!" Rani covered her mouth and coughed emphatically. "Mrs. Tippins, you are so blessed to have one of each."

Drake grinned. "One genius and one space cadet. That one," he pointed at Klara, "pees her pants."

Mortified, Klara looked at Rani, but Rani was looking at Drake, smiling cordially.

"It is a common misconception, young samurai, however, there is no scientific proof of a medical connection between micturition and acumen."

"Whatever." Flicking his curly bangs, which bounced and covered his eyes, Drake strutted back into his room, closing the door behind him with his felt slippers.

"What you said… what does it mean?" Klara asked.

"It means that there is no connection between a person's intelligence and their ability to hold their urine—which is absolutely true."

"Yes…" Mother looked at Luna licking Klara's leg, then at the puddle of water at Klara's feet. "A podiatrist you say?"

"A pediatric surgeon, yes. For many years I worked at a hospital in Mumbai, then at St. Mary's Hospital for children in the city of New York."

"Ah…" Mother took a sharp breath in. "And Klara won't be too much trouble for an elderly person, such as yourself?"

"I've found it is seldom the children who are the trouble."

Mother rearranged her string of pearls. "If you say so."

"So when, Mrs. Tippins, would you like me to bring Klara back? Five-thirty?"

"Six o'clock." Mother let go of her pearls and straightened. "And the dog goes too."

The two women locked eyes.

Rani blinked a few times. "You are quite exceptional, Mrs. Tippins. Six o'clock it is, and I will take the dog."

"Miss Rani?" Klara moved closer. "You might want to ask my mom for the Upanishads."

"But the book was a gift."

"My mom won't let me read it. I'd hand it back myself, except she took it and I don't know where it is."

"How silly you are, Klara." Like a deflating camel, Mother let out a long, exasperated exhale. "The kitchen had a mishap is what happened. You see Ms… Ratty."

"Rani," Rani corrected.

"Yes… a mishap. So I moved it to a *safe* place. That's what I did. I did not *hide* it." She turned to Klara, daggers in her eyes. "I would never take something from you, you know that. I'm your mother. Mothers don't do that."

11

Walking down the marble staircase to Rani's apartment, Klara carried a most fidgety Luna in her arms. It might have been that the echo in the Gothic stairwell unsettled the little critter, or the fact that Klara wore a down jacket without tucking her inside. Perhaps her unease came from having to share space with her own harness, leash, and doggy parka, along with Mother's hat. Then again, it might be that Klara was not paying enough attention to her, focused as she was on walking down a flight of stairs and chatting with Rani (who, incidentally, carried all of Luna's toys, Luna's food and food bowl along with the entirety of Luna's poofy bed, as well as Klara's flashlight—no Upanishads. Mother evidently forgot where she put it).

"What of the neighbors?" Rani asked. "Are they friendly?"

"To be honest I don't see them much. Me and Mia Rasmussen were friends, but then Mother told her I didn't like her playing soccer so she began to avoid me. Before we could sort it out, she'd moved."

"Did you mind?"

"What?" Klara tried placing Luna's head on her shoulder, but her own hair got in the way.

"Did you mind her playing?"

"Of course not. That's just Mother being Mother. She wants me to herself."

"Good heavens, why?"

"I don't know. We have fun sometimes; we'll go shopping or she'll take me to lunch. But I'd like to have my own friends too."

"We all have a right to make friends, Klara. What of your mother, does she have her own friends?"

"She has people she talks to on the phone. Mostly she complains."

"Ah."

Luna peered over Klara's left elbow, then curled up to bury herself under the right elbow. "Goodness gracious!" Klara arched her back to keep Luna from falling. "How about some patience?"

"Some patience or she will be a patient." Rani said, opening the door to her apartment.

Stepping into Rani's entryway, Klara held on tight to the dog while letting all the doggy stuff drop; the little legs pumping feverishly as she lowered her to the floor. "Happy trails!" she called out as Luna sped off into the living room. "And good riddance… though not really… Love you!"

Rani's apartment was not as big as the Tippins' and lacked hallways. And while the Tippins' apartment smelled of bleach and polyurethane, Rani's place smelled of caramel and summer sandals. The Tippins had tidy furniture and tiny plants; Rani had plush furniture with curvy legs that seemed to dance and huge tropical plants, some taller than Klara. It was a lot to take in.

As Klara hung up her jacket, Mother's hat fell on the floor. It made no sound, still Luna's ears perked up. Sniffing the air, she bared her teeth and growled; her growling escalating to a full-blown concerto as she bolted straight for the unsuspecting head apparel.

—*yap, yip, yap, yap*—

Grabbing hold, the tiny canine fiercely whipped the hat right and left, then tossed it in the air, pouncing on it as it landed.

"My dear goodness," Rani exclaimed. "I do not think Luna likes your hat very much."

"It smells of Mother."

Rani looked at the hat, then at Klara. "How about you and I go to the Ice Festival? I hear they have vendors there selling all kinds of things and most probably we can find you a new hat."

"But Mother will be there!" Klara bit her lip. She'd forgotten about the dentist. "I mean… the hat is fine."

Rani looked down at Luna, now contently resting on the remains of her kill. "My dear, I do not think that is still a hat."

"I'm fine," Klara insisted. "Spring is coming."

"Klara, spring will not be here for many months, even *I*

know that. How about we have lunch while we think it over? I made a special Indian meal for you."

"But you didn't know I was coming."

Fine lines spread across Rani's cheeks as she smiled. "You like buttermilk?"

Klara sat down at the small bistro table under the kitchen window while Rani was at the stove, sighing deeply with her nose over a boiling pot. "Punjabi-style chole with lots of curry. Nothing else smells this heavenly. I hope you like chickpeas, Klara. I tried not to make it too spicy." She licked a spoon from the pot, then pointed it towards a small table that Klara had been eyeing, covered with a plethora of sacred items: brass statues and framed deities, candle holders with votive candles, incense burners, flowers, a brass bell, bowls and silver plates, some fruit and, everywhere, draped necklaces. "Most probably one should not have one's altar in the kitchen," Rani granted. "But it is my kitchen, and they are my family, so I keep them here."

"You have a nice family."

"Yes, my celestial family. Perhaps your flashlight would like to join them? You know, Klara, it is not an ordinary flashlight and they will make room for it, I'm sure."

Klara nodded, then fetched her flashlight from the entry-way and placed it next to a colorful picture showing a devi with four arms sitting on a swan playing a banjo while balancing an upside-down cone on her head. Despite her predicament, the devi looked content.

"Saraswati." Rani walked over, picked up the frame and handed it to Klara. "She is a goddess of knowledge. Whenever I study, I consult her."

"You study?"

"Of course! What about you, you like school?" Rani brought the pot from the stove over to the table. It smelled rich.

"Learning new things is great, but not in school. I still remember my first day. I was so excited. Then the teacher asked me what two plus two was and I told her it depended on which two you ask, and she laughed. They all laughed and they're still laughing. Like I'm *that* hilarious. Like they can't believe their luck because, no matter how stupid they look, none of them is as dorky as I am."

"Have you told anybody that they laugh at you?"

Klara shrugged. "I used to talk to my mittens, though I'm sure that's not what you mean. Now I talk to starbeings from the Galactic Federation. Or used to. They were toy figurines that my brother threw in the blender. That's why I took a shower."

"Goodness me."

"I thought high school would be different and that, as long as I didn't open my mouth, I'd be fine. I even decided to trust people and was doing alright, when, out of nowhere, every-one began avoiding me again. Like I suddenly grew frog skin or something."

Rani brought a basket with steaming hot bread to the table and sat down. "Does your brother also go to this school?"

"There's only one high school in Pennington."

"I see…" Rani spun her bangles. "My guru always told me to leave people as they are, to see my own value and not the one others give me. 'Not everyone has the capacity to be kind,' he would tell me. 'People are not in your life to fulfill you, they are not here to be who you need them to be; they are here as they are and not everyone is in your corner—not friends, and not even family.' It is a hard truth, but I have come to think he was right."

"My grandpa says that. He tells me to know my own worth and not let others define me. But how do you do that?"

"An excellent question, Klara. For me it is done in meditation. That is how I get away from my narrow self. Or I ask my brook. There is a beautiful brook nearby that always gets me in touch with my strength. And, of course, the Upanishads. The Upanishads remind me that who I am is Self, and not what others project on me. 'The sun shines brightly even when it shines on that which is tainted,' the Katha Upanishad tells us. 'And just like the bright sun, the Self within us is unharmed by the failings of the world, for this inner Self is luminous, and cannot be harmed.'" Rani picked up a piece of flatbread and pressed it between her palms. "Family is the first ones to show us, of course. However, to be fully real, we have to know who we are beyond our roots. We need to know the *totality* of the landscape that we are."

Not paying attention to her food, Klara put a heaping spoonful of the curry dish in her mouth. She grabbed a flatbread and shoved it in her mouth. "Buh beh ish goo." She swallowed. "The bread is good." With a tearful smile she added. "It makes the curry less... assertive."

"I made it too hot."

"It's hot, but I like it." Klara pointed to a small metal object on the altar. "What's that?"

"A vajra." Picking it up, Rani handed it over. Shaped like a bow tie, it was small enough to fit in Klara's hand, its lacy skeleton making the loops look like royal crowns.

"It buzzes!"

Rani nodded. "The tiny ball between the loops represents Bindu. Bindu is the unmanifested state of cosmos and the smallest particle in existence. To think that cosmos' potential is within its tiniest part is quite marvelous and certainly a cause for buzzing." She leaned forward. "The tale of the vajra is most interesting. Long ago, good gods and not-so-good gods were fighting. An especially bad serpent god was king, making people miserable, so a human agreed to let the good gods take one of his bones to make the first vajra and defeat the king."

Klara turned the vajra over in her hand. "Like Adam using one of his ribs to create Eve?"

"Precisely!" Rani laughed. "Making something from one's bones is precarious as one never knows how powerful it might become."

"Did they conquer the serpent king?"

"Vajra is a Sanskrit word with two meanings: diamond and thunderbolt. Diamond, for nothing can harm it, and thunderbolt because nothing can stop it—So yes, they defeated the bad king."

"Is the Bindu part of cosmos, or is cosmos part of the Bindu?"

"Exactly both, I think. That is a very good question. I believe the universe is holographic and that consciousness creates existence in a feedback loop; the Bindu, then, creating from what its creation tells it. If that makes sense."

"All is consciousness?"

"Yes."

"And you can listen in?"

"If you are perceptive, yes."

"This morning an espresso machine told me it was broken and then a Bible let me know about a box." Klara handed the vajra back to Rani. "Does that sound crazy to you?"

"Not at all." Rani gave the metal bow tie a kiss and placed it back on the altar. "All you have to do is listen."

Scooping up a large portion of chole on a piece of bread, Klara shoved the whole entirety into her mouth. "Is so good," she mumbled, tears streaming down her face. "So good."

12

It was downhill from Mountain Manor to the Pennington fairgrounds. Downhill—and curvy. Squinting her eyes, Klara took a firm hold of Luna with one hand, the passenger seat with the other.

When agreeing to go with Rani to the festival, Klara had not considered that Rani had lived in big cities and not needed a car, that it wasn't until she bought a cottage that she saw the need for one and that, when confronted with a purchase, she'd seek to buy the smallest car imaginable—a Fiat 500. To further the insult, Rani played loud music, talked nonstop and gesticulated wildly. Klara dug her fingers deeper into the seat and squeezed her eyes shut.

"I play Boléro by Ravel to calm my nerves," Rani shouted. "Boléro has to be loud. You do not mind, do you?" Klara did a yes/no head-bob which seemed to satisfy Rani's peripheral vision. "So you know, I only failed my driving test three times. Which goes to tell you, one is never too old to acquire new skills."

"You failed your driving test?"

Rani gave Klara a sharp glance. "At the end I did not fail. You persevere with something and in the end it will not matter where you started."

The fairground's parking lot was a large grass field that worked well as a parking lot on dry summer days. For this event the frozen ground had been plowed. Or, rather, had been haphazardly plowed with good intentions.

Rani slid to a halt, only slightly merging with a snowbank. She nudged Klara. "You can breathe now."

Holding Luna, Klara squeezed the two of them through the jammed door; the fairground's crackling speakers greeting them by loudly announcing the schedule for carving competitions, dueling chainsaws (whatever *that* was), live yodeling, something undecipherable, and award ceremonies.

Rani stood waiting, hands on hips. "First we find a hat."

Quite a few vendors were at the festival, each vendor huddled in their own pop-up canopy tent. Some vendors sold jewelry, others wooden toys or pottery. Only one vendor sold hats: crocheted hats in garish colors, tragically matching the potholders offered.

"Oh dear," Rani put a protective arm around Klara.

"Yes?" An elderly woman poked her head up. "If you're looking for hats, there are more in the back. My daughter, Tilda, knits what she calls 'pixie' hats."

"Pixie hats," Klara's heart missed a beat, "with long ties

and pointy tops that topple?"

"Those would be the ones."

Making their way to the back, Klara first noticed Tilda's red hair, then the cavort of pixie hats surrounding her. Seemingly grown from Earth itself, the hats had names such as: Dreamy McMeadows, Mr. More Moor, and Sunset Pigeons.

Tilda looked at Klara, her green eyes glistening. "One hundred percent wool and hand dyed," she said. Klara nearly fainted.

"I can't choose," she gasped, shaking her head. "They're all extraordinary."

Rani picked up Miss Amble Woods, a forest green hat strewn with tiny red dots, like berries. She placed it on Klara's head. It was warm and the ties mingled nicely with her wild hair. It was perfect!

"Do you like it?" Rani asked.

Klara nodded, too speechless to speak.

"Klara!" Klara turned and saw Uncle walk towards her, arm-in-arm with Aunt Frida and Pontus; all of them rosy-cheeked. "Almost didn't recognize you! Not with that hat."

"It's adorable," Frida marveled.

Pontus pulled something out from his coat pocket and showed her. It was Kalanna wearing a red scarf.

"You gave... him a scarf? How sweet."

"Yeah." Pontus' rosy cheeks got even rosier. He put the doll back and, pulling out a bar of white chocolate, held it out to Klara. "Heard you like it."

"Thanks!"

"Who is your friend?" Aunt Frida asked, nodding towards Rani who stood with her back to them talking to Tilda.

Rani turned around. "I am—Pastor Bloom! My dear goodness, to meet *you* here of all people!"

"Ms. Ghaiwal! My, oh my…" Otto blushed. "I thought you were in the City this time of year. You're not staying at the cottage, are you?"

"No, not the cottage. Though I have to tell, once I retired, I no longer live in the City. Wanted peace and quiet but the cottage is too chilly." Rani illustrated with a shiver. "Very fortunately, I found a place in Pennington and moved in just a few days ago. That is how I met Klara."

"My, what a small world." Uncle clucked his tongue. "I'm Klara's uncle and this is my sister, Frida. She and her son Pontus moved up from Florida to stay with me."

"Florida…" Rani mused, using the same intonation one use when saying *Vasari Classic Artists' Oil Colors,* or *embroidered silk slippers, or chocolate mousse.* "That must have taken some adjusting."

"Tell me about it." Frida laughed. "Every time I freeze my ears off, I'm just as flabbergasted."

"You could wear a hat, you know," Uncle teased.

"What? And mess up my hair!"

Klara was laughing along with the others when something caught her eye: In a sea of fairgoers a Russian hat bobbed towards them. Discreetly she moved to stand behind Rani.

Rani, however, raised her hand and waved. "Mrs. Tippins!" she hollered. "Mrs. Tippins!"

Some twenty feet away the fur hat ducked behind a food truck.

Frida looked out over the crown, stretching her neck. "You know my sister?"

"We met only today."

"I see." Aunt Frida cupped her hands. "Mrs. Tippins behind the hot dog van. Yo-hoo!"

Klara cringed as the Russian hat, along with Mother, emerged from behind 'Hot Diggity Dogs.'

"My, oh my!" Mother exclaimed, a grin plastered on her face. "Ronda, how lovely to see you, my dear, and… ALL of you." She made a theatrical sweep of her arm. "Long time no see—ha, ha. Otto, Frida, let me introduce Doctor Ronda Gershwin, a dear friend of mine." Good-naturedly, Mother enunciated the botched names with great emphasis. "Doctor Gershwin is a renowned brain surgeon from Mount Sinai Hospital."

Rani opened her mouth. Then she closed it. She and Frida exchanged looks.

"Thank you again, Ronda, for letting Klara spend time with you." Mother placed a gloved hand on Rani's arm. "Exposing children to strange cultures is so important."

Chuckling softly, Rani withdrew her arm, "My dear goodness, Mrs. Tippins, I do not think you need *me* for that."

"Ha, ha." Mother wilted her hand like a limp leaf of

spinach. "She calls me 'Mrs. Tippins,' ha, ha. It's a little joke between us."

"Love your hat, sis!" said Frida.

"Yes," agreed Otto dryly. "The *hat* is lovely."

Mother gave them a coquette smile. "Bruce bought it for me in St. Petersburg. He's so thoughtful. Travels and works hard to provide." She cleared her throat. "We're getting sub-zero temperatures, did you hear? Lucky me to have this hat." Glancing at Klara's hat, Mother grimaced and shook her head ever so subtly.

"Sub-zero!" Frida rubbed her hands together. "Now I really miss the clammy subtropics."

Everyone laughed—everyone except Mother. Mother's face was still and empty. Then, without warning, it blazed with radiance. "Speaking of the tropics, you'll never guess what happened to me this afternoon."

Dumbfounded, they gawked as their eyes slowly adjusted to the floodlight. "The tropics?" Otto finally asked, shoving his hands deep into his pockets. "Do tell."

"Holy mackerel, I thought you'd never ask," Mother gasped as if she'd held her breath. "Mr. Griffin, Bruce's boss, told us it's all set—we're going to Malaysia!" To everyone's astonishment, Mother then wiggled her hips.

Klara was the first to regain her wits. "Malaysia?... I'm going to Malaysia?"

"No, not you, Klara." Mother propped up Klara's pixie hat to stand up straight. "Me and your dad. Only for a few months.

Your brother will look after of you."

Mother kept talking, surely Mother kept talking, except to Klara it was as a distant murmur. Could it be true? It couldn't, could it… her *brother*—That'd be absurd.

Then, as through a tin-can telephone, Klara heard the echo of Mother's chatter. "*Isn't it fabulous? Bruce is going to be head of the research department and we'll live in an exclusive community and probably have maids! Everyone will be so impressed with my knowledge of Malaysian culture. We'll visit tropical rainforests and sand beaches; eat squid and cuttlefish and snails and octopuses, and—*"

"Jeez, sis…" Auntie's cutting voice brought Klara back. "That's really something."

"Yes, yes," Mother twittered. "Quite so. Thank God I can finally tell someone. It's been dreadful with all the hush hush."

"How long will you be gone?" Otto asked.

"Twelve months."

"Twelve! That's a year!" Uncle rubbed the back of his neck. "So, when are you leaving?"

Getting on her tippytoes, Mother rapidly clapped her hands. "In two weeks on the dot!"

"What!" Klara jolted. Her head spun.

"I know—finally! I'm so excited! To top it off, Mr. Griffin is taking me and Bruce to the Windley Inn this evening to celebrate. The Windley Inn, can you imagine!" Mother fanned herself. "I've been in a tizzy all afternoon. Doctors eat at the Windley Inn, and executives—all the royal people."

Auntie stroked Luna, still in Klara's arms. "Gosh, sis... really... you really didn't tell *anyone?* Not even your children?"

"Klara understands." Mother tried to stroke Klara's chin, but Luna got in the way. "Imagine if I told and then it fell through—who could survive that?"

Pontus put a hand on Klara's shoulder.

"My dear." Rani straightened. "Instead of burdening your son, who I am sure is very, very busy, why not let Klara stay with me?"

"Out of the question." Squinting suspiciously at Rani, Mother adjusted her hat. "A generous offer to be sure, Dr... Gumdrop, but in our family we take care of our own."

"But, sis," Otto interjected, "Rani is a neighbor of mine. If Klara stayed with Rani, we could *all* look after her."

Mother squared her shoulders. "Our dear Drake will care for Klara and that is that. Klara couldn't be in better hands. I'm the mother. I know."

<h1 style="text-align:center">13</h1>

By the time Klara had seen the dueling chainsaw competition and finished three cups of apple cider, it was time to go home. (Disappointingly, the chainsaw competition was about quickly chopping ice, *not* surviving a duel with chainsaws, which had been Klara's assumption.)

They had cast their votes for the best ice sculpture. Klara voted for a pair of glasses resting on top of an open book. It'd reminded her of the Bible she planned to read that evening, while Rani voted for a large elephant, not only because it was gorgeous, but also for the artist's gumption to create such a thing.

Finally, walking back to the car, they'd watched the sculptures lit, all at the same time, creating a brilliant wonderland that'd given Klara such a feeling of homesickness she'd had to sit down, her frozen cheeks burning from her warm tears. She'd been at a loss for words and Rani had not pryed.

"On Friday the newspaper will announce the winner. I have paper subscription." Rani turned the ignition key. "It will be the elephant. You will see. Everybody loves an elephant."

Back at Mountain Manor, they parked without incident, greeted the Western Gate, then brought Luna to the courtyard to do her business. Right as they entered, Klara spotted a man standing by the fence, his wonky contour clearly defined by the city lights below. Earflaps down and smoking a pipe, there was no question who it was.

Klara nudged Rani and pointed. "That's Mr. Tippins."

"Your dad? You call your dad 'Mr. Tippins'?"

"He's never around. He comes and goes and maybe *he* feels at home, but home isn't home when he's there, you know, it's like having a guest. Though I would never call him Mr. Tippins to his face, that would be rude. I only say it in my mind."

"And what do you say when you want his attention?"

"I walk up to him and start talking."

"And with your mother, what do you call him when you mention him to your mother?"

"Why would I mention him?" Klara shrugged. "Though sometimes I wonder if he's noticed."

"Noticed what?"

"That he doesn't have a name."

As they approached, Mr. Tippins startled and nearly dropped the pipe dangling from his mouth. The pipe was unlit and this was odd. Even though it could be expected for Mr. Tippins to forget to light his pipe on occasions, to go outside for a smoke and then not light it—that was odd even for him.

"Bruce Tippins," he said, extending a hand to Rani. "Klara's dad."

"Rani Ghaiwal. Glad to meet you."

"She's the lady who gave me the book," Klara volunteered.

"I see… That was kind of you, Ms. Ghaiwal."

"I was more than happy to pass it along, and to such a keen scholar. But then, as I am sure you will agree, she is no ordinary child. It has been a great fortune for me to have spent today with her. Your wife was ever so generous."

"Was she now…" Pensively bobbing his pipe up and down Mr. Tippins watched as Luna squatted, then jerked up as the cold snow touched her tush, squatted, then jerked up again. He raised his eyebrows. "We have a dog?"

"Not ours." Klara untangled Luna from the tangled leash. "We're doggy-sitting Pontus' dog while he and his mom go to Canada."

"And congratulations, Mr. Tippins," said Rani. "I hear you are going to Malaysia."

"Call me Bruce."

"Yes, Bruce, if you have not been to Malaysia, let me tell you it is a wonderful place. I have wanted to go back since 2007. And to think you'll be doing research."

Mr. Tippins took a long drag from his barren pipe. "Mostly I'll be teaching a master's program. It's for sustainable solid waste management."

"That is magnificent! Just recently I read about a company

looking to turn *all* waste matter into plastic. All waste—even chicken bone! Can you imagine?"

Mr. Tippins' jaw dropped and the pipe fell out. "That was written by a colleague of mine in Israel! You read his article?" Mr. Tippins delicately picked up his pipe and, recognizing it was dead, stuck it in his coat pocket. "Tell me, Rani, what were you doing in Malaysia?"

"I went with Doctors Without Borders to Kuala Lumpur to improve health services for the refugees. This was in 2004. Quite a successful operation, I must say, as only three years later we had improved the capabilities of the infrastructure to where local organizations could manage on their own."

"Now there's a fine organization," said Mr. Tippins. "I've always admired Doctors Without Borders."

"Indeed. And, if I may ask, sustainable solid waste management, what is that about?"

"It's about creating a generation of scientists who can manage our planet better than we have. Quite invigorating being part of something bigger than oneself, would you agree?"

Klara picked up Luna, who—finally—had done her business. Despite her doggy parka she was cold and Klara swaddled her into her own down jacket. She glanced at Mr. Tippins. Mr. Tippins did good things? How had she not known?

A frigid wind picked up and Mr. Tippins pulled his collar up. "It was three degrees below zero when I last checked," he told them. "It may go down as low as minus twenty-eight before morning."

"Celsius?" Rani asked.

"No, Fahrenheit. Twenty-eight below Fahrenheit if you can believe it. That's unusual even this far north."

"The climate has gone completely batty," Rani fretted. "Just last week I listened to a program—"

"Alright, you two," Klara interrupted, "keep talking if you will, but I'm bringing Luna inside."

"No, no I shall go also." Rani turned to Mr. Tippins. "A pleasure meeting you."

Mr. Tippins snapped his legs straight and gave a small nod. "Pleasure all mine. All mine."

14

Hugging herself hard, Klara bit into her wrist. Stupid. Stupid. Stupid. The pain felt good and it wasn't until her jaw ached that she realized she might break the skin.

"Are you okay?"

For a moment Klara felt disoriented. Then she remembered that Rani was with her, carrying Luna. "I don't have my key. I forgot to take my key with me."

"There is a doorbell you know." Placing Luna on the floor, Rani took the doggie parka off. "Even if Mr. Tippins is outside, surely somebody is home. I hear music."

"The music is the problem." Klara picked Luna up and smoothed out the tousled hair, then pressed the button. "And doorbells have consequences."

As feared, Drake opened.

"Klara," her brother jeered, "did you forget your key—again? How many times is it now?" He looked knowingly at Rani. "It's an ongoing tissue we have with Klara."

"You mean 'issue'?" Rani corrected, unawares.

"Sure." Smiling wryly, Drake adjusted his cowlick. "It's a

sad thing, but my sister was never right after mom threw her across the room."

"Mom never!" Klara protested.

"Right across the room she flung you. Of course, you were too little to remember."

"You're lying!"

"Then why did Grandma Nelly move in?"

Luna yelped and Klara realized she'd been smothering her. "Sorry, Luna."

"Luna?" Drake's face lit up. "As in 'lunatic'? What a perfect dog for you." With a courtly chuckle he strolled to his room and closed the door. Seconds later, the clamor of his music shook the walls. This was war. A war only Mother could stop. And where was Mother?

A lamp glowed in the kitchen window, but the only thing at the sink was a pile of dirty dishes. Mother never left dishes…

Klara had just begun to worry when a staccato of fake laughter broke out inside the bathroom, loud enough to overpower the music. Mother was practicing for the fancy dinner, of course she was. The laughter stopped, the door opened and Mother erupted in a belch of hairspray, wearing stiletto heels and a black dress tight enough to show off her thin figure.

"Mother!" Klara coughed. "You're home!"

"Of course I am." Strutting down the hallway, Mother failed to acknowledge Rani standing there and Klara decided not to ask for the missing book. She banged on Drake's door. "Too loud!" The music stopped and Mother pranced back to the bathroom.

"What's for dinner?" Klara called after her.

"Make something!"

Rani nudged Klara. "I could stay?"

"I'm fine. Thanks." Klara put Luna down. "I can make myself an omelet."

Reluctantly, Rani handed Klara the flashlight and Luna's bags. "You have my number?"

Klara leaned in for a hug. An entire year with Drake and no Mother to rein him in. How was she to survive?

Rani kissed Klara's forehead, encouragingly squeezed her shoulder, departed and the front door closed. A heavyset old door, rigid and immovable—like Mother. For a long while Klara stood there looking at it. Then she walked into the kitchen.

There were no eggs for an omelet, so she made toast with cheese and marmalade instead. While Luna ate her dog food in a bowl on the floor, Klara took her plate to the kitchen table, then grabbed a deck of cards from behind the kitchen curtains and began a game of Klondike solitaire. It was her way to check how well aligned she was with the world. Though Klondike has one of the lowest rates for success of all solitaire games, Klara almost always went out. Not tonight though. Tonight, something was off. She put the cards away in their tattered box. It was quiet in the kitchen. Not peaceful.

But quiet.

Quiet, even as Mr. Tippins came home. Klara heard him move about as she cleaned her dishes, the long ties of her pixie hat flung neatly over her shoulders. She did the tall stack as well, the one left by the sink. She couldn't say why she did it, it was just something she did.

In the entryway she collected her flashlight, the bar of white chocolate she got from Pontus, and all of Luna's stuff. Carrying everything close, she and Luna turned the corner to the hallway only to stop short when Klara noticed a bright light shining under her door. How was there a light coming from her room? And why was it so bright? Apprehensively, they approached.

With arms full, Klara pivoted the handle with her elbow, then pushed the door open with her shoulder. One step in and everything dropped from her arms. The flashlight hitting the floor with a clang.

This room—not her room—was cold and smelled funny. It had white walls, a white ceiling with a bright fluorescent light, and no trace of a gondola. Even the chandelier was gone, along with the teahouse.

Then the flashlight caught her eyes, laying on the floor by her easel. Picking it up, she could see it had a dent, a rather large dent, but the glass was intact. She placed it on the night table along with the white chocolate. She meant to pick up Luna's things but decided to leave them as they lay, scattered on the floor. It's where they belonged anyway. Keeping her pixie hat on, she changed into a pair of flannel pajamas, then turned the fluorescent light off and went to bed, finding Luna already snug under the covers.

As Klara made room for herself, Luna settled down between her feet and did not stir, not even as Mr. Tippins came to say goodnight. He, on his part, did not ask about the dog, nor about all the doggy stuff on the floor. "Rani seems nice," he said, looking regal in his tux. "I'm glad you didn't make her up."

"Right you are." Klara let their silence settle as dishes clanked in the kitchen. Evidently Klara hadn't cleaned them well enough. She took a deep breath. "What happened to the Upanishads?"

"Please, Klara, don't pester your mother with that."

"It's *my* book!"

"Why upset the household when you can easily borrow it at the library?"

"You do realize, don't you, that as far as my birthday goes: I lost one telescope, one bar of chocolate, and one book—all because of Mother. I thought birthdays were about *receiving* gifts. Or do I have that wrong?"

With a closed face, Mr. Tippins reached down and patted her knee. Then he adjusted his bowtie and left.

Soon after, Mother stopped by. From the doorway she eyed Luna's things on the floor, then the pixie hat on Klara's head. "Behave," she said. "And don't forget to wear the hair clip our dear Drake gave you. It'd make him happy."

"Sure… I'll behave."

"And Klara, from now on, no more visits to Miss Raisin, okay? She's too old to care for a child like you. You can be quite a handful, you know, so promise me you won't disturb her again."

"Her name is Rani."

"What I said. You exhaust her and I will not have it." The hallway light made Mother's bouffant hair shine angelically and Klara wondered how it'd all gotten so wrong. "I saved you some cake. I put your name on it and everything. It's in the fridge."

Was that a bribe or an apology?

"Did you see it?" Mother tapped her fingers on the doorframe.

"No, I didn't, but thanks."

"Didn't want you to be without."

"Yes. Thank you." Klara looked closely at Mother. Was this the moment to ask her? If she didn't ask now—when? She took a deep breath. "Drake says that, once when I was little, you threw me across the room. Is this true?"

"I'm surprised he remembers. And no, you never hit the wall so that's not why you're strange, you just rolled across the rug."

"But I was an infant. How could you—"

"You bit my nipple, you little brat," Mother chortled. "Boy did that hurt. If you have a child—which I don't think you will—don't ever let them bite your nipple."

"Why wouldn't I have a child?"

"You're not interested in children, dear. You're interested in dogs. By the way, where is the dog?"

"In the room somewhere," Klara said truthfully.

"Well it's not allowed in your bed, okay? I'm gracious enough to let the critter into our home, but in bed? No."

"*In* the bed?" Klara ventured. "As in the *actual* bed?"

Mother shook her head, then caught herself and lightly checked her hair with her palms. "Half the time I don't know what you're talking about. Now, go to sleep." She gave the doorframe a couple of taps, then left.

So Mother *had* thrown her. What kind of person throws a baby? What mother throws her own baby and still, thirteen years later, feels no remorse?

"Don't wait for us!" Mother called from down the hallway. "We're going for drinks afterwards."

Klara stared up at the assaultingly white ceiling. Of course, in the dark, she couldn't tell that it was white, but of course it was. Drowsily, Luna crawled up from under the covers and curled into the small of Klara's neck, the soft hairless tummy smelling sweet, like vanilla…

Vanilla! Of course! She could savor the white chocolate while… reading the Bible!

Turning her flashlight on, she checked under the bed— still there. She gave it a kiss, puffed up her pillows, propped the flashlight on her shoulder, and leaned back.

This was the night. This was the night Klara Josefina

Tippins would read the Bible. Contently she sank into her pillows. She had something excellent to do.

The black cover was supple and the book opened on its own, unfurling to a part called 'Proverbs.'

"This is going to be amazing, Luna." She ruffled Luna's head. "You'll see. Piles and piles of wisdom."

15

Klara opened the wrapper to the white chocolate and broke off a piece. To her delight, the piece was slick with an embossed bunny. Closing her eyes, she placed it in her mouth. Soapy at first. Then, as it melted soapier still—Oh, fuddlesnucks!

Unceremoniously, she let the half-melted piece slink back into the wrapper. "Luna?" Luna poked her head up. "Luna, we shall not speak of this to anyone, you hear? Not ever." With a sigh, Luna plunked her head back down and Klara kissed the downy head, then fluffed up her pillows, grabbed the flashlight and resolutely aimed it at the Bible.

As before, the flashlight self-illuminated certain things. One word almost glowed. It was the word "trust" in Proverb 16:20. How peculiar. She aimed it around the room to see if the anomaly was caused by some sort of reflection; but no, moving the light did not change the phenomenon.

Trust… Trust what? The proverb said to trust the Lord. In fact it claimed that 'trusting the Lord' was the *only* way to be happy. But that didn't make sense. She stared into the muted light of the flashlight. "Please explain yourself." Then, starting at the beginning, she flipped the pages, one by one.

As she thumbed through Genesis, two more words stood out: The Journey… Trust the journey? Now that made sense. She nudged Luna, but Luna was sound asleep. "Okay then," Klara pulled the covers over the little dog, "I'll read on my own."

Genesis was easy to follow, even if some things were perplexing. For instance, why must man be ignorant and not able to tell bad from good? Seemed like the perfect setup for conning someone. But who'd want to con humans?

Although this was never explored, she kept reading and did okay until she got to Exodus. Exodus was not perplexing; Exodus was infuriating.

This Lord, the one that she was supposed to trust, promised to free a bunch of slaves in Egypt, but then changed his mind and kept them for himself to build an army. For forty years his henchman, Moses, dragged them around a desert, turning the children of farmers into warriors so they could kill some giants in Canaan.

He and Moses threatened them, gaslighted them, and when they asked for necessities like food and water, Moses shamed them, telling them they were not worthy.

"I know people like that, Luna. I know people who withhold necessities to gain power. People depriving you of love, attention… having you beg for scraps, then kick you as you… This perverted mind-twisting-shit-thing! IT'S CRAP!"

Hurling the book across the room, it hit the bookcase with a smack, slackened and landed spread eagle on the floor, causing a startled Luna to shoot out from under the covers.

—*Yip!Yip!Yip!Yip!Yip!*—*Yip!Yip!Yip!*— Her legs stiff, her body shaking—*Yip!Yip!Yip!Yip!Yip!Yip!Yip!*—Catching her breath she turned to Klara, a crazed look on her face.

"That's right, Luna. That's right. You tell that Lordi Boy to stay the hell out of my life."

As the book stayed flat and did not move, Luna soon ran out of steam—so did Klara.

She knew she ought to put the Bible away. She ought to do a lot of things. Instead, she closed her eyes. How tired she was.

How tired she *is*… then a hum from deep within; a hum as from a thousand monks chanting… and a scent of basil. She smiles knowingly—it's Buxtin, her grandfather's spacecraft.

And there he is—the legendary Captain Gompsie Writtum—as buoyant as ever with his voluminous crystal-white hair, bright gray eyes, and a long wide nose on his short wide face. At the tip of his nose his spectacles balance, not because he needs them, he tells her, but because he likes the feel of folding them.

The moment she is with him—she never left.

16

22,236 MILES FROM EARTH
— In a Geosynchronous Orbit —
Saturday, February 13, 10:48 p.m. EST
As Per: Klara Tippins, aka Kalanna Boon

«Tidings, Kalanna,» her grandfather beams. His voice, as always, clear in her mind. «I made you a park in the dreamscape.»

"You made a park?"

«So you won't get spooked when you come here.»

Klara regards the bio-interfaced walls of her grandfather's study, presently shimmering like shells of abalones. "Grandpa, your place could never spook me."

«Trust me, the longer you are on Earth, the more foreign this place will seem. For instance, I notice you no longer show up in your dragon form. This is why I made the park Earth-like.» His arms fall to his side. «Would you prefer I call you Klara?»

"Mostly," she admits, "I want a hug."

«Of course!» Her grandfather coils down to her height and extends his extendable arms in an embrace. It's a long thorough hug; a hug where all her meridians align, even the ones she didn't know she had. He uncoils and looks her over. «You look splendid. A bit worn perhaps. Is it worn up or worn down?»

"Worn down, Grandpa."

«Yes, of course. Down would make more sense. Later I will introduce you to Ma'iinac Zook, our new communications specialist; she can help us with the 'down' thing. Are you ready to see your park?»

"Can't wait."

Leaving the captain's study, they move through Buxtin's membranous self-illuminated corridors, the two of them making but the faintest of sound. After a brief moment, Grandpa Gompsie slows. «Here we are!» He gestures towards a rough section of wall where patches of iridescent bark fluctuate. «Please, female specimen first.»

"I don't remember how…"

«Allow me.» Looking expectantly at the wall, her grandfather claps his hands in rapid succession. The wall groans but does not change. He claps again, more assertive-like.

Leaning in closer, Klara detects some incremental, painfully miniscule, changes. "Does it usually—"

«No, this is all Buxtin. He's displeased with me right now. Only a tad. Naught to worry about.» A loud Humph! then a snap, and the wall is back to being bark. «Buxtin, please, not now. Klara doesn't have time for this!»

The wall sighs. The patch smooths and this time begins to shimmer like the back of a waterfall. «Go ahead,» her grandfather prompts. «The morphing is managed by tinker flies which are mostly friendly.»

Klara begins to step through the wall. "Wait!... most friendly or mostly friendly?"

«A joke. Please, go ahead.»

As expected, stepping through the wall is like stepping through a waterfall—a dry waterfall.

Her grandfather wafts in behind her. «So,» he blushes, «what do you think?»

She looks around. The park is lovely enough. There are green trees. In fact the trees are altogether green. Bright green and surprisingly rubbery as they twist and flail, seemingly trying to catch birds. There is a pond with several clattering fountains and benches running around chasing each other.

"This is… quite something." Klara squeezes his powdery hand. "How kind of you to make it."

«Can't tell it from the real thing, can you?»

"Hardly… Except, benches are for sitting. You know that don't you?"

Gompsie looks befuddled. «The body folds?»

"It does."

«Of course! How silly of me—Halt!» In an instant the benches stop. So do the fountains, the trees and the birds— they all turn to look at him.

"Also," Klara adds, "Not everything on Earth is competing."

«Right you are.» He claps his hands. «Shanti, shanti everyone!» At the sound of his call the landscape quiets and the benches and the fountains begin moving in harmony with the birds and the trees.

"Seems like Buxtin has become more cooperative," Klara observes.

«Not even Buxtin can resist shanti. And how are you my dear?»

"I threw a Bible." She expects him to wince, but he doesn't. "And I lost a telescope. I'd hoped to look at Aldibain but—"

«I know.»

"You know?"

«I hired a new surveillance company. It's called Owl Watch Always; still AI-free but their owls don't sleep all day and are more...»

"In your face?"

«... informative.» Over the rim of his glasses, her grandfather studies her. «He freaked you out, didn't he?»

"A bit."

«I am sorry. It's not like you don't have enough trauma. I should have listened to Buxtin.»

"It's fine, grandpa, really, the owl is growing on me."

Gompsie gasps and clutches his heart. «Where! Oh, for heaven's sake!»

"No, not actually 'growing.' I'm getting used to him. It's a manner of speech."

«Dear heavens... I felt so bad for you when you lost your

telescope, and so relieved when I managed to convince Otto to give you the flashlight. All I want is to make life easier for you, and then, to think an owl—»

"So you fiddled with the flashlight? That explains a lot."

«Indeed.» Gompsie squeezes one eye shut in a fair impression of a wink. «I infused it with my personal agape using an Essence Transference Device. It was the first time I used the dang thing and I didn't need help from anybody. It works through electromagnetism. Everything is electromagnetic these days. Did you know they have electromagnetic tilt projectors?… Anyhow, I contacted your uncle Otto in his dreamstate and through elevated info-streams compelled him to bring it to you.»

"Thank you, grandpa. It was wonderful to see my Uncle again."

«Certainly.» Gompsie scratches his jaw with one of his long claws. «Would you say you feel close to him?»

"Sure. He's more of a dad to me than Mr. Tippins."

«Don't tell anyone I told you this but,» Gompsie glances right and left, «Otto's primal self, Ortet, is your Otimian father. He's your dad and also my son-in-law.» Letting his claws tap lightly against each other, he straightens.

"And Rani?"

«Your Otimian mother, Rativett.»

"So Rani and Otto are married?"

«In a manner of speaking, yes.»

"And you have told me this before?"

«Yes, even though I'm not supposed to; Prime Directive, and all that.»

"Wow... I wish they were my parents on Earth. Do you know Mother and Mr. Tippins are going to Malaysia, leaving Drake to 'babysit' me?"

«We're looking to fix that. Though, of course, everything has a price. One day, I hope you can forgive me for... for this entire mission. Naarlet warned me not to allow them entrance to Earth, but I did it anyway.»

"Who?"

«Naarlet Ulkvadd, our commander-in-chief.»

"No, I mean who came to Earth?"

«The Thubans.»

17

Folding his glasses, Gompsie looks out over his pond and sighs. «When the Thubans heard about Earth and demanded we give them the address, the Federation said no, but I… I wasn't so sure. The Thubans had been horrible to us, yes, but what if they wanted to come to Earth to make amends for what they'd done?» Her grandfather straightens and clears his throat. «Silly me not to realize they'd want to come here to exploit the planet; to cultivate and sell fear-frequencies for the galactic market. Evidently there's a demand for the stuff. Beats me, but they're making a profit.» He snorts and a plume of smoke escapes his nostrils. «While working behind our backs they've managed to obtain more and more of the stuff by artificially increasing the psychopathy numbers through gene-manipulation, creating a terrible situation.» The robust feathers at the end of Gompsie's tail slap the ground repeatedly. «Naarlet warned me not to let the Thubans come to Earth. But did I listen? No, I defended them. I insisted Thubans deserved a second chance. I might even have told her she was being snooty.»

"You called our commander-in-chief 'snooty'!"

«Not one of my finest moments. I still believe everybody deserves a second chance. My mistake was that I hadn't noticed they never asked.»

"Asked for what?"

«To be forgiven.»

"Oh."

«Seventy thousand four hundred and ninety-three years later I get a message from Naarlet telling me the human civilization needs help.» Gompsie taps his folded glasses against his forehead. They get stuck in one of his eyebrows and, cussing unsparingly, he yanks them out. «In all that time you'd think the Thubans would have dealt with their karma, but no, they let their souls grow stale, as stale as cheese puffs.»

"You've heard of cheese puffs?"

«I have. In one surveillance footage I saw an owl nearly choke to death.» Gompsie shudders. «Anyhow, the reason we need to clean up now is because of the zap-cloud and what the Thubans might do to the humans before it... before it...» Her grandfather looks at her quizzically. «Am I to assume you've forgotten about the zap-cloud?»

"Yup."

«Alright. The zap-cloud is a highly charged electroplasmic cloud that's floating around in this galaxy. It is approaching Earth and will undoubtedly intensify things, most notably the emotions; both positive and negative. By the way, it was Naarlet who thought to call it a 'zap-cloud.'»

“That was clever of her.”

«She is ever so proud.»

“Duly noted.”

«Now, the polarity will keep intensifying the closer Earth gets to the cloud until, in one moment, the universe can no longer hold the two polarities together and the one Earth becomes two Earths.»

“Two Earths?”

«Being a holographic universe, that's not uncommon. One planet will host those who understand the interconnectedness of things and the potency of the present moment. The other planet will be for those who wish to further explore the intricacies of Judgment, Separation, Guilt, and Shame.»

“I see… Open-hearted and closed-hearted?” Klara thinks of Mother.

«Yes. The challenge for us is to help humans make their hearts as open and joyous as possible before they get zapped. Our quota is to raise ten percent of the population to a baseline frequency of 8 Hertz.»

“Is that a lot?”

«The Earth has a baseline frequency of 7.83 Hz. It’s called the Schumann resonance in case you’ve heard that mentioned in your science class. The natural frequency of the human body is slightly lower, at around 7.5 Hz, so to raise it by 0.5 Hz may seem like a lot, however, just one hug can raise someone’s frequency a whopping 0.9 Hz. Even if hugs are temporary, you get the idea, and, as I mentioned, we only need to do ten percent of the population. If it wasn't for me allowing the Thubans to come here, it'd be a cinch.» Gompsie begins to pace and a couple of flowers duck out of his way. «To grow Fear for profit should not be allowed. We need stricter infringement laws, but not only that, it's time for the neophobic gene to be neutralized. When I bring this up with the council, they insist the neophobic gene can only be rectified by those who initiated it and those folks don't want it tampered with. What a dung mountain of bureaucracy!» Abruptly, he stops pacing and looks on as the high-strung flowers collapse. «Sorry. Got carried away.»

"What's a neophobic gene?"

«The neophobic gene makes humans suspicious of anyone looking different from themselves. It came in handy for the various groups who did gene manipulations on humans, ensuring that their various experiments didn't get contaminated by crossbreeding.»

"Did it work?"

«Ha! It worked so well the males and females wanted nothing to do with each other. If they hadn't amped up the sex drive the whole thing would have flopped.» Glancing at her sideways, her grandfather adjusts his glasses. «It was, of course, never their intention to cause all this violence. Even though, in my opinion, they should have foreseen it… But who am I to speak of foresight?» Gompsie begins to play with a reluctant tuft of grass. «Something as simple as an unfamiliar headgear can throw a human into a tizzy. Not only that, but *it's so ingrained no one ever questions the absurdity.»*

"Then why am I not scared of odd things? I mean, how come 'Klara' isn't?"

«Your neophobic gene was never activated since you went through the Arcturian gate as you incarnated. The Arcturian gate is a preparatory configuration portal specifically set up for entities who wish to incarnate on planets steeped in fear.»

"Then why doesn't everyone go through it so no one has to deal with the neophobic gene?"

«Because it makes you feel out of place during your incarnation, which can make the incarnation overly challenging. For instance, Otto and Rani did not take that route. They feel quite at home amongst humans but don't remember enough of themselves to come and visit me in their dreamstate. Of course, I visit them, but it's not the same.» Grandpa places a light hand on her shoulder. «It's a bit of a doozy, I hear, going through the gate, but I'm glad you did it as it lets you experience the nature of things more clearly.»

"It makes me cry."

«Yes?»

"Seeing how Mother and Drake fail to notice even the most obvious of wonders, like sunsets and ice-cream swirls. It doesn't seem fair."

«The universe has room for all sorts of experiences.» Her grandpa removes his hand. «And, just for the record, not all Thubans create hardship, many of them work with us and are a great resource.» His face brightens. «Noburu, for instance, he's a Thuban who's been with us for years.»

"Who's Noburu?"

«My new assistant.»

"You have a new assistant?"

«Of course, I had to find someone to take your place when you left. He came highly recommended.»

"By whom?"

«Himself. I think he's still in love with…» Her grandfather hastily looks down at the ground.

"With you?"

«No.»

"Then who?"

«I promised not to tell.» Gompsie extracts and retracts his claws a few times, then looks up. «Remember the communications specialist I mentioned?» He clears his throat. «Buxtin? Buxtin, if you have a moment, would you be so kind as to call Ma'iinac Zook to the dreamscape?» A sudden ripple runs through the park, like the stifled burp of a rhino. «Yes, Buxtin, I understand. I only hoped you wouldn't mind.» Gompsie shakes his head. «I have to treat him with tecton gloves. Sure was nice when one's equipment wasn't bio-neural and so darn opinionated.» The craft jolts. «And when it didn't eavesdrop!» Gompsie huffs. «What moron thought a conscious craft to be a good idea? I'll have to talk to Naarlet about this… unless that moron is Naarlet.»

Abruptly, the tinker-wall cracks and pops, making Gompsie wring his hands in excitement. «I believe our lady is *arriving.»*

The wall section falls open with a zung and a toad-shaped dragon emerges, his smooth-scaled purple tummy bulging between his large, clawed feet. He smiles at Gompsie and gives a small nod. The smile is wide, endowed with fangs, and would not seem courteous if not for the long whiskers, arching from under his sizable nostrils, like an aristocratic mustache.

At the sight of her, the scales below his red conical hat (looking not at all like a lampshade) deepen to a well saturated maroon. «Mz. Kalanna Boon, what a delight!»

"Kalanna? Why am I called Kalanna?"

«Kalanna is your primal self as originating from Otim Dorum. Klara is the name you were given when you incarnated on Earth.» In one grand swoop he removes his hat and Klara catches her breath for the familiarity of his eyes. Pressing his hat to his chest he bows, revealing a large birthmark, the shape of a... a singular quotation mark... a cashew?

With a twinkle in his eyes, he peers up at her. «During my life in Japan, some 16,500 Earth years ago, that birthmark inspired the famous Magatama symbol. Some people say the shape represents the moon overlapping the sun thus symbolizing the vitality of the human spirit. Not sure of the connection, but it sounds good.» He straightens and looks bemused as he whisks away some tinker flies. «What on Zoobrit happened to the mess hall, Captain?»

«Noburu, I did not expect... Klara, let me introduce my new assistant, Mq. Makoto Noburu, your first husb... someone who is still... I mean, who is most loyal to you... to us.»

With a raised eyebrow Noburu looks around. «Not bad,» he muses. «But what's with the four-legged birds?»

«Picky, picky. How about you create the dreamscape next time?»

«It would be my pleasure.» With a dapper twirl of his roundness, Noburu turns to face Klara. «Do you like Japan? We had a lovely incarnation there, you and I.» He bows, his head nearly touching the ground, and, still bowing, begins walking backwards towards the wall. Before he reaches the tinker flies, he straightens, puts his hat back on and winks. «Nice to see you again, your highness.»

Taking his glasses off, Gompsie rubs his temples.

«And Captain,» Noburu adds, «our commander-in-chief would like a word with you on the holographer.»

«When?»

«Pronto.»

«Pronto?»

«Yes, I'm fairly sure that was the word she used.»

«What rotten timing... Noburu, will you keep Klara company?»

«Of course.»

«I shouldn't be long.»

18

22,236 MILES FROM EARTH
— In a Geosynchronous Orbit —
Sunday, February 14, 12:13 a.m. EST
As Per: Captain G. Writtum

«ThIngs aRe gOing weLL?» The holographer's static reception turns Naarlet's voice into a jagged shriek and her violet complexion and green bioluminescent hair into a disturbing light show. Gompsie sighs. He is no more fond of holographers than of pigheaded spacecrafts.

«Things are fine.» Squinting his eyes, he looks for a knob to adjust the setting. «…except for a minor upset.» The knob seems to be missing. «…or two.»

«I aM AwaRe, CaPTaiN.» Above the black electromagnetic box, ragged lines of green and purple strike out, like an unhinged aurora borealis —P' KAW chsssssssssssssssssss!— The dubious contraption goes blank. «CaPTAIN WRITtum? I bElieve wE loSt ConNecTioN.»

«I wish.»

A numbing light burst and her image pops into place— sharp and clear as zim drops. «Captain Writtum, I heard that!»

«And so you did.» He wipes his eyes.

«I forgive you your insolence, Captain. No need for tears. Simply verify my intel regarding Incarnet Klara B-pcc7, if you please. It is correct that Dwinn, known to Klara as the brother Drake, had his genetic code compromised in-utero by Thubans?»

«This is correct.»

«Chromosome 2?»

«Afraid so.»

«And Kalanna incarnated—without my approval—to be a sister to Drake, foregoing the customary thirty-eight years of prep time?» A shudder goes through Naarlet—or is it static?

«This may be so, however she managed to go through the Arcturian Gate.»

«Gate or no Gate, this was wise?»

«I don't think it was wisdom that... what I mean to say is—»

«Spare me, Captain, you know full well that thirty-eight years is the minimum, the bare minimum in prep time for joining a family with Minimal Parental Guidance. You can't just jump down to Earth willy-nilly. Everyone who incarnates on Earth has to be Reared By Self. It's part of the anti-indoctrination protocol. She should have been aware. To change a system one has to remain outside of it, yet belong; goldfish in a fishbowl and all that.»

Gompsie grits his teeth. Why is she telling him this when it was he who wrote the bloody protocols! He swallows hard.

«I was not aware you had knowledge about goldfish, Commander Ulkvadd.»

«Certainly. In fact, we had a briefing about their situation not long ago. Now, I agree that the requirement for incarnets to be RBS was originally a fine idea. Our present issue is that Thubans use MPG families to magnify the toxicity of their psychopaths. Thus, not only do new incarnets have to be Reared By Self, they also have to deal with psychopathic siblings. Perhaps this was not considered when the recommendations were drafted?»

«Are you asking?»

«Of course not.» Naarlet's bioluminescent hair sways hypnotically, triggering sparks on the holographer. «We have reason to believe Dwinn may have overreached the MPG-factor, inadvertently drawing attention from Thubans.» She stops speaking.

«You're asking?»

«Of course!»

«Mother is 95.3 Red, G-major.»

«Ouch! And the father?»

«21.8 Blue, D-minor.»

«Not much life in that one.»

«He works for a biotech company that promotes environ-mental sustainability. It's good work.»

«All good work and never available to his children.» Naarlet snorts unabashedly. «You do realize that if Klara doesn't survive this parental wasteland, we will not meet our quota. This was considered?»

Gompsie takes a deep breath. «Are you… asking?»

«No! Regret to inform you, Captain Writtum, but due to Kalanna Boon's ill-considered actions, Code Nine has been implemented.»

A sudden nausea comes over Gompsie; he focuses on his breathing. «Do we have to?»

«Afraid so.»

«When?»

«It's imminent.»

Naarlet's image compacts into sharp horizontal lines, then belches and swells out again—it's not flattering.

Warily, Gompsie clears his throat. «Are we… Did we lose connection?»

«No, I do not believe so.» Her voice unexpectedly softens. «You are getting along well with your spacecraft, Captain Writtum?»

«Me and Buxtin? Absolutely. He's most compliant.»

A rumble staggers across the floor.

«He mirrors your persona, Captain, you know that?»

«Say what!»

«He mirrors—»

«I knew that…»

«Gompsie?»

«Yes?»

«My therapist tells me I should forgive you.»

«Forgive me for letting the Thubans come to Earth? I can't

tell you how—»

«For standing me up. I waited two full narp-cycles on Bertfer. Bertfer of all places! The most godforsaken lump of rock this side of the Galaxy. Even the water is terrible.» The holographic image fizzes for a moment. «All the same, I forgive you.»

«That is good?»

«Yes. You know, you and I should try again sometime— to hook up, I mean. I—»

With a pop, the holographer abruptly blinks off.

Rubbing his temples, Gompsie sinks down in his hover chair (which for once does not move out of his way). «Was that you Buxtin? Did you turn the blasted thing off?»

A soft purr vibrates through the chair.

Leaning his head against the backrest, Gompsie closes his eyes. «Glad to have you back, my friend.»

19

22,236 MILES FROM EARTH
— In a Geosynchronous Orbit —
Sunday, February 14, 1:52 a.m. EST
As Per: Klara Tippins

Noburu is not as overbearing as Klara expected. In fact, with Gompsie gone, he's half decent and she's enjoying his stories about the Japanese deity Ninigi-no-Mikoto, Ninigi's wife Konohanasakuya-hime and the couple's three sons.

«One morning, Hoori, the youngest of the brothers, persuades his older brother, Hoderi, to lend him a fishhook. As Hoori's fishing, a giant fish snaps the line and swims away with the hook. All the same, his older brother wants the hook back, so Hoori must dive to the bottom of the sea and—»

A sudden ruckus amongst the tinker flies interrupts Noburu, followed by her grandfather's laughter. He's laughing? In silence she and Noburu watch Captain Writtum teeter through the wall, rosy cheeked and giggling.

«Buxtin… oh, Buxtin… too much fun… he, he… Hello there!»

«Greetings Captain, sir. I shall be on my way then.» Noburu tips his hat.

"But what happened to Hoori?"

«Not much, Miss Klara. At the bottom of the ocean, he finds the hook and meets his true love who follows him home. Once home, Hoori discovers she's a dragon. This makes her so embarrassed she returns to the ocean, never to come back.» Noburu soberly takes her hand, kisses it, then slowly lets it go as he walks backwards towards the wall. Without another word, he tips his hat a second time and is gone.

«Alrighty then,» Grandpa Gompsie says cheerfully, giving her a tap on the back. «I have you know Buxtin and I had a breakthrough.»

"I can tell. Is there something I should know about Noburu? He seems—"

«Not at all. Perfectly normal. And thanks to Naarlet no less. Seems Buxtin has a heart after—» Without a sound, the dreamscape explodes with the unassuming scent of rosewater. «My, oh my,» her grandpa fans his heart. «I believe she has arrived. So glad I made it back, and in the crack of time!»

"It's the 'crack of dawn' or the 'nick of time,'" Klara clarifies.

«Yes, yes, but look!» Gompsie points to the center of the silicon pond where a stately woman appears amid cascading fountains. With long white hair that flits around her shoulders like a unicorn's mane, she's not only stunning in her own right but has the good fortune to wear a dress that adores her; the gown's train trailing behind her by many fathoms as she glides towards them. «Just so you know,» Gompsie whispers, «she always speaks of herself in plural.»

"What?"

«I wouldn't bring it up if I were you.»

Still a long way from shore, the Pleiadian stops and tugs at her dress, her garment letting out squeals of terror.

Gompsie grabs Klara's hand. «My apologies Ma' Zook. Apparently, Earth is not as synthetic as I presumed. My… Lieutenant Boon informed me as much.»

«That is quite all right, Captain,» Ma'iinac calls back. «A mistake well understood.»

By the time she reaches the shore, water drips from her chin and nose. Her dress—her magnificent dress—is ripped and seems visibly upset.

Smiling placidly, Ma'iinac bows her head, her wet hair straining against her back. «A delight to meet you, Mz. Boon.» She takes Klara's hand, then tuns it over and examines it. «Oh dear…» Placing a damp hand on Klara's head, she closes her eyes and draws a deep breath in, exhaling with a quiver. «Yes.» Her eyes twitch. «We shall perform a Comemeya healing. The healing, Mz. Boon, will gift you a necklace for the enhancement of your communication, both in regards to reception as well as expression, thus lessening the impact of the upcoming trial.»

"Trial? What trial?"

Looking at Gompsie, Ma'iinac blinks repeatedly. «You have not told her?» It's more of an inquiry than an accusation. «Following the Prime Directive, I presume.» Solemnly, she clasps her hands to her heart, then holds them out, revealing a hovering cluster of translucent blue orbs, vibrantly spinning.

Taking the largest orb, she places it over Klara's heart. A second one, almost as large, is placed at the base of Klara's neck. One by one, smaller orbs are added, creating a twirling incandescent necklace.

«Mz. Boon, please be advised that once you have reentered the Earth-plane, you will need a focused intent to activate the Comemeya necklace.»

"To help me communicate with my grandpa?"

«No, not him. With your primal self. The necklace will help you remember who you are.»

"And I will notice the necklace when I wake up from this dream?"

«No. The orbs' frequencies are not of Earthly origin. No one on Earth will see them.»

"But I'll remember they're there?"

«Afraid not.»

"I see." Klara looks down. "They're pretty though."

Ma'iinac places a hand under Klara's chin, this hand is dry and wispy. «The most important thing to remember, Mz. Boon, is to be kind. As stated in the Isha Upanishad: The Self that dwells within is hidden, not shown. It can only be known to those who have released their fears and their false selves;

those who have learned to see with their heart.»

Klara bites her lip. "And when I see with my heart, I'll be kind to all people?"

"I would think so!» Ma' iinac looks pleased.

"What about people who hate me, who take my kindness and use it against me? Am I to be kind to them as well?"

«Kindness may not be what you imagine, Mz. Boon. Giving to those who use your gifts poorly is like feeding sugar to a diabetic, or alcohol to an alcoholic; doing so is not kind. You have to be discerning and use patience, insight, and tact. If you meet their anger with anger, they win; if they crush you with their anger, they win. Defeat their unkindness—not by combat, but by changing the rules.» The Pleiadian communications specialist smooths out her gown and smiles as the dress gives out a sigh. «And, Mz. Boon, do not be afraid that your brother's hatred will harden you. When you are kind, your mind is serene, and hatred has nothing to offer a serene mind.»

Glancing at her grandpa, Klara clears her throat. "Ma'iinac Zook, why do you refer to yourself as 'we'?"

«An 'I' would be focused in a singular dimension, Mz. Boon. Our focus is not singular. You are not singular either. You have your focus in many lifetimes, in many dimensions, however you are only, at this moment, aware of this one focus. We are aware of our many focuses.»

"Thank you."

«Anytime.» Ma'iinac Zook crosses her arms over her heart,

smiles warmly, cocks her head, and is gone.

Taking in the lingering smell of rosewater, Klara and her grandpa stand there for a moment.

«Are you ready to go back?» he asks.

"Of course not," she replies. "Though I might be if you give me another hug?"

«Always.»

Engulfed in her grandpa's embrace, she grabs him tight as she's hurled through layer upon layer of inter-dimensional space.

—Kalanna!— she faintly hears him calling —Tell Luna I'm so sorry—

20

PLANET EARTH
— Terra Firma —
44,5956°N, 75,1691°W
Sunday, February 14, 1:53 a.m. EST
As Per: Klara Tippins

A sharp jolt and Klara found herself in the confines of a body… her body? The heart clutched itself, it was hard to breathe. With a gasp she woke—a dream still clawing at her. Something important—Luna!

Where was Luna?

She lit the lamp on her night table and looked around. No Luna by her pillow. She threw off the covers—No Luna. Crouching on the floor she looked under her bed, then behind the curtains then under the bookcase and dresser. The door was closed so Luna had to be there—except—she wasn't. It made no sense… Grabbing the flashlight, she set out to search the apartment.

No Luna in the bathroom.

She checked her parent's bedroom even though she doubted Luna would be there. The bed was untouched. No

Luna under the bed.

"Luna!"

Drake's door was closed. His music was either muted or he wore earphones—most likely earphones. Best leave him alone. At least for now.

No Luna in Mr. Tippins office. No Luna in the kitchen. No Luna on the living room couch or anywhere in the—

Looking through the glass door to the balcony, something caught her attention; a dark creature on the snow-covered balcony floor, bracing itself against the wind. Or was it debris?

As Klara approached, Owl looked up startling her; his huge wings spread oddly across the floor, his black eyes fixed on hers. Was he hurt? She walked closer and he took off. He was okay, yet her heart stopped when she realized he'd sheltered something… something white and wispy and small.

"LUNA!!"

Jerking the door open, arctic winds whipped her. The little one with a nose so white… so very, very white. She drew her close but nothing stirred and she rushed inside, found Mr. Tippins' blanket and wrapped her in it—still no movement. No chirpy little sounds. No heartbeat. Nothing. The nose remained as white as…

Rocking back and forth at the edge of the couch she burrowed her face in the blanket, willing life back. There was no response. Nothing but nothingness.

Oh god this could not be…

"What the hell did you do!" A brother stormed in, the soles of his slippers slapping against the wooden floor — slap, slap, slap — like meat pounders. "You killed it? For god's sake don't tell me you killed it, you moron."

The sound of a key turning a deadbolt. Clatter and cheerful voices ambling towards her, disjointed and nonsensical.

"What are you two doing up?" a mother's voice rang out. It sounded tipsy.

The brother: "Klara killed the dog."

A father: "What!" The father walked towards Klara.

The mother: "Not with your shoes on, honey."

The father: "What happened?"

The brother: "She must have let the dog out. I didn't know until I heard her scream."

The mother: "Is the dog dead? Shit! Frida will kill me!" The mother stumbled into a doorway. "Bruce, make sure it gets out of here before it stinks!"

The father gently opened the bundle, sighed and closed it again. An arm wrapped around her. "I'm sure you didn't mean for this to happen."

"The owl tried to save her." The words might have been hers.

"Of course." The father removed a strand of hair from her face. "I'll get the cooler and you'll make it nice for her. She'll be safe in the cooler."

"Owl won't hurt her."

"Of course not."

The father left and came back, placing a small cooler by Klara's feet. Clutching the bundle to her face, she drew in the solace of wet warm wool. Though the wool was warm—the bundle didn't stir.

The brother was in the kitchen now, talking to the parents. She heard him tell them how she must have walked in her sleep. Such tragedy. He sounded so sad it made her wonder.

But she didn't walk in her sleep… did she?

Pulling back a corner of the blanket, she kissed the tousled fur on Luna's head, then gently placed the bundle in the cooler and sat, staring, waiting for when she'd be able to close the lid.

In the end it was the father who closed the lid. He was the one to carry the cooler out on the balcony; the one to guide her to her room. Once in bed, he wrapped her bedding around her and left her sitting, leaning against pillows.

She did not lie down. If she laid down, she'd drown.

A light knock on the door and Drake peeked in wearing his soft brotherly face. *Oh god, not the soft face…*

"May I?" Without waiting for a reply, he strolled to her bed and sat down, leaving her door wide open. He didn't say anything, but even with her head turned away, she could feel him studying her. This was the suffocating phase of the Brotherly Talk. This would last until she turned and faced him.

"I am sorry, Klara." Without wavering, his probing eyes urged her to succumb. On a normal day she'd play along. On a normal day she'd steel herself and submissively meet his gaze while quietly reciting the Periodic Table.

But not tonight. Tonight, she couldn't give him the servitude he craved. Tonight, he would never leave and she would die here in her bed.

"Remember today when you lost your key?" His voice halting and meek, he spoke as if to a wounded animal. "I know I tease you, but the fact is… normal people don't do that. Normal people don't lose keys. Our parents don't. I don't. Have you ever known us to lose our keys? Of course not. Mom and dad won't tell you, but…

"…you're chronologically damaged."

Chronologically damaged?…

In the midst of it, Klara almost burst out laughing. He meant 'psychologically' damaged. Like what Otto had said. *Good grief!*

"And now you walk in your sleep," her brother trudged on. "I fear you're only getting worse. Just imagine how upset Pontus and Auntie will be when they find out you killed their dog."

In one instant her world crumbled and she snatched into the smallest of breaths, desperate to disappear. Then, a voice in her head: *Those who know themselves to be all beings…* all beings—she was not this tiny. She wasn't tiny at all!

"ENOUGH!" she bolted. "GET OUT OF MY ROOM!" For

a moment, Drake seemed lost. "NOW!!!" she bellowed.

At the door he turned, looking unconvincingly abhorrent. "You're crazy, you know that? You really are crazy."

Then he was gone and the bed caught her, for now she could not sit anymore. And maybe her tears would never stop, and maybe she would drown.

21

Klara did not drown. Instead she blew her nose. She was tired. Very tired. There was not a bone in her body that did not beg for sleep. All the same, she was not sleeping.

The sound of their front door closing caught her attention—so soft, it was more like a puff of ether than an actual sound. She listened intently but heard nothing more. Not even a wind from outside.

She'd nearly dozed off when something rammed into her window. Bolting upright, she discovered it was Owl; his beak frantically tapping the glass, his massive wings thrashing against the window. Their eyes met. Then he was gone.

Pulling her window open, Klara watched as Owl circled the courtyard, round and round on soft wings. "Thank you," she called out. "It was kind of you to—" She cut herself short as she caught sight of a man walking towards the Eastern gate. What an odd hour to be out walking. With tilted body and rigid stride, he seemed almost robotic.

… Mr. Tippins? No, not Mr. Tippins. The person was too short and too wide to be Mr. Tippins.

… Drake?

She rubbed her eyes and looked again. It *was* Drake. Drake walking outside in the middle of the night, wearing nothing but his robe and slippers. Crazy! His robe wasn't even tied. Was *he* sleepwalking?

She might not like her brother, but she wasn't going to let him freeze to death. With a quick move, she closed the window and grabbed her flashlight. In the entryway she put on her snowsuit and boots, tied her pixie hat tight, and dashed out the door.

The lampposts in the courtyard were lit and Owl was easy to spot, his silhouette stark atop a statue. Expanding his wings, he gazed at her, then majestically swooped down and, skimming the snow-covered ground, coasted towards the Eastern gate.

"Good evening," said the Eastern Gate. "And who have we here?"

"I believe it's morning," said Klara. "Just very early."

"As you wish," said the gate.

Crooked and rusty, the iron gate stood wide open in the deep snow. "Hot damn," Klara remarked appreciatively, "for a sleepwalker, Drake sure got muscle."

Turning on her flashlight, she could see footprints trail off into the woods. She thought of his worn slippers and his thin pajama pants. Additionally, she thought of her knees, and how far she'd have to pull them up to make it through such deep snow. Pondering further, she dared to venture the crust might hold her and that, trodding carefully, she could skim the surface all the way to the woods.

Inside her mittens she crossed her fingers.

Step one—Did not hold.

Step two—She surveyed the terrain but found no signs of wolves, bears, or trolls. Just trees. Tall looming pine trees cordially huddled together—also, no sounds.

Step three—It sure was silent. Hopefully Drake hadn't gone far.

Step eight—She could see why no one walked this way. Only eight steps in and the snowy silence had snuck into her bones, laid her bare, and never even asked. Quite clearly, this kind of silence demands a quiet heart and her heart was anything but quiet. She wiped her nose against her sleeve.

Step nine—Maybe she should have woken her parents.

… Step two hundred thirty-eight and the sky suddenly pulsed with an orange glow. City lights? But why were they pulsing?

Up ahead Owl hooted and she hurried her steps, straining to keep the flashlight above the snow as she stumbled. Then, sprawled on her tummy, she looked ahead.

It wasn't the town that made the sky orange.

It wasn't the town at all.

Gently rocking, the circular craft hovered some ten feet off the ground with orange lights streaming underneath, round and round, in a soothing, eerie-kind-of-way.

As Klara moved closer, her face prickled. Closer still and her chest began to reverberate to where it was cumbersome to breathe. Looking to the ground it seemed the bedrock should be windswept but wasn't. Instead, Drake's footprints could clearly be seen leading to the craft.

With a sudden—*woosh*—the lights spun faster. The craft wobbled and rose.

"Don't you dare leave with my brother!" Heedlessly and without a second thought, she projected onto the ship.

The first thing she noticed was the disproportionately large head, then the spindly arms and the three long fingers. The Grey ET sat alone in some kind of control room. He did not notice her at first—and then he did.

«What are you doing here!» he shouted into her head. «We are within protocol.» He pushed a button on the console in front of him. Soundlessly a door slid open and a second being appeared: slightly taller and with the skinniest of skinny hips. The two beings reminded Klara of the sort of ETs people dress up as: the Roswell Greys. And though neither one appeared to be wearing any clothes, they also did not seem naked.

«What is *that* doing here!» The newcomer looked straight at her. «Evaporate!»

Evaporate?

Without turning her head she looked around, then pulled back as she caught her reflection. Holy petunia, no wonder she could see without turning—She was an orb! A bright luminous orb that, not only could see all around, but could also perceive feelings. The Greys, they were afraid of her …of *her*? No reason to 'evaporate' then, was there?

Moving effortlessly through a nearby wall, she found herself in the back of a theater with row upon row of Greys sitting with their backs to her, intently watching a screen. A theater of all things. Clearly, this ship was larger on the inside than the outside. And there, on a narrow stage, was her brother with his untied robe, wearing a helmet with tiny nibs that blinked on and off.

And what were they watching… a home movie? She looked closer and realized they were watching the hallway of the Tippins' apartment… What the heck! And there *she* was. On screen. Soundly asleep with Luna by her side.

Who had taped this?

And when?

On screen, Luna quizzically perked her head up. Klara, next to her, did not stir. A hand grabbed Luna—Drake's hand?

… Wait? Drake taped this! With his cellphone?

Drake on screen reached out his other hand… both hands? So there was no phone…

While Luna on screen was muzzled, Klara's eyes were drawn to the stage where the lights on Drake's helmet blinked ecstatically. This was no movie, was it? This was the Greys tapping into his memory…

Stunned, Klara watched as Luna was brought to the balcony and placed on the snowy floor, winds lashing her fur. The door closed. It closed… Frantically, Luna scratched the glass, but the door did not open, instead Klara could hear Drake on screen chuckle.

The screen went black and the Greys applauded.

They applauded! How could they celebrate such cruelty! Klara felt suddenly nauseous.

At the opposite end from where Drake stood, a door slid open and a fiercely muscular creature swaggered onto the stage. Clearly reptilian, he had red scales and exuded a musky odor that made her queasier still. With a twinge, she felt his mind encroach on hers. He pointed a clawed finger at her. «Seize it!» he bellowed.

As effortlessly as she'd left her body, just as effortlessly she was pulled back in. Unfortunately, the body had been left on the bedrock and she couldn't get the chilled limbs to work.

In a panic she called out, feeling talons dig into her shoulders as Owl swung her to her feet. She turned towards the ship and, on shaky legs, braced herself as the ramp lowered and the scaly one stormed out; his muscular feet hammering the swaying ramp as he raced towards her. She screamed at her body to run, to move, her heart pounding to where there was no room to breathe. Was this her end?

Incredulously, at the bottom of the ramp, he stopped.

Glaring venomously at the snow, he let out a hideous string of growls and hisses, then turned theatrically and lumbered back up, his short tail twitching as her brother squeezed by.

Drake, with robe untied and no helmet, stepped onto the ground. The ramp retreated, the orange lights spun, the craft shuddered—and was gone.

"HOW DARE YOU!" She bellowed. "How dare you blame me, when YOU killed her! YOU'RE A DESPICABLE... SORRY LUMP OF A CREATURE!"

Drake charged and she ran. No longer paralyzed, she bolted into the dense night, the deep snow pulling at her. Then lights—actual city lights.

Somewhere above, Owl made a racket, screeching and hissing. A push from behind. Her hands grasped... nothing...

She heard the trees mumble. Then a sickening crack of her head. An explosion of pain and—

22

22, 236 MILES FROM EARTH
— In a Geosynchronous Orbit —
Sunday, February 14, 4:02 a.m. EST
As Per: Klara Tippins

All around, the air exudes love.

Not the kind you give and receive, but the kind that breathes with you; the one that structures life itself.

Also, it smells of basil…

Did she die?

Opening her eyes makes no difference. The room is dark. As her eyes adjust, she recognizes the lustrous walls of her grandfather's study. But where is her grandfather?

Sudden voices outside his room. One deep, like whale song and somewhat familiar, the other crisp and light—her grandfather's.

«Did you get a hold of Mz. Zook?» her grandpa asks.

«Indeed,» replies the whale voice. «Said she'd be here in a few of those… what do they call them… minutes? Maybe ten.»

«Do you have any intel on what happened?»

«Apparently the owl did a fantastic job mitigating the fall. Says he managed to fling the body onto a ledge.»

«This is a two-pound owl we're talking about?»

«Correct.» The whale voice seems to clear his throat.

«And he... flung... the body?»

«Those were his words, sir.»

«Very well. Go on.»

«The owl predicted extensive head injuries and summoned Rani, who brought Klara's unconscious body to a hospital where it remains, still unconscious.»

«Are they severe?»

«The injuries? Rani is providing healings. However, one can presume Klara's dreambody has been traumatized— Perhaps it's best I go in.»

«I'm her grandfather and the captain of this vessel.»

«I'm less goofy looking. This is no time to frighten her.»

... ...

«What of the Japanese dreamscape?" her grandfather asks. «Did you finish it?»

«All, except for the lake.»

«There's a lake? Ma'iinac Zook is not to appear on a lake, is she?»

«She likes a grand entrance.»

«We shall skip the lake.»

«Altogether?»

«Altogether.»

«I created a teahouse next to the lake. It's nearly settled

and should be fine,» the whale persists.

«Skip that too.»

«It's lovely.»

«All the same.»

«I planned a tea ceremony…»

«I say no.»

Soft shuffling, followed by a succession of rapid clicks and she notices the aroma change—still familiar, still sweet, though not quite basil. A morning dawns and she makes out a steep decline. Cautiously, she moves away from the edge; and not just an edge—she is standing on top a mountain peak. Breathtaking. And how peculiar that she can't remember this place, yet she knows it. Like a song she knows by heart the moment she hears it—too important not to belong to her. And what of the sacred dance between the wispy mist and the steadfast mountains, between knobby trees and their delicate flowers… What do you call that?

«You call it Japan.»

She twirls around and nearly trips. It's Noburu! Noburu looking dashing in a black layered kimono. "You're the whale song!" She looks at her feet—no wonder they feel wobbly— she's wearing clog-flip-flops! Not only that, she's in a tight kimono! Excitedly, she pats her head. Sure enough, her wild locks are arranged into a tidy Geisha hairdo full of trinkets. She does a little dance and nearly trips again.

«I've been named many things, but never 'a whale song'… are you alright? I mean after what happened.» With a wide sleeve he gestures towards a blossoming cherry tree under which an old wooden bench has appeared. «How about we sit down?»

Though the bench is only a short distance away, the roots are large and numerous—this will be interesting. A chickadee lands on top of her hair-extravaganza, then flutters on to settle among the blossoms, the blooms greeting it with flickers and cheers. Was that a pep talk?
"If I trip, you'll catch me, won't you?"
«Sure,» he chuckles, «on a good day.»
She tries to turn and glare at him, but, alas, kimonos are not good for glaring.

With a multitude of tiny steps, she flounders forward— step step step step step step step—reaching the bench both rumpled and in tears. "It's all so much," she blurts out. "First Luna dies, my dog... well, Pontus' dog. Then I find out my brother killed her. And he tried to trick me to believe I did it! I only discover the truth 'cause I follow him onto a spacecraft with Greys and watched him do it and I got chased by a devil. I don't know why, but I think the Greys were scared of me. Bah—scared of me and not the devil!"
«Of course you scared them. Your aura was probably bigger than their entire ship!» Noburu looks at her affectionately and sits down on the ground next to her.
"But I was a tiny orb."

«All the more reason for them to be frightened. Showing yourself as an orb means you've come to recognize yourself as a spark of the eternal.»

"But I have not done that."

«A part of you has. The orb you saw was the conscious fraction of creation that holds your unique experience as manifested into form through a singularity, the very singularity that makes up our universe. You see, reality—»

"I'm sorry Noburu, I don't think this is a time for metaphysics, I can't—"

The mountains hum softly then and, as her mind relaxes, bright discs appear above a ridge. Immensely slim, they lay stacked one on top of the other in seemingly infinite numbers. Whichever disc she looks at grows brighter. Reflexively, she knows what they are—They're alternate versions of reality.

Klara unfolds her arms and laughs. "The world is flat after all!" Looking down at her okobo shoes, she notices the red straps and how nice they look against her white toe-socks and the yellow fabric of her kimono. She lets the wooden flip-flops clunk against each other, finding the sound comforting – thomp, thomp, thomp – "So… I mean… why flat?"

«Because they're static.»

"They're static… why static?"

«I thought you didn't want to—»

"I don't. I mean, I'm not here very often and… I was just wondering."

«Remember the Bindu?»

"The tiny particle that's the unmanifested state of cosmos?"

«That's the one. You see, not only is it the smallest particle in existence, it's also the fastest. Moving so fast, in fact, that it can be in all places at once. Like snapshots: POW! this configuration of reality, POW! that configuration, one static layer after another. Static, you see, as any movement would create a new configuration. Formation upon formation upon formation.» Noburu moves his arms to illustrate, his sleeves creating quite a breeze. «Time, or rather the illusion of time, is thus created as consciousness travels through these layers, these potential realities, leaving emotional impressions on the soul as memories.»

"Memories?"

«Of course. And to forget things is to no longer resonate with its imprint. In fact, we can use this to our advantage and intentionally let things go. When we do, some elements of our reality will be different, or disappear altogether.»

"Disappear?"

«By the way, when you run into someone you've traveled with through the discs, you think of them as soul-mates or, more apropos, as surf-mates—like Pontus.»

"What!"

«As stated in the Isha Upanishad: 'Stiller than still, yet swifter than swift, It cannot be comprehended by the mind for It is perpetually ahead of the mind, creating and sustaining the physical world.'» Noburu smiles. «Do you know who wrote that?»

"The authors are unknown."

«Not to me they're not.» He gently takes her hands. «It was you who wrote that.»

"Me…?"

«Indeed, your highness, you are wiser than you know.»

23

In fits and starts, the air in front of Klara forms itself into a bright column. A huge bulb is added on top… Grandpa?

«Schnatdoodle and ficklestix!» exclaims the light-phenomena, sounding like her grandfather. «How am I supposed to do this?»

«Captain Gompsie!» exclaims Noburu. «You came!»

«… Or not! Having trouble manifesting into your dream-scape. What if… shoosh, that did not work! Oh, hi, Klara! Hold on… I think I got it.» A sudden flicker. «Nope…»

«Captain, sir, you might want to—»

A bright flash interrupts and there he is: nine feet tall, too bright for words, and swaying somewhat. An exquisite rush of chimes tingle down Klara's spine at the sight of him.

«Hello, Klara.» His voice is non-local and, like the chimes, reverberates within her. «I am your grandfather. And your captain, I am also your captain.» His brightness dissipates, or is she adjusting? «You did an excellent job, Noburu.» He squints at the bird still in the tree. «Two legs and everything!»

Noburu bows politely. «Very kind of you to say, sir.»

«And your garments! My goodness, you thought of everything.» Behind the captain, countless light-beings gather. «I asked for reinforcement. If the light bothers you, Klara, I can ask them to tone it down.» He looks inquiringly at her.

"No... no, it's fine." She wants to say more but the love emanating from the beings chokes her up. They smile. ALL of them. Oh, this is awkward.

Her grandfather continues to study her. «You look splendid, my dear. Not at all what I expected. What did you do, meet your maker?»

"Sort of. I saw discs of possible realities, stacked like pancakes."

Gompsie rubs his chin. «Ah, the fields of information that project your holographic reality... I suppose they could be pancakes.»

"Noburu said that as you travel through the layers, you can make things disappear, like, maybe I could get rid of my brother?"

«You want to get rid of Drake?»

"Hypothetically, how would I do it?"

«Let me think... the first thing to understand is that, even though the singularity builds physical reality, it's not the creator; much like paint is not the artist. In fact, the Bindu is the only thing in existence without consciousness.»

"I know paint. I have oil paints and an easel."

«Good. Do you paint?»

"I mean to."

«Hmm… So, the Bindu is not the creator—consciousness is. And consciousness—as you—have thoughts and feelings which dictate which pancake you will be on in any one moment. To not be on the same pancakes as your brother, you'd have to let go of your angry feelings towards him, let go of your fears of him, and let go of your expectations of getting hurt by him. It's that simple. Letting go of all the things that bind you to him will put you in a state of reasonable harmony and, since your brother is never in harmony, circumstances will keep you apart. You'd be incompatible.»

"We already are."

«Yes, but the Universe would agree.»

"Are you saying that if I loathe my brother, he'll be in my face, but if I accept him, I won't have to deal with him?"

«This is correct.»

"And if I'm frightened and believe no one loves me, I'll be alone, but when I'm strong, everyone will be there for me?"

«So glad you understand.»

"I'm not understanding, Grandpa, I'm being facetious."

«Klara, the universe isn't trying to be troublesome; it's how it works is all. You won't see your brother when you're accepting, because he's not accepting. And when you think no one loves you, those who do can't reach you. The universe isn't ornery; you've simply forgotten how it works.»

"But—"

Her grandfather raises his enormous brows. «Reach for

kindness, Klara. Be compassionate; both towards others and towards yourself. Compassion is your best defense, always. Besides, I hope you can see that being Drake is not much fun.»

"Sure it is."

«It may seem like fun, but trust me, being nasty is… nasty. You get to be the catalyst for everyone else's growth, while you yourself are stuck—and not a word of thanks.»

"I'm still not feeling it."

«What are you not feeling?»

"Sympathy."

Her grandfather's shoulders slump. «Klara, sweetheart, I am so sorry. How about a group hug?»

"Grandpa, I didn't mean—"

«Everyone,» he calls out to the light-beings, «please step forward.»

Klara braces herself.

24

Panting and wheezing is heard below the ledge and Gompsie averts his eyes. Noburu takes a deep breath, adjusts his wide kakuobi belt and steps forward while Klara follows and peers down the mountainside from behind him.

There, amid a cloud of dust, a giant ice-cream-swirl-of-a-hairdo bobs towards them. «Ma'iinac Zook!» Noburu calls out. «Glad you made it!»

Looking flushed, yet smelling of rosewater, Ma'iinac heaves herself over the edge, her hair in tatters; one single chime and two strings of flustered petals scarcely hanging on. Blowing the flowers out of her face, she sighs and, with the help of her closed parasol, pushes herself to a standing position. With a rigid bow of the head, she acknowledges Noburu, causing her hair to flop forward, then back, then off to the side, where it rests, the wind chime tinkling with fright. «Our apologies,» she says, tenderly patting her yellow obi-belt which staunchly holds her disheveled kimono together. «The original idea was to glide across a lake, however, our plan changed when we were informed the time-space-sfuxus for the frequential water had not been solnified.»

«Quite so.» Noburu bows.

«Walking is good. No complaints. It was just very... uphill.» She forces her parasol open causing dust to cascade around it. While it rasps and gasps, she hands it to Noburu. «Position this device, if you will, above Mz. Boon's head. We aim to do an assessment of her luminosity.» She motions for Klara to move closer. «The chromaticity of the auric field has most definitely been compromised.» Ma'iinac pensively taps the tip of her nose as she looks Klara over, then steps back and places her hands on her hips. «We believe, most firmly, that it is time for tea.»

Gompsie gulps. «'Most firmly,' you say?»

Noburu beams. «An excellent idea!»

Turning away from the edge, they inch their way down a gentle slope crowded with chatty shrubbery, Noburu at the lead.

"I'm pretty sure these aren't hiking boots," Klara grumbles.

«I'm pretty sure I can't hear you,» Noburu chuckles.

They find the teahouse nestled amongst lush greenery at the edge of a dry lake. It looks odd with the water missing, though the house itself is lovely. Made of dark wood and white paper, «it's built to depict the fine balance between spirit and matter,» Noburu explains.

Leaving her shoes outside, Klara crawls through a low door and ends up in a small room where light sifts through *paper making the space free of shadows.*

A cast-iron kettle dominates the space, a sculpted ladle delicately balancing on its rim, a row of small teacups neatly arranged beside it on silky straw mats.

Noburu is last to enter, the door making a 'clacky' sound as he closes it behind him. He bows to the door, walks over to the kettle, bows to it, then turns and bows to the group. «Welcome, friends.» Graciously, he sits down on his knees, a fantastic feat considering his anatomy. «Everybody, on your knees please, and keep your backs straight.» He looks at Gompsie and nods, then pulls a napkin from his belt and, with the fluid motions of a magician, folds it and places it beside him. «Attending a Japanese tea ceremony is more than just sitting down for tea, it's about doing simple tasks with utmost care, finding harmony, purity and tranquility within.» Barely touching the objects, he then begins to prepare the tea. Having turned a cup clockwise three times he hands it to Ma'iinac. Ma'iinac gives it to Klara together with a small cookie.

«The wagashi cookie first,» she whispers. «The tea is bitter. Together they will help you rest.»

Klara turns to her grandfather. "How long will I rest?"

He pats her hand. «Take as much of the stuff as you need.»

Her dream will soon end, she notes, and she will leave them. These beings gathered just for her, creating this teahouse from the loveliness of their hearts. She looks at her tea. In contrast to the gray cup, it's shockingly green. The pink cookie is soft and pasty. They all watch as she takes a bite. Bland at first, the flavor quickly morphs into something complex. As she takes a sip of tea, her eyes water and her mind gets foggy—the tea is bitter. Gently her thoughts melt away, along with her bitterness, until all that remain is—rest.

25

PLANET EARTH
— Terra Firma —
44,5956°N, 75,1691°W
Tuesday, February 16, 10:27 a.m. EST
As Per: Klara Tippins

Waking up was brutal. Although her head rested on a pillow it felt hollow and strained and her face was silly putty. The nose functioned, but all smells were wrong: no wet wool, crushed pepper, or red marker—just prickly residues from a sterile world. She thought to open her eyes, but her eyelids tugged on her brain so bad she decided to keep them closed— indefinitely… or till someone brought her water.

She tried to sneak back to where she'd been, but even if she'd remembered where that was, the sounds would not let her. Random and obtrusive, they were too loud, too long between the loudnesses, and always out of context. Klara quickly dubbed them 'lost clanks.' No soothing birdsong or wind, just the occasional clank, along with the occasional chatter—always at a distance.

Though not *all* at a distance. Close by was a stream of

melodic snores, highlighted with birdlike chirps. Though tempted, she stoically ignored them until, inevitably, curiosity took over and she begrudgingly opened one pained eye.

It was Mother; Mother sleeping in a hospital chair over by the wall clutching the beaded handle of a purse, her legs spread in an unladylike fashion. With her head slumped to one side, drool dribbled down her chin, soundlessly dappling her skirt.

There was a window in the room, but the shades were drawn and Klara couldn't tell if it was nighttime, daytime, or morning. It felt strange not to know. And why were greeting cards propped up on the windowsill? And flowers? Whose hospital room was this? And why on earth was Kalanna there wearing a red scarf? Suddenly tears stung her eyes, her throat tickled and she needed water.

On the hospital table next to her bed was a styrofoam cup with lipstick marks along the edge—no liquid.

She would not cough and wake up Mother, this was a given, but maybe a timid clearing of the windpipes would do…

And then… maybe not. Klara coughed and laughed as the timidness quickly turned into the absurd squawkings and gruntings of a piglet being thrown into a henhouse.

Mother, understandably, shrieked, causing nurses and doctors to come rushing.

Not one of them brought water.

Finally, a nurse named Andrew gave Klara a cup and the water was so, so good. Who would have thought hospitals had the best water?

After checking her vital signs, the doctors asked if she knew who she was. "I'm a holographic prism in the kaleidoscope of life," she told them. They all laughed and wanted to know who she was 'other than that.' She told them and, after answering a few more of their questions, they cheerfully left the room.

"It's just awful that you ended up in the hospital." Mother drew a sharp breath in, shuddering as she forced the air out. She was pale and poised in a structurally unstable way and did not look well. "It's been dreadful with you here. People calling. Having to tell the same story over, and over again, for—what is it—two days now?"

"It's been two days?" Klara realized she hadn't questioned being in a hospital. It'd seemed expected. How strange...

Mother stood up, snapped the curtains open (it was morning) then walked over to Klara and kissed her on the cheek, nearly hitting Klara on the head with her purse. "What in heaven's name were you doing in the woods?" She patted Klara's hand absently, the way Klara had seen her pat salt into fish. "Were you sleepwalking again, sweetie?"

"Again?"

"Oh dear, you don't remember?" Mother let go of Klara's hand and walked to her chair. "They told me this could happen." Grabbing the armrests, she dragged the thing all the way to Klara's bed, without a doubt making the most aggravating noise in the entire building. After positioning it in some kind of perfect angle, she plopped down, grasped her purse and began twiddling the handle like a rosary. "Remember Luna?"

"Of course."

"She froze to death on the balcony. It seems…" Mother picked up a discarded candy wrapper from the floor and looked around.

"I did not walk in my sleep."

"But sweetheart, you must have. How else would Luna end up on the balcony?—Don't they have trash bins here?" With a sigh, Mother stuffed the wrapper into her abandoned styrofoam cup. "Anyhow, our dear Drake is all broken up, says he should have suspected." She took a firm hold of her purse. "Of course, no one blames you." Mother screeched her chair closer. "Ms. Runty? That silly woman said an owl led her to you. Can you believe it? An owl!" She shook her head. "That old crone is not quite right in the head." Again, Mother fiddled the handle. "And your dad, he too has lost it. Told me Drake's slippers were wet. 'So wet,' he says, 'there were puddles all around them'. What's that supposed to mean? Crazy thing is, he no longer wants our dear Drake to look after you. Says you're to stay with Runty or we're not going to Malaysia. Have you heard of such nonsense? I've insisted he tell me why, but he says I don't want to know. Ridiculous, of course I want to know!"

While Mother fiddled her handle, Klara, on her part, wanted to shout with joy. Her life—her entire future would include Rani! To hide her jubilation she grabbed a pillow, covered her face…

… and promptly fell asleep.

How long had she slept? Though no one talked, someone besides Mother was in the room. Without stirring, Klara squinted her eyes open. It was Mr. Tippins—Sir Tippins, sitting by the wall in the hospital chair, his chainmail armor partly visible from behind a newspaper.

Mother, meanwhile, was pacing the room, a steaming cup in her hand. "I am not going over to that ompous brother of mine." She paused and managed a tiny sip through her pinched lips.

Mr. Tippins yanked open his open newspaper. "You mean pompous, don't you; or do you mean onerous?" No smoke rose from behind the paper. Probably smoking wasn't allowed.

"Excuse me!"

"Oh, *ompous*," he backpedaled. "The onerous pompous ones."

"Yes…" Mother paced again. "That goes for his sister, too."

"Who incidentally is your sister as well."

"Stop correcting me. I know what's what and to be frank, I don't care if our plane crashes and I never said my goodbyes to that no-good brother of mine and his no-good sister with her half-breed."

With a humph, Sir Tippins wrestled his newspaper into a mad bundle and slammed it against the armrest. Disfigured, it flopped to the floor. Mother looked shocked; so did Sir Tippins. He took a deep breath. "His name is Pontus." The words came with the exhale. "Isn't it time you let bygones be bygones?"

For a moment Mother's universe seemed to teeter, then it imploded: "WHAT!" Twirling on her heel, she showered tea all over Sir Tippins' chainmail cardigan. "Forgive that slut of a sister for sleeping with a savage!"

Sir Tippins looked at his soiled cardigan, then at the crumbled newspaper. Grimly, he worked his way out of the chair and stretched his legs. Picking up the mangled paper, he snapped it into a semblance of shape, whipped it under his arm, and, with his knight's cape flapping, left the room.

As soon as he was gone, Mother burst out laughing. "What on Earth got into that man!" Then she noticed Klara being awake. "And a late morning to you, sleepyhead. I was talking, then—Boink!—you were out."

Klara took a big swallow of her lovely water. "What day is it?"

"Tuesday."

"And I've been here two days, you said?"

"I know! Thank goodness you woke up when you did. We're leaving next Saturday and who knows what we'd have done if you'd still been sleeping." Mother peered into her cup, sighed, and placed it on Klara's table. "You'll be going straight to Ms. Ransom once you're out of the hospital. No reason to come home, us being so busy and all. Crazy how much there's to do!" Mother reached down and patted Klara's hand. Klara tried not to think of flounder. "I packed your things, so don't worry. Thank goodness you don't have much. It's not like when *I* was your age, I had so much, it'd have taken days to pack." She teasingly puffed up her hair. "I told them not to, but everyone kept giving me stuff, me being so popular and all." With a tilt of her head, her face sobered. "Just so you know, your brother is upset with you. He doesn't like that you don't trust him."

"But that was… that was dad."

"No matter, Drake insists you not set foot in the apartment, okay? Too upsetting." Mother walked over to the windowsill and began fussing with a bouquet. "Also, he's to have your house key. I assume you found it."

"I haven't looked." Klara let her head sink deep into the pillow. "Been indisposed as of late."

"Too bad the head injury didn't fix that."

"Fix what?"

"You being a brat." Mother snatched Klara's cup from the table and brought it to the windowsill where she began to water the potted plants.

The door opened and Sir Tippins reemerged. He had a fresh newspaper under his arm and the front of his cardigan was free of tea stains, albeit a bit wet. "You woke up!" At the sight of her, tears welled up in his eyes. "Thank heavens…"

Aghast, Klara stared at Mother, but Mother kept fussing over the flowers. *I woke up from a coma and you didn't tell him!* Sir Tippins sat down on her hospital bed, looking open and vulnerable. "I did," she said, not wanting to hurt him. "Just now."

"Yes, Bruce," Mother twittered, "isn't it wonderful? And the doctors tell me she's doing remarkably well."

"They visited while I was in the bathroom?" Mr. Tippins' expression was hard to read but mostly he looked incredulous.

"I heard I'll be staying with Rani," Klara cut in.

"Yes…" Sir Tippins righted his glasses. "I think that's better. Compared to Drake's cooking, the food will be better for sure. Rani tells me you like Indian cuisine."

"I do…" Klara thought of Rani's altar. "Does either of you know what happened to my flashlight?"

"What flashlight?" Spilling water on the windowsill, Mother wiped it with the curtain.

"The one I had with me."

"How could you have had anything with you, you were sleepwalking."

"So where's my flashlight?"

"Sweetheart, you never had a flashlight. Your brain is playing tricks on you, is all. The doctor told me so."

"I got it from Pontus on my birthday. It was just the other day."

"Bruce, did Klara get a flashlight from Pontus?"

"Not that I know of."

"Not that he knows of? Of course not!" Sudden heat flared in Klara's frostbitten face. "He wasn't there! He didn't even know we were doggy sitting! Ask Drake. Or did Drake find it in the snow and now you're protecting him?"

"I will tolerate no ambush from you, young lady." With a thud, Mother slammed Klara's empty cup on the hospital table. "Time to go!"

Mr. Tippins straightened. "See you soon," he said, his cape askew.

"We're leaving next Saturday," Mother reasserted, clutching her handbag.

As Klara arduously propped herself up it dawned on her—they'd never done this before; they'd never said goodbye. She sighed. Probably she'd flunk this the way she flunked everything homo sapien.

"No walking in your sleep." Mother pinched Klara's tender cheek. "And don't exhaust Ms. Raspy with your jabbering. Talk like a normal person, okay, or she won't like you."

Klara bit her lip. She knew she should tell them she'd miss them. It's what people said. "Have a nice time," she managed.

"You just say that." Though Mother looked dismissive, there was a brittle shard in her mockery. "I'm sure you can't wait to see us go."

Mr. Tippins did not look at Klara. He faced her as if he was looking, but he was not. She thought to give him a hug but, as the awkwardness might kill them, she only smiled.

On their way out, Mother paused in the doorway, her chin high. "You didn't say you'd miss me." She tried to slam the door but, for obvious reasons, hospital doors don't slam. All the same, Kalanna-the-dollhouse doll fell over.

Klara nodded. "My feelings exactly."

26

The hospital continued its disjointed noises. Nevertheless, a pattern emerged, like that of food carts zigzagging down a hallway. Klara crossed her fingers, hoping the food would be just as fantastic as the water.

Before long, the wide hospital door swung open and Rani stepped in carrying a tray. Klara could hardly contain herself. Lovely, beautiful Rani. "I'm gonna live with you!" Sitting up, she quickly made room for the tray on the hospital table.

"I know! You will take my room and I will sleep in the living room. I got a new, and most comfortable, daybed."

"Your bed is—almost—comfortable?" *Why had Rani done that?*

"Why tears?" Rani took Klara in her arms.

"I'm an intrusion," Klara sniffled. "Everything is better when I'm not there."

"Not true! My goodness child how I worried. How can you think… Dear me…" For a while they rocked. Then Klara's tummy grumbled and they both laughed. "Let us see what I brought." Rani expertly flipped off the lids to the various items. "We have… let us see… a soup of some sort, orange juice… looks good, though I would not have the orange juice with the stew, if I were you. Someone in the kitchen is being very funny." Rani laid out a napkin, then swung the table to where it hovered, right in front of Klara.

"The table can do that?" Klara blew her nose in the napkin.

"It can." Gently, Rani kissed Klara's forehead. "Make sure you do not eat too fast and chew well even though it is a soup." She brought the chair over and sat down. "How do you feel? Any numbness or tingling?"

"Did you find my flashlight?" The soup lacked salt. It was almost warm.

"Sorry, no."

"But I had one, right?"

"Your flashlight is very special." Rani ruffled Klara's hair. "It will find you."

"Did the elephant win?"

"My goodness, no, not the elephant. The seal pup. Evidently everybody loves a seal pup." Rani quickly glanced up at the ceiling. "Once you are finished, we would like to give you healing."

"We? Who are 'we'?"

"One is bright and tall. He tells me he is your grandfather. Also a stout man, and a tall lady with long white hair. Behind those are many others."

"I think I've met them."

Rani righted the tray and tapped it. "First you eat."

Not unexpectedly, Klara fell asleep during the healing session. When she woke up, Rani had left and the tray was gone. In its place stood a brown paper bag folded like an owl. It held a note in its beak:

Dear Klara,

Mr. Tippins and I have talked and we both agree it is important that you should have a cellphone. I hope you do not mind that I asked Otto, Pontus and Frida to add their phone numbers to the address book.

I am so glad to have come to know them. They are lovely people, as you know.

Precious Greetings,
Rani

PS. If you do not like the cover to the phone, no problem, we get you a new one.

Klara flipped back the owl's head but saw only strips of crinkle-paper. As she plowed her way down, the shreds scattered on her bed and she laughed. How had all that paper fitted inside the bag? Finally, nice and square at the bottom, lay a white cellphone with a big pink heart.

It was perfect.

She pushed a button and, as it swirled to life, it let out a short jingle. Klara quickly turned it off. Then she turned it on again. And off… and on…

Probably she should use it before she broke it. She should… call Pontus!

She should call Pontus and ask him about his trip to Canada. Klara felt proud—such a normal thing to do. Also, she should tell him how very sorry she was that his dog died.

How did people do those things?

First, she supposed, she'd need to dial.

She heard Pontus pick up. "*Hello?*"

"This is your number?" Klara did a facepalm. That was the kind of stupid thing that Mr. Tippins would ask.

"*Klara? Mom! Mom! It's Klara! Klara's on the phone! She's awake!*"

Loud shrieks in the background. A breathless Frida up close telling Pontus to run get his uncle. Then Auntie on the phone. "*Klara? Is it you Klara? Holy smokes have we worried. Worried sick I tell you. Rani told us you woke up but needed rest or we'd have been there in a jiffy. How are you, dear? Feeling okay, and what do the doctors say?*"

"I'm fine, thank you." Overwhelmed, Klara pressed the phone to her heart. How could her aunt care so much?

"*Are you okay?*"

"What?"

"*Are you okay?*"

"Just a bit overwhelmed."

"*Pain medications will do that. We'll make it short.*"

"No, it's not that. It's just… you all care so much and—"

"Of course we care, Klara… we love you."

Methodically, Klara gathered the scattered crinkle-papers into a heap. "How was Canada?"

"Decided not to go. Did a lot of praying together with Otto is what we did. I may not believe in a god, but I do believe in prayers. Oh, here's your uncle."

"Klara?" Uncle's voice sounded husky. *"Klara dear, what a blessing. I'm so relieved… All the same, I understand you need rest so I won't pry for details. Just know we love you very much. Can't wait to give you a hug."*

"Love you too, Uncle."

…

"Hi, it's Pontus."

"Hi."

"So, Klara, what's it like being back to life?"

"You wouldn't think a couple of days could turn things upside down, but everything is different now. Our bodies are an assemblage of tiny parts in an ocean of tiny parts, but I'm not a raft, I'm the captain, you know. My consciousness is."

"Oh shucks, I'd completely forgotten about that."

"About what?"

"About you answering a question of how to rig a gondola by explaining time, space, and the coordinate points of reality."

"You remember?"

"How could one forget?" Pontus cleared his throat. *"So why did you walk off a cliff? Were you trying to kill yourself?"*

"I…"

"Cause if you ever are," his voice faltered, *"I'd like to know."*

She let the phone drop. It hadn't occurred to her someone might see it that way. From under the big pile of crinkled paper her phone mumbled. She picked it up. "Pontus? Hi! Yes… I realize it must seem strange, you know; me, walking in the woods in the middle of the night. The thing is… I saw Drake outside in his robe and slippers and thought he might be sleepwalking, so I followed."

"He *walked in his sleep? What's up with your family?"*

"Hey, *I* never walked in my sleep."

"Okay. So what happened?"

"What happened was one of those weird things no one believes."

"Try me."

Klara pressed a strip of crinkle paper into a spring and let go. Quite improbably, it shot well past the bed, landing almost by the wall. "Fine," she granted. "What happened was…" She took a deep breath. "Drake walked onto a spacecraft and I followed. Not as a person, mind you, I followed as a ball of light." She exhaled.

"I buy that."

"You do?"

"Sure."

"Okay… So when I was inside the craft there were these ETs watching a movie, a whole bunch of them, they had grayish skin, large heads, big freaky eyes and short spindly bodies."

"Heard of them. Go on."

"The footage showed Drake killing Luna. It showed him bringing her out on the balcony and… and they were all so pleased and it made me sick to my stomach, though I didn't have a stomach. Then this devilish creature spots me and I shoot out of the craft and he chases me and I know I'm done for, but at the end of the ramp he stops. He stares at the snow then walks back and out comes Drake. Now I'm in my body and I am livid. I'm furious at Drake for killing Luna and I know I only had her for a short time but I loved her and I am so sorry Pontus and I was so very mad and I screamed at him and he chased me and I fell off a cliff.

"Also I dropped the flashlight you gave me and I don't know where it is. So, I'm sorry about that too."

…

"Pontus, was that too much?"

"It's not what I expected. Give me a moment."

Outside her window an owl hooted. A barred owl with large white tufts above his eyes. Klara gave him a wave. "Thanks for saving me."

"Did you say something?"

"Just talking to my owl."

"Right… So in school last week we learned that atoms are mostly empty space and how everything is pretty much a void. The lunch bell goes off. Everyone's excited, but I sit there and

I'm like... why eat? Why put empty space into empty space?"

"Shoot..."

"I know. It was quite the drop. I mean, if I don't understand the most basic thing about my existence, how can I know anything?"

"Right."

"Next day, as I walk to school, I see a squirrel stashing nuts. He doesn't stop to ponder his existence and it dawns on me that I'd exist, whether or not I know why. I can be completely wrong, it doesn't matter, I still exist. All these beliefs people have, they're just there for their stories to make sense. They're like souvenirs we pick up on our journey; if we can't remember why we have them, then we can get rid of them and, if we do, then we open ourselves to experiences far outside of what most people experience because we're not hindered by our beliefs. I went from 'Holy crap, I don't know anything' to 'With nothing being certain, imagine the possibilities!'"

"You thought that?"

"Yeah, I did. So like, if you chased your brother onto a spacecraft as a ball of light, then I believe you because I can hear in your voice that you're telling your truth. And that's all I need."

"Pontus?"

"Yeah?"

"You blow me away." She could feel him grinning. "I have a confession to make."

"What?"

"Not only did I lose the flashlight, I also threw the Bible."

"You threw a Bible?"

"I did. At a wall. And I'm not proud of it. Turns out the Bible was not the easy read I thought it'd be."

"You thought the Bible would be an easy read?"

"I got as far as to the end of Moses, then I got pissed. This Lord told people it was up to him to give them worth—such fiddlesnots. I flung it square across the room."

"How big a room?"

"Enough to make a dent."

"In the wall or in the Bible?"

"Both."

"Jeez."

"I know, right? No doubt, as we speak, a little hell is being assembled just for me."

Pontus chuckled. *"I've heard of the Bible having an impact on people; however, I've never heard of anyone having such an impact on a Bible."*

"You're going to tease me, aren't you?"

"Afraid so."

"And you're telling Otto?"

"Wouldn't want to leave him out."

"Pontus?"

"Yeah?"

"… Nothing."

"Nothing to you too," he said.

27

PLANET EARTH
— Terra Firma —
44,5956°N, 75,1691°W
Friday, March 19, 8:08 a.m. EST
As Per: Klara Tippins

Sitting on Rani's balcony, Klara used one hand to pull her sleeping bag close while the other warmed itself with a hot cup of cocoa. She glanced at Rani reading the Pennington Gazette while draped in a floral quilt, steam rising from her mouth. Conceivably, they'd gotten ahead of themselves having breakfast outdoors in the middle of March, but the air was nice.

"This summer they are doing a youth camp at the amphitheater. *The Wizard of Oz.*" Squinting against the rising sun, Rani brought the newspaper to her face. "The sign up begins…" the paper touched her nose. "… next week!" She placed the paper on the patio table, a spot of ink at the tip of her nose.

Letting the paper lie, Klara blew into her mug, feeling warm steam graze her cheeks as cars down in Pennington drove through puddles of melting snow – *slush, slush, slush* – Spring was coming and, after that, summer. A theater camp was something she'd never considered. Probably a lot of camaraderie went on in theatre camps. And self-expression. Precious things. Things Drake would destroy.

"I would pay, of course." Rani interrupted her thoughts.

"What?"

"The theater camp; if you wish to go."

"Oh, sorry, no." Klara looked at Rani. Rani's face was quiet. "Thank you, though."

"Okay." Rani leaned back and closed her eyes. Her fingers tapping the arms of her chair. "I can hear spring coming. The crows are cawing."

"Crows always caw."

"That is true. But now they are happy."

On the table, next to the Gazette, lay a huge postcard with 'Malaysia' splashed across it in gaudy letters and a photo of an enormous statue, golden, and so big it dwarfed the trees around it.

Three weeks her parents had been gone and not a word. Not even a call to let her know they arrived. She'd thought to call Mr. Tippins' cellphone but decided against it. She wasn't going to play their games. She was being punished for not worshipping dear Drake and for being difficult and falling off cliffs and making Mother look bad. Sometimes Klara wondered what she was to Mother: a sock in a sock drawer to warm the feet? Well, she wasn't some sock.

Klara tried tucking a strand of hair behind her ear, forgetting she'd had it cut short. She took a deep breath. It had to be asked. "Rani, did your mother love you?"

"My goodness child, what a question." Rani clasped her hands in her lap. "I believe my mother thought she loved me. That is what I like to think. As a child I assumed she did, as all children must trust those things, though as soon as I became independent, I could see she did not love; not me, not herself, not anybody. Feeling cheated, I grew angry with her. Then I spoke to my guru. He said I was grieving an imputed loss of something promised that had never been promised and that, instead of blaming my mother for not being who I needed her to be, I should love her for who she was. If you want a good mother in your life, he said, then you become that mother. And I did. I never had children of my own, but I always tried to be there for my young patients. He said it is important that I love my mother and my family because, like it or not, they are all part of me and I cannot fully love myself without loving them. He said I do not have to like them. I do not have to approve of what they do, or who they are, but he proposed very highly that I love them. The Vedas teach us we are all related and so I asked him about that, about loving all the people and he said this is true, but I should begin with my family; the ones who are close and difficult and then the rest will follow. Take care of your relationships, he said. You don't have to get along with every person but do get along with yourself in regard to every person. Love is unconditional, he said. No one should have to earn your love. All the same, everyone should earn your friendship. It was good advice."

Klara reached for the post card and turned it over. Seeing the address, she chortled. "Hey Rani, you're Runny Graywall, did you know that?" Squinting her eyes, she continued reading:

Klara,

Your dad, Mr. Jolly Poppins, bought this postcard for me to send you.

What can I tell you? Customs was a nightmare. All those colored people rummaging through my things, and not even asking! Then they made me clean up. ME! When THEY made the mess! I told them as much but they just stared at me.

All the same, I'm staying positive. Did you know squid is as rubbery as eyeballs? I won't touch the stuff. Your father loves it though.

Ta-ta from the mother you so rudely discarded. Hope you're having fun with Miss Ranting, the two of you chatting away. Precious, precious, like you never did with me.

P.S. Your father says Hi!

"Is everything good with them?" Repositioning herself in the chair, Rani pulled up her quilt.

"They're good. It's just... the food wasn't what she'd expected. And... I think she might be jealous."

"Jealous? What of? Isn't she the one who went to Malaysia?"

"I know… I think she makes small things big just so the big world stays little. She's pretty good at it."

Rani let her fingertips dance along the stitched edge of her quilt. "I have a proposal: What do you say we stay in my cottage this week?"

"Your cottage?"

"I think it would be good. If you like, we could pack up after breakfast and leave as soon as this afternoon. Pontus is out of school and you can see him in person instead of talking on the phone."

"You know about spring break?"

"I have my sources. I know he's been looking forward to seeing you. What do you think?"

Leaping up from her chair, Klara tripped and nearly tipped her mug, caught it, grabbed the table, then knocked the mug over again.

"Oh, dear," Rani laughed. "Is that a yes?"

"Don't take this personally." Klara pinched Rani's arm. Rani winced. "Good. You are real."

"You know, it is customary you pinch your own arm."

"But that would hurt."

Rani laughed. "So glad my pixie is all better."

The doorbell rang. "I'll get that." Klara brought her mug to the kitchen sink, picked up a rag for the spilled cocoa and went to the front door. Who would call on them so early on a Friday morning? A Jehovah's Witness? A neighbor in need of milk, or eggs?

It was Drake. Drake, looking surprisingly bashful. "Hi Klara. Hope you're feeling better."

"Uh-Huh." Klara folded her arms across her chest, wishing she hadn't soaked the rag.

"Wanted to let you know my class is throwing a dance party at the high school tonight. A guy from India will be there… Ahmed. He knows a lot about the… Urpinads. I thought you might like to meet him. He even knows the old language… pebble writing? No, that's not it… sand script!"

"A Vedanta scholar?"

Drake ran his fingers through his hair. "Yeah, yeah, one of those." Without faltering he held his thoughtful gaze, making her head spin. So this was why everyone liked him. To be the center of someone's universe—how lovely.

Slowly, her cynicism began to subside. He looked so sincere, it couldn't be fake, could it? Perhaps he was regretful. Maybe he got shook up when she ended up in a coma? Maybe, at the thought of losing her, he'd come to appreciate her? What if, all this time, she'd been wrong about him? On the other hand, she'd told Rani she'd go to the cottage. Thirteen years of pestering wasn't going to be undone by one soulful stare. "Perhaps another time."

"He leaves on Monday."

On Monday! Klara bit her lip. What if she and Ahmed were destined to connect? Maybe Rani could pick her up after the dance? That would be a win-win. "I'll check with Rani," she said.

Drake smiled triumphantly, or was that his way of looking supportive? Klara's head spun so bad she couldn't tell. All the same, she did her best to return his smile before closing the door.

"Ahmed, you say his name is?" Rani looked puzzled.

"That's what Drake told me."

"Ahmed is a common Muslim name. I do not know many Hindu people with that name. And you say he's a Vedanta scholar?"

"Yes, he knows Sanskrit and everything."

Rani still did not look convinced. "It does not make sense for Drake to make this up. I am just surprised to not have learned of this young scholar. I have a friend at the faculty and I do not know why she has not told me. What of you? You go to the same school as your brother, have you heard of him?"

"No," Klara admitted. "But then I don't hear about a lot of stuff."

"That is fine. I will give her a call. If I can, I would like to meet this young man myself."

"He leaves on Monday."

"He leaves in a week? Mid-semester?"

"I suppose it would be in the middle of the semester. I didn't think of that."

"Let me call Britt right now."

Klara waited on the balcony, counting crows. It was not easy. They are dark, of course, and keep moving about.

Luckily, the conversation ended quickly and, before long, Rani stood in the doorway, her eyes squinting the way they did when she was annoyed. "They do not have any exchange students at the high school this year. None."

"What?"

"For some reason, Drake wants you at the party."

"Why? Why would he want me at the party?"

"That I do not know. Though, to tell you honest, this whole thing makes me uneasy."

"There is no Ahmed?"

"Klara, listen, do not go to the party."

"Okay."

"And do not tell Drake you changed your mind."

"Okay." A sudden shudder went through Klara.

"Come here." Rani held her close. "You will be fine. We will be fine. We are fine. We are all fine."

28

The black road in front of Klara zigzagged through a billowing landscape, like a snake on a white pillow. Confidently, she lowered her window, allowing the crunching of the sodden road to drown out Rani's Boléro while air, full of thaw, rushed in. Somehow, she'd acclimated to Rani's driving; either that, or she'd become used to the idea of dying young.

"In only a day or two all the snow will be gone." Rani checked her rearview mirror. "You will see."

Klara doubted the snow would be gone that quick, though she had no doubt someone from the City would think so. When Rani checked her mirror a second time, Klara turned and looked. Close behind them a motorcyclist followed, wearing no helmet. No wonder Rani was edgy. Klara took a second look and realized the biker had an uncanny resemblance to Drake. But it couldn't be Drake, could it? Drake didn't have a motorcycle. He wasn't even sixteen. She must be getting paranoid. Except... "Rani, what day is it today?"

"The nineteenth day of March."

"Oh, for the love of cabbage, his birthday is today!"

"Whose birthday?"

"Drake's!"

"Surely he does not expect—"

"Oh, he absolutely does," Klara squinted to get a better look, but the motorcyclist had dropped back and disappeared behind a curve.

A few more miles and Otto's white farm showed up on the left; Pontus and Otto out front polishing a very large and very red pickup truck. Though the truck stood in the middle of a muddy driveway, it was strikingly clean. In the warm weather, Uncle wore bib overalls and mud boots, Pontus, a pair of jeans and a hoodie.

Klara tucked a strand of phantom hair behind her ear. "Otto got a new truck?"

"Exhaustingly new, what can I tell you. Unless you are wildly interested in windshield wiper technology and suspension construction, do not ask him about it." As Rani drove into Otto's driveway, Klara turned to watch the motorcyclist go by; an orange backpack drawing her attention. Not only was it similar to one Drake had, there was something sticking out of its side pocket. Something that might be a thermos—or a flashlight!

Rani sharply turned the Fiat and brought it to a halt. She rolled down her window.

"Hey," Otto pointed to Rani's tires, "be careful with my

mud, would you? I spent all morning getting it right."

"Yes, that is evident by your boots. Do you have nothing better to do, old man, than shuffle mud around?"

Uncle let out a hearty laugh, then bent down and poked his head through Rani's window. "Klara, your hair shrunk! Is that a side effect of being cooped up? Looks great by the way."

"… Thanks?"

Outside Klara's window, Pontus showed up and she startled. What happened to the petting zoo? What happened to the rabbit teeth and the calf eyes?

"So, my dear niece, how does it feel to be out and about?" Rani nudged Klara, even though it was Otto who'd asked the question.

"What?"

"How does it feel to be out?"

"Mostly disorienting."

"I bet." Appreciatively, her uncle tapped the roof of the car.

"Everything seems new and glossy." She leaned towards the steering wheel to see him better. "Like the world went through a tumbler. You sit and marvel, but then you try to walk and realize you went through the tumbler too, only it didn't make you shiny, just wobbly."

"Believe it or not, I understand." Otto peered into the backseat. "A lot of stuff you got there. Planning to stay the whole day?"

In the tiny space of the Fiat, Rani crossed her arms. "Keep

making fun of us and you will not be invited for dinner. Besides, with the good weather coming, we are not staying for just a day but for the entire week."

"They say it might snow."

"No, Otto. No, they are not saying that. Only you say that."

Otto winked. "If it gets cold, you're welcome at my place."

Rani started the Fiat. "Dinner at six and not a minute late." She nodded towards the backseat. "We do not want our seven-course meal to get cold."

Pontus leaned in close. "You'd think they're married or something."

"I know, it's weird, isn't it?"

Rani began to back up. "Six o'clock sharp, I tell you. Ask Frida also."

29

Rani's cottage was not far from Otto's house, just over a knoll and down a hill. In fact, the cottage had once been part of the Hayes family farmstead and used to house the extra farmhands needed during harvest months. When Uncle took over, the farm stopped growing crops and he decided to rent out the cottage. For years he tried. Then, Rani, bless her heart, came along and bought it.

It was an odd place to vacation at with nothing around but farmlands and many miles to a beach. All the same, Rani had felt drawn to it, and that had been that.

"Here we are and not a cloud in the sky!" Stopping the car, Rani skid only slightly in the dry gravel. "I am grateful to Otto for shoveling my driveway. That was kind. All the same, the poor man knows nothing about weather. Look at this sky!" She pulled out her phone. "One pizza, or two? With Pontus probably three… maybe four. Two pepperoni and two mushroom?"

"We're ordering pizza?"

"That is our seven-course meal, yes."

"And they deliver?"

"We may be in the woods, Klara, but we are still in the United States; of course they deliver. Only it takes a while."

Well hidden behind a pair of knobby apple trees, the tiny cottage would have been overlooked if not for its splendid green color. Peering around a corner, Klara noticed a tottering outhouse in the backyard. "Is that…?"

"Fully operational, but a bit drafty on the buttocks. Ready to go inside?" Rani flung the front door open.

"You don't lock?"

"What are people going to steal—toilet paper?"

The one-room cottage was surprisingly airy inside with white walls and ceiling. In fact, even the floor seemed to be white, though an oriental rug covered most of it. The main furnishings were a large kitchen table and a wrought-iron stove. In the window at the head of the table was a porcelain deity and, on the table, a vase with fresh flowers. A kitchenette covered the back wall but for a glassed door. The wall opposite the table was mainly covered with drapes, except for the narrow walls on either side, each with a door, but… where were the beds? Behind the drapes? How could there be two beds behind the drapes?

"What do you think?" Rani asked.

"It's comfy and yet it sparkles."

Rani pointed to the door closest to them. "This is the closet. Behind the other is the bathroom."

"But you said—"

"That the outhouse was drafty. Which is why indoor plumbing is a blessing. Both plumbing and electricity, though Otto warns me not to use the toaster when I iron. But who irons?" Rani took off her shoes and carried them to the closet. "Please, no outdoor shoes indoors. Frida has the same rule. She crocheted a large quantity of slippers for me, all quite pink. She tells me they can expand to a men's size eleven. Which, incidentally, is the size of Otto's feet."

"And where are the beds?"

"Behind the drapes. A bunkbed. So far, I have only used the extra bed for pillows. One can never have too many pillows." Rani walked to the table and pulled out a small card from the bouquet. "It says that by watering one another's path, we blossom… so true. Also it tells us welcome to Pinebrook. Otto signed it, Frida and Pontus as well." She stuck the card back in the bouquet then picked up a pocket lighter from the windowsill and lit a votive candle that was next to the deity.

Finely painted, the figurine was a foot tall and depicted a devi on a lion. The devi wore a beautiful red dress and balanced an elaborate crown on her head while holding a plethora of weapons in her many arms. Klara recognized a trident spear, a knife, one bow-and-arrow, a big club, a metal disk with spiked edges… also a lotus flower and a seashell (two items her grandfather, no doubt, would find useful).

"This statuette is the only thing I took with me from my childhood home in India." Rani bent forward and kissed the figurine. "All this time she's kept me safe. Her name is Devi Ma Durga, mother goddess of protection."

"A good friend to have," Klara agreed.

"Want to see the beds?" Crossing the room with a couple of strides, Rani pulled the drapes apart revealing a sturdy-looking bunkbed; the bottom bunk wider than the top, the top covered with silk pillows. Reaching up, Rani grabbed one and brought it to her nose. "Damp as a drenched daisy. You and I will start a fire, right away."

The stove was small with stubby legs and had a glass door with wire-whisk handles. A pair of unwieldy mammoth-sized gloves lay on a wood pile next to it. Klara found the gloves formidable. How dangerous was this?

Over by the closet she took off her shoes and put on a pair of Frida's slippers. They slid right off so she fished a couple of rubber bands from her pocket and looped them around her feet. Being tiny, she'd learned to never go anywhere without rubber bands.

"Help me crumple paper," Rani beckoned. "Once we have a good amount, the wood will be placed on top. There is nothing to it, except for the flue. The flue must be open. If you forget, there will be so much soot, even the toilet paper will be black."

"I take it you've done that?"

"Many times. And bring the matchbox, will you? The one

in the small window by the front door."

The matchbox had a faded tiger on the cover. Klara shook it. "There aren't any matches in here."

"I will get the lighter then."

Klara pointed to the matchbox. "Can I have it?"

"You want the empty matchbox?"

"For the flies."

"We have flies?"

"Dead ones. The windowsill is full of them and I'd like to bury them in the backyard."

"Of course."

"And a pen if you have one? I'd like to write on the back. Something like 'Blessed are those who seek the light.'"

"Right you are. Pens are in the top drawer of the kitchen; a shovel is in the back shed."

Klara had no sooner stepped outside when Pontus came walking up the driveway.

"Hey, Klara!" He called out. "What you got there?" She slid open the matchbox. "You're gonna bury them?"

"Wanna come?"

"To a funeral? Sure!"

For such a small cottage, the backyard was surprisingly large—large and flat with pussy willows along the periphery, their fuzzies already showing on their tall dark branches.

The shed (or sort-of-shed) was not easy to spot; deep in

the willows and covered with vines, it was a marvel to still be standing.

Holding up a branch, Pontus squinted at the door. "Is it locked?"

"Define 'locked.'" Klara pointed to a lanky vine that snaked its way through the hasp. "We'll need a pruner."

"Ah," Pontus laughed, "you mean the pruner that's inside the shed? Not to worry, my lady." Bowing theatrically, he pulled a Swiss Army knife from his back pocket and presented it to her.

"Mine squire!" Fanning herself, Klara took the pocket-knife then rubbed her thumb over the logo. "This belonged to your dad?"

"Yup."

"You miss him?"

"He wasn't nice when he drank."

"But do you miss him?" She cut the vine and handed back the knife. "It's got good vibes, Pontus. Reminds me of the Bible Otto gave me."

"Is it still on sabbatical, you know, after its untimely run-in with a wall?"

"It was a bookcase, not a wall and, yes, the Bible is feeling better, thank you. Besides, someone at the hospital gave me a new one. A priest did. He stopped by to see if I wanted to talk. I suppose they send them out whenever someone jumps off a cliff."

"Sure. What did you tell him?"

"His name was Father Gordon. I told him I was fine and that I have my grandfather to talk to. He asked if my grandfather lived close and I told him he was on a spaceship."

"Was he surprised?"

"Perhaps. He seemed to take an awful lot of deep breaths. I told him my grandfather was thousands of years old and very wise, but that did not calm him. 'The church has a lot to offer,' he said. 'Not the priesthood,' I said. 'Not if you're a woman.' He agreed this was unfortunate, but Jesus had talked to the men, so…" Klara watched Pontus' jaw drop. "And since it was the dumbest thing I ever heard, I concurred."

"Wait! You agreed with him?"

"Agreeing is always superior. 'Of course Jesus talked to the men,' I said. 'The women already turned the other cheek, did no harm, and loved their neighbor. It was the men that needed a talking-to.'"

"You'd say that, wouldn't you."

"He started it."

"Did he get mad?"

"I think, more than anything, he was stumped. There was an elderly nurse in the room. She was trying very hard not to laugh and I think he could tell. All the same, when he found out my Bible was on sabbatical he gave me a new one."

"Black?"

"It's like a terracotta red."

"Nice."

"He said I shouldn't worry about hurling my Bible at a

bookcase and that people don't go to hell for being passionate."

"That was nice of him."

"He seemed nice. For all that our understandings didn't match, Father Gordon was quite sincere." Klara dragged the door open, making a deep gouge in the soggy ground, then stepped back as the full-bodied scent of fermentation overcame her.

"Holy pintails!" Pontus exclaimed.

Klara laughed. "You sound like me."

"I know. But check it out!" Top to bottom, the shed was stacked with rusty tools and wrecked lawn furniture. There were flowerpots, ropes, hoses… and a bike! "I see it! I see the shovel. It's in the back."

"Of course," Klara groaned. "Of course it's in the back."

Grabbing the seat and handlebar, Pontus carefully pulled the bike out. Once outside, he pensively leaned it this way and that. "Good bones."

"Eyeing to fix it?"

"Nope."

"Its name is Sir Galahad?" Klara tempted.

"It's a women's bike."

"Oh, because it belongs to Rani?"

"No, because it's a women's bike. You never had a bike?"

"If I rode down the hill from Mountain Manor, I'd never make it back… hmm, maybe a bike *would* be a good idea." While Pontus admired the bike, Klara stepped into the shed. Halfway in, she grabbed hold of a rake and reached for the shovel. This did not work, so she swung at it—missed tremendously and watched, dumbstruck, as the rake knocked over some lumber which toppled a stack of terracotta planters causing a shelf to slant and an iron pot to crash to the ground; the iron pot making quite a dent as it hit the dirt floor.

She thought it was over when several rusty pipes fell. Gradually tipping, they took the shovel with them and, in near slow-motion, placed the shovel in Klara's outstretched hand.

"I'll be darned," Pontus said.

"It was my circus trick in a previous life."

"Any survivors?"

"Ha, ha." Klara brought the shovel outside and pricked the ground a few times with the tip of the blade. The ground was not entirely thawed, but it was also not frozen solid.

Pontus watched. "It's a matchbox, you know, we don't have to dig deep."

"I know."

He began twirling his Swiss Army knife like a small baton. "I'm glad you and Rani—" The baton flung out of his hand. He quickly picked it up. "That you came here for spring break."

"Feeling much better, thank you. It was time to get out." Klara glanced over at him. "The other morning I played Klondike. It's a game of solitaire."

"I know."

"Well, since I went out seven times in a row, it seemed I've finally aligned myself back into life."

"Aligned yourself?"

"With the beat of cosmos and stuff."

"Seven times in a row… that's like one chance in… I can't even wrap my head around it!"

"Yeah," she agreed. "It was a bit much. Almost got me spooked. So, do you want to dig the grave or would you rather cut willow branches for decoration?"

"How about you dig the grave? Not sure the shovel would listen to me." Pontus looked towards the road. "And we should get going, I hear Galileo's truck."

"There are tons of trucks on these roads."

"None as new as Galileo's."

Seeing as they were burying a matchbox, the grave did not take long to dig. They placed the matchbox in the hole, tiger side up, then covered it with dirt.

"We never buried Luna." He kept his eyes fixed on the grave; a cross of pussy willows laying on top. "The ground was frozen solid so we had her cremated. We should have done a ceremony… Don't know why we didn't."

"Would you like to add a few words now?"

"Not sure what to say."

"How about the two of us hold space in silence?"

And so they did. It was quite touching. For several minutes. Then Klara farted. And not just any fart, this was a haunted house tour. They both laughed. "Another circus trick of yours?"

"What can I say, I'm a natural."

After they'd straightened up the mayhem in the shed and rolled rusty Sir Galahad back to where she'd been, Pontus secured the hasp with a twig, then the two of them walked around front to where Otto's big truck stood in the driveway next to Rani's Fiat.

"Instead of digging her car out of the snow later, he should have parked over it." Pontus bent and looked under the truck. "Plenty of space here for a Fiat."

"It's not going to snow."

30

"Hey, kiddo, close the door!" Sitting at Rani's table, Aunt Frida chewed gum with gusto, her hair oddly flat on one side, an untouched slice of pizza on a paper plate in front of her. Though she wore a plush robe over a sweatshirt over a turtleneck, the most startling thing was the sunglasses.

Pontus, however, did not seem taken aback. "Great seeing you too, mom."

Rani got up. "I will add wood to the fire." Looking intently at Klara and Pontus, she nodded for them to take a seat at the table though, possibly, there was more to the nod than that.

"Who's this?" Frida asked, looking straight at Klara.

Otto and Rani exchanged looks. Otto cleared his throat. "That's Klara," he said with slow emphasis. "Your niece. She got a haircut."

"Oh for heaven's sake! Don't talk t'me like I'm'n infant." Aunt barely stopped chewing to let the words out. "I forgot m'contacts s'all. Anybody gonna gemme coffee?"

Klara picked up the coffee decanter placed in front of her aunt and poured her a cup.

"'Couse I knew 'o yo'are." Her auntie put a clammy hand on Klara's wrist. "Quit smokin' anit make me i-irritable isall." A foul odor snuck out from behind her aunt's peppermint breath. Sitting down, Klara discreetly withdrew her hand.

"Mom." Pontus looked cross. "I don't think smoking is your problem. It's been two years since you quit."

"I know!" Auntie squealed. "An' you-know how illitating that is?" She took a swig of coffee, grimaced, then spit it back into the cup. "Who ga'me coffee? Eryone knows yo'can have coffee with pepplemint!" She slammed the cup on the table, took her chewing gum out and stubbed it into a napkin like a cigarette butt.

Rani sat down next to Frida. "How is your head?"

"Life threw me a curveball is wha' happen. Whack me, right 'ere at m'head." She pointed to the right side, then changed her mind and pointed to the back.

"I know." Otto took his sister's hands into his. "Life does that sometimes. But right now, sis, that's not why your head hurts. Right now, your head hurts because you drank too much."

"I don't drink!" Frida jolted. "How'cn you say that? You stab me righ' 'ere in m'heart and if I wasn'…" she looked out the window "… on the firss floor, I'd jump right outta that window!"

Otto laughed. "For goodness sake, Fry, look at yourself. You're as bundled up as a baby in Siberia. We could drop you from a mile high and all you'd do is bounce!"

At that Frida too laughed, then Rani, then all of them. After a while, Klara couldn't remember what had been so funny, only it felt so good to laugh.

"So, Klara," Otto dabbed his eyes and reached for another slice of pizza, "what would you like to do while you're here?"

"Milk a cow."

"Milk a cow? Really!"

"It's on my bucket list."

"Some bucket list you got. Well then, you're more than welcome to milk Rose."

"Yeah," Pontus grinned. "Rose will kick your bucket for sure."

"Come now, Pontus." Otto folded the sides of his pizza and took a bite. "I'm sure Klara will be fine."

"Twenty bucks she wouldn't?"

Tapping his bearded chin, Otto looked Klara up and down. "How much do you weigh?"

"What?!"

"Let's make it ten."

"You only have ten dollars' worth of confidence in me? Who is this Rose? Is she going to kill me?"

Pontus nudged Otto with an elbow. "Not as long as you wear hockey gear." He reached for his third slice. "I'll lend you mine."

Otto wiped his beard with a napkin. "That's mighty kind of you, Pontus. So, Klara, apart from getting roughed up by a cow, what else is on your bucket list?"

Klara looked at her paper plate. The whiteness made her think of a pillow and of how sorely she needed rest. They were all having so much fun and she wasn't built for it.

"I'm sorry." This was Uncle. "You look tired. And you haven't had any pizza."

Klara took a deep breath. "I like mushrooms."

"Absolutely." He gave her a big slice. "Head still hurts?"

"Off and on. It's mostly… I'm not used to this. To people… to having…"

"That's understood. Give it time. Be easy on yourself and accept whatever feelings come up. You've been through a lot."

"They teach that at the Quakers?" Klara asked. "How to cope?"

"Kind of."

"I think, while I'm here, I'd like to know more about the Quakers."

"Is that on your bucket list?"

"Sure."

Otto clasped his hands over his stomach. "First and foremost, I should mention that Quakers won't teach you what to believe. It's more about finding your own path. In fact, the freedom to pursue one's beliefs is the very reason they broke away from the Church of England back in the mid-17th-century. It was to move away from doctrines and get back to Jesus' original message of seeking truth, not from outside ourselves, but from within."

"You know," said Pontus, chewing on his sixth slice of

pizza, "You might want to check out Otto's Quaker youth group. There's only four of us, me included. We talk about everything. Next meeting is tomorrow at the Friends' meeting house in Pennington."

"Not so." Otto said. "Furnace sprang a leak so I'm forced to cancel. Never got to tell you."

"Or," Pontus leaned forward, smiling sweetly at his uncle, "we could have it at our place."

"So it's 'our' place now? I like the sound of that."

31

A noise. Or maybe not a noise, maybe a distant rattling of the earth, like a muffled warning. Perhaps a warning and a sound both, as from a buzzing you ignore until you realize it's a wasp. And it got louder. It got so loud they all went silent. Then the motorcycle stopped and that was even worse.

Klara hugged herself tight as the *crunch, crunch* of heavy boots made their way up the gravel to their door—the door Rani never locked.

Though she knew it was coming, she jumped nearly a foot when the front door flung open.

"Here I am!" Sporting a slick leather jacket and a smooth pirate's grin, Drake squared his collar, then pranced into the cottage, leaving behind a trail of dirt and the door wide open. "Aw, you guys got pizza for my birthday. Thanks!"

Looking at her soiled rug, Rani stomped over to the door and slammed it shut. "Why do you come here?"

"It's my birthday and I want to see my family."

"How did you find my house?"

"Whoa, what's with the altitude? Mom told me to keep an

eye on miss 'space cadet' here. Okay? I'm only following orders."

"Plenty of people keep an eye on me," Klara retorted. "I don't need you. Last I heard I wasn't allowed in the apartment. I wasn't even allowed a key."

Drake chuckled. "Of course you can be in the apartment, Klara, it's your home." With a meek smile, he addressed the group. "She tends to get paranoid."

"And where did you get the bike?" Klara demanded.

"Where is this and where is that? Where is the sweater you promised me, huh? I know it's why you cut your hair."

"The bike," Klara pressed.

"It's a Harley."

Otto's eyes lit up. "A Harley you say? What model?" Frida sent her brother a furious glare, having perked up considerably since Drake arrived.

"The Roadster. Latest model."

"Damn…"

"Where," Klara took a deep breath, "did you get the Harley?"

"Mom bought it. She just doesn't know it yet." The pirate grin was back. "I mean, how else was I to keep an eye on you? Oh, and Otto, you should hear the things people say about your youth group."

"Really?" Otto looked pleased, if perhaps a bit surprised. "Didn't know it was talked about."

"Oh, for sure." Drake grabbed a slice of pizza. "Is it *every*

Saturday in Pennington?"

"The third Saturday, and actually—" Otto looked bewildered as Frida pelted his side with her plush belt. "Actually, tomorrow I'm hosting it at my house. You're welcome to join if you like. If you can't make it, we meet on Sunday at the Ski Lodge for brunch, so you can always catch us there."

"Schweet." Drake nodded approvingly.

"Oh, for chrissake!" Frida let go of her belt and pressed her hands to her head. "You're denser than Aunt Edna's fruitcake!"

Drake grinned. "I see where Klara gets it from. And yes, Otto, I'll be there." He reached for another slice, one with mushrooms.

Frida slapped his hand. "That one is Klara's."

Drake shrugged. "No mind, time to head over to the daaance paaarty." He looked at Klara. "Are you coming? I'll give you a ride."

"On the bike?" Klara stalled.

"Yeah, on the bike."

"Not with no… with no helmet," Rani spluttered.

"Got one to lend."

"I…" Klara began. "I got a headache. Thanks anyway. Took a bad fall and all that. Still healing."

"Ahmed will be disappointed. I told him all about you."

"Tell him I said hi."

Drake's eyes narrowed. He looked at her long and hard. Klara felt her eye twitch. Grinning, he snatched the last two mushroom slices and shoved them in his pockets, then turned and headed out the door.

"How dare you!" Before anyone could stop her, Frida grabbed the porcelain deity and flung it. Spinning through the air it looked sublime and Klara thought 'maybe.' But then it hit the doorframe and shattered, showering the floor with thousands of white, red, and golden shards.

Hardly breathing, Rani stood motionless, a fist pressed against her lips.

"Oh, god." Frida collapsed in her chair. "What have I done? Rani, I am so sorry. I'll get you a new one."

"No." Rani's voice was strained and even. "It is family… There is no way."

Frida stared down at the broken pieces. "I'll clean up. Let me at least clean up."

"No!"

Otto put an arm around his sister. "Fry, it's time we leave."

32

PLANET EARTH
— Terra Firma —
44,2042°N, 73,9932°W
Saturday March 20, 12:22 a.m. EST
As Per: Klara Tippins

Being in the top bunk, Klara hit the ceiling pretty hard as she startled awake. Good thing she wore her pixie hat, but—why awake? Gently massaging her bruise, she could hear the house settle against the cold and a couple of owls hoot outside. Other than that, no sound. And yet… and yet, something caused the hair on her arms to stand on end.

"Rani?" she whispered. "Rani, are you awake?"

A mumbling came from the bunk below, sounding like a long-winded rendition of the word 'no.'

"I think I heard a noise." Klara climbed down the ladder.

"Why is a lot," Rani remarked as Klara's feet touched the cold floor.

Pulling the drapes open, it was shockingly bright. No doubt the floodlight outside had been triggered. She walked to the stove. It was ice cold. The fire was out and there was no wood in the woodpile. She supposed that, if she went outside and was not instantly killed, she should bring logs back from the woodshed. That would be normal. She closed her eyes and, standing in the middle of the light-flooded room, upgraded her pixie hat to a 'good luck hat,' then put on her boots and jacket, grabbed the poker from the woodburning stove, took a deep breath, and—the floodlight went out. With no city lights around it was amazing how dark it got. "Sure would be nice with a flashlight right about now," she told the Universe (in case it was listening). Then, somewhat patiently, she fumbled in the dark until she found the switch to the porchlight, flipped it on, and stepped outside.

The snow surprised her more than anything. At least ten inches, it covered the newly shoveled driveway and all of Rani's car. As she trudged around the corner she found herself in the shadow of the porchlight. Surrounded by darkness she tapped the wall to find her way; lightly at first, then more forceful the darker it got and the longer it took, grateful to have an iron poker, if not a flashlight.

Rounding the corner to the backyard she triggered the floodlight. Holy sneakers it got bright!

Shielding her eyes, she noticed that the door to the shed was wide open. As she walked closer, she saw footprints and, over in the pussy willows, the shaft of a flashlight sticking out of the snow. The Universe *was* listening! She ran over and pulled it out—It was hers! The lens was fogged, but it worked.

On the ground, footprints were everywhere; either from the same person, or from different people wearing the same shoes. Though stomped out erratically, many lead to the deck. Klara turned, noticed the barrage of stuff surrounding the back door, staggered backwards and tripped.

Tall poles leaned on either side of the door with black feathery things tied to them. Between the poles, and above the door, lay a plank, precariously balancing some big black monstrosity… oh, god no, not the cast iron pot from the shed!

Through the glass, Klara saw lights turn on inside and Rani walking towards her, carrying the empty wood pail. Oh, no… no, no… no, no, no, no… Frantically, Klara waved but noticed with horror how this only made Rani hurry her steps.

And there it was: Rani would open the door, the iron pot would crash on her head and there was nothing, nothing Klara could do to stop it.

And yet, in one instant, an impulse came bolting through, both shocking and familiar. "NO!" she roared and threw a ball of urgency at the door. As Klara watched the invisible-thunderbolt-of-Zeus hurl through the air, a raccoon, out of nowhere, charged for the deck. At the very moment the thunderbolt ran into the door, the raccoon tripped a pole and everything came crashing down: poles, plank, feathers, the cast iron pot; it all tumbled down in a tremendous calamity. The raccoon, clearly spooked, scampered under the house.

Behind the glass, a wide-eyed Rani opened the door. When she saw the cast iron pot in the snow, her face paled.

"The door. It was rigged!" Klara panted, zigzagging through the debris. "But then a raccoon showed up."

"Rigged?"

"I saw you walk to the door and I thought… but then, I don't know, it was as if the dimensions recalibrated, like the melody in the air changed."

"You hear a melody in the air?"

"Sometimes. Should we call the cops?"

At the mention of 'cops,' Rani's ER-persona triggered and she quickly regained her color. "Not right now," she said authoritatively. "We call tomorrow. No one is on duty in Pinebrook and the Pennington police station is only for actual emergencies. Thanks to you Klara, we are all okay."

"Thanks to dimensional recalibrations and one disoriented raccoon."

"Yes, we must thank the raccoon."

"How about pizza?" Klara suggested. "I believe there's a slice left."

"Good idea. We will give it some pizza. Then you and I shall rest."

"Rest?"

"We start a fire, place our mattresses by the stove and bring over some hot cocoa and biscotti." Rani put an arm around Klara. "I am glad you got your flashlight back."

33

PLANET EARTH
— Terra Firma —
44,2042°N, 73,9932°W
Saturday March 20, 7:08 a.m. EST
As Per: Klara Tippins

Klara's butt was cold. Apparently it'd slid down to the icy floor during the night. She repositioned herself, careful not to bump the flashlight on her pillow.

… her flashlight! She hadn't dreamt… Oh dear… it was true that her brother found it. Walked home and never told anyone. Leaving her there…

Her own brother…

Then, darker thoughts: Did he push her? Did he hate her that much? If it wasn't for her, would he be happy? Klara felt nauseous.

Rani stirred. "What is it, Klara?"

"You're awake?"

"Kind of." Rani propped herself up on her elbows, her hair in disarray. "Is something the matter?"

"What if I broke something… or someone? What if I

broke someone and I can't fix them? What if I broke my brother?"

"Broke your brother? My goodness, the thoughts we think… You, Klara, see things more clearly than anybody I know, making some people uncomfortable. But that is all and that is okay. Truly, if you live your life correctly, there should be at least eight people who would really, really, rather not run into you. So, tell me, what are your plans for today?"

"I thought I'd milk a cow."

"Brilliant." Rani sat up, making biscotti crumbs spill from the open box on her stomach. "My good heavens, we have not called the cops!"

'The cops' was one good-humored Deputy Sheriff Reilly, sporting a trapper hat, duck feet (size fourteen no doubt), and an unfortunate garlic breath. "Oh, dear," he said as he surveyed the grounds. "Could have ended badly." He took hold of the cast iron pot and lifted it a few times. "Twenty pounds, maybe more." He looked at the dead crows tied to the poles. "A local biker gang calls themselves The Ravens. Have either of you ladies heard of them or have any connection to them?"

"No," Klara and Rani answered in unison.

"Did you hear any motorcycles last night?"

"My brother has a motorcycle," Klara said. "We heard him. That was earlier in the evening."

"I see." Deputy Reilly took out a small notepad from his

jacket. "Is your brother part of a biker gang?"

"I wouldn't know. It's as likely that he is as it is that he isn't."

"I see… Do either of you have any idea who might have done this?"

"Maybe," Klara admitted.

"Yes?" Deputy Reilly rocked back and forth in his giant boots, flipping his pen against his notepad. When the tapping settled into the beats of a march he abruptly stopped. "Are you going to tell me?"

"If I tell you, will you question him?"

"We might."

"Even if that makes him dangerous?"

"Looks to me like he's already dangerous. You wouldn't want him hurting anybody else, would you?"

"What if he's only after me."

"Someone is after you?"

"It's likely he pushed me off a cliff. And he killed my friend's dog."

The deputy got his pen ready. "Was it reported?"

"No."

"But you saw him push you? Did you see him kill the dog?"

Klara hesitated. Had she seen it? "No," she conceded. "But I know it was him."

"I see." Deputy Reilly rocked so extensively he nearly went on his tippy toes. "Any evidence or eyewitnesses?"

"No witnesses, but there's a flashlight as evidence."

"Tell me about the flashlight."

"I lost it when I was pushed, then found it here last night. Right over there in the snow." Klara pointed to the spot, now partly thawed.

"I see." Deputy Reilly sounded hesitant. "Does the flashlight have any distinct markings?"

"A dent. Also, it's old, if that makes it distinct. Besides, I know it's mine."

"Look, I'm not... Any reason this person would be upset with you?"

"Being born. Being his sister—I mean... What I meant was..." Klara bit her lip.

"So it's your brother? Look... emotions run high in most families, sometimes they even result in violence, but this here..." He gestured at the explosion of debris. "This took some plotting and that's a different bag of beans." He smiled sympathetically and tucked his pad away. "This might be attempted murder; it might also be a very bad prank. As no one got hurt it's not a crime scene, but you may wish to file a report for trespassing and destruction of property?" He looked at the iron pot. "Such as it may be." Rani shook her head. "So you know, your statements will be in my report all the same."

"Thank you," Klara said.

"Yes," said Rani. "Thank you for coming."

Deputy Reilly tipped his hat. He tipped his hat as well as any man can tip a trapper hat.

34

Following a hearty breakfast of pancakes with pineapple and shredded cheese (Rani tended to serve unconventional toppings), Klara hauled her bedding up the ladder and placed it back in her bed. Curling up under the covers, she pulled out her phone; her stomach full, herself slightly out of breath.

"... *Klara?*" Pontus sounded drowsy.

"I woke you, didn't I?"

"*What time is it?*"

"Time to milk the cow?" Klara crossed her fingers.

The phone went silent. Then an explosion of moans which was either a stack of half-filled styrofoam cups being simultaneously crushed or the disgruntled mutterings of a tarpit—followed by: *"Seven-thirty!?"*

Klara checked her cellphone. "Actually, it's seven thirty-two. That *is* when you milk the cows, isn't it?"

"*Ten. And there's only one.*"

"You milk her at ten?! I thought cows got milked when the rooster crowed. Isn't that why farmers have roosters, to know when to milk the cows?"

"I don't know why farmers have roosters… No, actually, I do. Anyway, how would you know when a rooster crows, you don't have one."

Klara looked at her phone. This wasn't at all how the conversation was supposed to go. She flung the phone at her feet. Then, with the help of both big toes, she hung up. "He can call me when he's in a better mood," she muttered, after which she curled into a tight ball and sobbed. She was wrong of course. She knew she was wrong and also unreasonable. Pontus had not antagonized her. All the same, she felt antagonized and couldn't help it.

At the far end of the bed her phone rang. She threw her pillow at it, then her comforter. It still rang and she had nothing else to toss. "Suits you well, Klara," she shivered. "Suits you well to lose all your comforts—you're too callous to have friends." She heard Rani down below, chatting on her phone. A lot of 'yes, yes,' and 'no, no,' and 'Yes, absolutely, of course.' Someone was coming over? Klara checked her eyes with her hands, they were puffy from crying. This was not good, Rani would ask. And what if Pontus came? He wouldn't ask, he'd just stare. Maybe laugh.

Sitting on her bed, she smelled coffee brewing, then heard the distinct sound of Otto's truck in the driveway. There was the quiet *thop* as his fiber-reinforced thermoset door was closed, followed by the sound of crunching gravel, the stomping to get snow off of boots, the clearing of a throat and, finally, a knock on the door.

Leaving her phone buried under her pillow, she climbed down the ladder and pulled open the drapes.

It was Otto. Only Otto and no Pontus. She might have been relieved, or she might have been disappointed; she was too disordered to tell.

"Good morning, Rani." Uncle held up a small piece of wood and a long twine of braided grass. "I brought you some palo santo and some sweetgrass." He dug into his pocket and handed Rani a small brass bell. "Don Ricardo is sorry you lost your heirloom and wants you to have it. Says it should dispel any lingering negativity—Oh, hi there, Klara." If her uncle noticed she'd been crying, he didn't let it show.

"That is very kind of him." Smiling, Rani pointed at Otto's boots. "Those will have to come off. Then both of you to the table, I warmed up some puri bread."

Klara sat down and grabbed a bun. Despite the pancakes, she felt famished. "What time is it?" She looked at her uncle. "Has Rose been milked?"

"She won't be for another hour. There's still time if you—"

"No! I mean, I…"

"Please, Klara, don't be upset by anything Pontus says before ten in the morning. He's not himself until he's had his… whatever it is… *Frosted Flakes*? Anyhow, he can be quite a bear and wants you to know he's sorry."

"He told you!"

"… because he was concerned."

"Well, *he* wasn't a bear."

"So, you'll milk her?"

Klara took a bite of her bun but couldn't swallow. "You said you brought sweetgrass and… something else."

"Yes, sweetgrass cleanses and palo santo calls in light spirits. Palo santo is Spanish and means 'holy stick.' It grows in Peru. Don Ricardo gave it to me when he heard what happened last night. I hope you get to meet him, Klara, he's got quite a story to tell. Like many growing up in the Q'ero Nations high in the Andean mountains, he got struck by lightning. Unlike most, he survived—twice! Once he'd recovered from the second strike he became a paqo, which is both a kind-of healer and an interpreter of natural spirits; a bridge between the seen and the unseen. Kind of like you, Klara. Someone who listens to the natural world so fully they can speak to it. Some paqos are said to make water flow in dry streams, to teleport, and to shapeshift. I don't know if Don Ricardo does any of those things. When I ask, he just smiles. If you'd like to meet him, he'll be at the farm today to check on my goats."

"He is a long way from home." Rani remarked. "What brought him here?"

"Love." Otto placed a hand on his heart. "Our local reporter, Sarah Lindsten, went to Peru to write about the Q'eros. That was forty years ago."

Holding a coffee pot, Rani reached over to fill Otto's mug.

"No. No, thank you," Otto said. "Just stopped by to bring you the incense and the bell. Hope to see you later, Klara."

He left and Rani picked up the sweetgrass and sniffed it, then handed it to Klara. It did not have a strong scent but smelled surprisingly of leather. "Otto said to start with the cleansing." Rani took back the sweetgrass. "Is there anything you like to tell me, Klara?"

"What?"

Rani tapped the table with her slender fingers while Klara repeatedly failed at tucking hair behind her ear. "Okay fine. I was unfair to Pontus and don't know how to fix it. Now, it seems, if I don't fix it, we can't clean up this place."

"Ah," Rani's face softened. "Tell him you are sorry."

"Sure, saying it like that makes it seem obvious."

"It is obvious, but not if you are used to people rejecting you with: 'Oh, *now* you are sorry!' or 'You should have thought of that *before* you did it.'"

"How did you know?"

"Old age." Rani swept crumbs from the table into her coffee cup. "Pontus is not a person who wants you to feel bad. Quite the opposite; most people are quite the opposite. You can trust me on that."

35

The snow from the night before had all but melted and the sodden road merrily chanted *cronch-clonch-cronch as* Klara marched towards Otto's farm.

Halfway there, the wind picked up and she wished she'd worn a windbreaker instead of a sweater. She'd picked the sweater 'because of the colors'—*Snurpeldum and frizzelbroot for being such a dabbeljang!* she shuddered.

She was so annoyed she could have *snurpeldumed* all the way to Otto's, and probably would have, if it hadn't started to rain.

Kindly at first. Then not-so-kindly.

Giving the raindrops the evil eye, she pulled down her pixie hat. "Stop competing," she snarled.

The rain, of course, did not listen.

By the time she knocked on Otto's door and Pontus opened, her clothes were so soaked her sleeves nearly touched the landing and her pants clung to where she could hardly bend her knees, and Pontus? Pontus wouldn't stop laughing.

"Oh, dear," said Aunt Frida, joining him in the small entryway. "Come in, come in. Take off those soggy shoes and put these slippers on. I'll fetch some dry clothes. Oh, and give me that." Auntie pointed to Klara's pixie hat. As Klara dragged it off her head, water dripped on the floor. "You poor thing." Shaking her head, Frida took off for the kitchen.

Pontus grinned. "It's a good thing you didn't melt."

"Apparently I'm not as witchy as all that." Unable to meet his gaze, Klara struggled to get rubber bands around the slippers. "I'm sorry I hung up on you. I felt a bit raw after my brother tried to… after he…"

"No need to apologize. Otto told me what happened."

"You're not mad?"

"Of course not."

"You're sure?

"Well… keep asking and I might get irritated."

Otto's living room was just as she remembered. His armchair, now worn, stood by the kitchen door and the two couches that she and Drake used to jump on (both from the ugly part of the 70's), were, as always, facing each other. The couch below the staircase had an abrasively orange fabric (some things simply refuse to fade). The other couch, the one Drake always chose, was upholstered in a toad-inspired leather. It stood under the large window and had indeed faded, quite unnecessarily.

On the far-off wall a fire burned in the brick fireplace and, feeling cold, Klara walked closer. The carpet was still the same mustard color, the fireplace just as sooty, and the blankets stacked next to it, still folded into pillows the way only Otto knew how. A couple of floor pillows had been added. That was nice.

Auntie came back carrying a faded blue towel and a pile of clothes reeking of mothballs. "Use my bathroom," she suggested. "It's at the top of the stairs. Your wet clothes can go on the shower rod."

Klara assumed the bathroom upstairs had remained in the same time capsule as the living room, with seashell soaps, plush toilet-seat cover and wallpaper that showed seahorses and goldfishes swimming together (this had clearly not been researched), forgetting entirely that this was Frida's bathroom now.

Not only were the seashell soaps gone, the entire bathroom had been transformed into a... a magician's hat! Most striking was the bold stripe wallpaper in pink and red with gold edgings. Baskets with hairdryers hung from the ceiling (Klara counted four!) and wall-mounted shelves displayed colorful bottles. Atop a mirror, nail polish and bright lipsticks balanced, perhaps in some kind of arrangement, and everywhere scarves: scarves draped around the doorknob, scarves (along with necklaces and bracelets) hung from a rabbit hook on the wall.

"If I flush, will I turn into a rabbit?" she called out to Pontus.

"It's happened, but mostly to witchy people."

"How witchy?"

"Don't worry, we have plenty of carrots in the root cellar."

Closing her eyes, she steadied her tittering heart. Then she flushed.

She did not turn into a rabbit.

It was nice getting out of her wet clothes and into dry ones, even if Frida's clothes were cold and a bit on the large side. Taking the rubber bands off the slippers and strapping them around the sleeves helped, even if it made the slippers floppy. As best she could, she wrapped the faded towel around her head, then exited the magical top hat.

Pontus, waiting at the top of the stairs, looked amused. "So you *did* turn into a rabbit! I'll be darned."

"Very funny."

"You wanna see my room?"

"Sure."

Pontus' room was right next to the bathroom and Klara had no time to decide what to expect. All the same, she was surprised. Never in a million years had she thought his room to be so dustable and so unremarkable. Unremarkable, even with the model airplanes. Airplanes were exciting, of course, but these planes paraded on bookshelves as if in a museum and hung so orderly from the ceiling it was as if no breeze ever touched them. Was this really his room?

"You want to be a pilot?" she asked.

"No, I… well, maybe. It's a silly dream."

"Or a really cool one. I wish I had a dream like that."

Reverently, Pontus picked up a plane. It was red. "The Red Baron, Baron Manfred Albrecht Freiherr von Richthofen became a fighter pilot with the German Air Force during World War I. He's credited with eighty air combat victories. This is his 1917 triplane."

"He must have been amazing at what he did."

"I thought it would upset you."

"That he killed so many? I don't think killing is what he was good at. It's just what happened." Klara picked up a framed picture that stood on a windowsill. It was the only picture in the room and showed Pontus with Luna, the two of them in a puppy pose with a ball between them. Pontus took the picture from her. "It's just what happened," he said in a low tone. Then he blew off some dust and put it back. "I think Rose is calling. We should go."

Even though the downpour had been reduced to a drizzle, Aunt Frida insisted that Klara put on, not only a raincoat, but fishing waders and a rain hat as well.

Wearing the waders, Klara pulled the waist out in front of her and sighed. Clearly, they were made for a five-foot-eight, two-hundred-pound Uncle. All the rubber bands in the world wouldn't make them fit. "Are you sure this is necessary?" She and her aunt stood by the open door while Pontus waited outside on the landing, his corduroy jacket barely misted. "Your son seems fine."

"I'm sure he's fine but I would never forgive myself if you got sick. Just out from the hospital and all."

"It's been nearly a month."

"Better safe than sorry."

"But what if I fart?" she objected, looking down into the waders. "What if I fart and the fumes knock me out?"

Doubling over with laughter, Pontus stepped back and tumbled down the stairs. At the bottom, he grabbed the banister, planted one foot in a bucket and—still laughing—plopped down, his butt in a puddle.

"Are you okay, Pontus?" Toddling down the stairs, Klara reached the bottom and gave him a hand, but instead of pulling him up, she too landed in the puddle.

"What did I tell you, Klara?" Frida hooted from the top of the stairs. "Didn't I tell you you'd need raingear? And you, Pontus, you should go inside and change."

"I'm good."

Bracing against Pontus to stand, Klara spotted a tree stump over by the barn with two nails sticking up. "What's that?"

"That's where our chickens say goodbye to their heads. Did you know that even without heads they run around flapping their wings?"

"No way."

"They do. Sometimes they squawk."

"With no head!"

"With no head. And I've heard of ones that open their eyes and see themselves running."

"Abort! Abort!" She covered her eyes. "Tell me it isn't true."

"It's absolutely true."

Taking another look, she noticed an ax leaning against the tree stump. "Do you ask their permission?"

"To take their life…?" Pontus eyed her. "That's something Don Ricardo would do. I don't, though I do apologize afterwards."

"Any other dinners running around?"

"Not at the moment."

While taking in the hearty, pungent smell of farm life, Klara considered the mud on his cheeks and the dark patches of damp on his shoulders and it struck her; it wasn't that his room was like a museum, it was that his room was out here.

Having run out of clever remarks, she simply said, "Yes."

36

It was dark inside the barn. The light bulbs trailing the ceiling were sparse and the few windows were small and set high on the wall. Somewhere in the barn two men were talking; one was Otto, the second voice Klara did not recognize.

"I met someone," Otto said.

Both Pontus and Klara paused their steps.

"About time, you old goat." There was a warmth to the other man's voice; deep and husky, it lumbered like a bear.

"She's not ordinary."

"Wouldn't think so."

"From the City and smart as a whip. Used to be a surgeon."

"Oh, my."

"I know. I wish I knew what someone like me could offer someone like her."

"What About Love?" sang the husky voice.

Otto chuckled. "It's not that easy."

"Sure it is."

Klara nudged Pontus. "Should we not be here?"

"No, it's fine." Over by a water spigot Pontus filled one

bucket with water, another with supplies. "They're at the far end. If we stay quiet, we can reach Rose without bothering them."

"Where are the animals?" Klara whispered.

"The goats are in the pasture."

"But isn't the ground frozen?"

"They got hooves."

"Pontus, is that you?" At the far end of the barn, Otto poked his head out from behind a stall door. "And Klara! Glad you came. Come over and meet Don Ricardo."

Pontus motioned her closer. "So you know," he said in a low voice, "Don Ricardo answers his own questions. If *you* answer them, you'll throw him off."

In the last stall, a staunch looking man sat cross-legged on the straw-covered floor with his back to them. The man, presumably Don Ricardo, was talking to Otto while stroking the very large belly of a white goat, an orange-striped hat lying next to him, presumably knitted by a young child.

Otto leaned against the half wall of the stall. "Klara, meet Don Ricardo."

Don Ricardo turned and squinted up at her, his eyes so compassionate they were unnerving. "You must be Klara. My, oh my, not from around here, are we? Thanks for coming."

"Eh… you're welcome?"

"Draconian?" Don Ricardo twisted to get a better look. "Yes, definitely a Draconian starseed." He nodded appreciatively. "I take it you meet with your star-family while you sleep? That's good. I too am a starseed, though I come from a different star system than you." Without elaborating, he turned back to the goat and to his conversation with Otto. "It's an emotional hunger that makes her overeat. You should play music. Brahms is good, though not the lullaby. You want her active. And whatever you do, don't let her eat with the others, she's a thief. Between feedings, give her olive oil with baking soda, that'll get things going. I'll check on the other goats before I go and then, this evening, I'll come back to check on her." Standing up, Klara found he was scarcely taller than herself but many times broader.

"This evening?" Otto ran his hand over his balding head. "I have a youth group coming to the house this evening around seven. Perhaps you'd like to join us?"

Don Ricardo picked up his hat and, without removing any straw, yanked it on his head. "You're doing a fire?"

"We could. The firepit is free of snow, so yeah, let's do a fire."

The tiny hat was snug on Don Ricardo's large head, making him look slightly unhinged. Why didn't he pluck the straw off, it had to itch like crazy? With effort, Klara pulled her eyes away and focused on her uncle. "Otto, can Rani come?"

"Sure."

"Rani...?" Don Ricardo absently stroked the goat. "A Hindi name if I'm not mistaken. Is she Hindu?" Klara waited for him to answer, but he only cocked his head.

"Oh, sorry, I was… yes, she is. She's Hindu and knows a lot, actually."

"Wonderful."

"I'll call her then." Klara held up her phone. "I have my own cellphone." She dialed and received a recorded message. *'Please state your name and the reason for you calling me.'* "It's Klara," Klara said. "Don Ricardo will be at the Quaker meeting and hopes to meet you." She hung up. "She wasn't there," she told them. "I left a message."

Pontus gave Klara's slicker a tug. "Ready to milk a cow?"

From inside the barn, Rose assertively let out a long, drawn-out mooing—or rather 'booing.'

"Is she always this loud?"

"Only if it gets past ten."

"Is it past ten?"

"Just barely. She's CEO at guilt tripping, what can I say."

Rose might have been bossy, but she was also stately; her white fur covered with brown markings that spread across her body like landmasses on a world map. In the cramped stall, she stomped her hind legs, unsettling the stagnant air and making it teem quite gravely of cow.

Pontus put hay in the manger. "This should keep her quiet."

Klara looked at their supplies: a bucket with warm water, Vaseline, a rag… "Is she giving birth?"

"Those are for cleaning her teats."

"Ah… and a stool for me and a bucket for the milk. That's a big bucket."

"Actually there's two buckets but you only need to fill one. Just remember to grab the teat firmly. Squeeze down with a pulling motion, top to bottom. Aim for the bucket. That's all there is to it."

One by one, Klara got out of Otto's raingears and draped them over the top of the half-wall, then pulled up the sleeves of Frida's sweater and sat down on the stool. "Here goes." *Grab, squeeze, pull, drag, aim… aim is important. Get the rhythm—Yikes they're slippery—Grab, squeeze, pull…*

"How's it going?"

"Like running up a muddy hill in Otto's galoshes," Klara said, not losing focus. "Perhaps I could clean out milk bottles instead? I bet I'd be real good at cleaning milk bottles."

"Trust me, you'll do that too."

Her arms tired after a while so she stopped, tilted the bucket, and peered inside. "Not bad. Probably enough for a baby squirrel, though I don't know that baby squir—"

"*MOOOOOOOOOOOOOOOOOOOooooooOOOOOOOOO!*" With excellent aim, Rose kicked the bucket from Klara's hands. Klara, in surprise, toppled and Pontus dove, catching her head before it hit the cement.

Flat on her back, and with her head cradled in his hands, she smiled sweetly at him. "You know, Pontus, when I promised to milk a cow, I never said how much."

"True." Pontus helped her up. "Very true." He straightened the stool, placed one of the buckets under Rose, sat down, grabbed a couple of teats, and patiently began milking. In no time he'd filled the two buckets—*two* buckets! Then he grabbed Otto's raingear and tossed them over his shoulder, picked up the milking paraphernalia plus one of the buckets and unlatched the stall's door. As he held the door open for Klara, she picked up the other bucket and followed him, her sleeves only slightly dipping into the milk.

<h1 style="text-align:center">37</h1>

Making it through the cantankerous barn door would have been a challenge even without raingear, soiled paraphernalia, and buckets of milk. Pontus kicked it hard with the back of his foot like a stallion, while Klara went for the stick-butt-out approach; all the while, the two of them trying hard not to spill the milk, or touch each other.

Some distance away a boy stood leaning against a bike, a humored grin on his face.

"Hi, neighbor!" Pontus called out. "Meeting isn't until seven."

"Bored," replied the boy. "Thought I'd come over and annoy you."

"All taken care of." Klara greeted, walking up to him. "I like your bike. It looks indestructible."

"Thanks! No doubt it's an excellent bike for clowns and country merchants. It was my grandpa's and, come to think of it, is a lot like him—both of them humorous and unwieldy. I'm Corny, by the way."

"Right…" Klara wasn't sure if he'd meant his name or his

person… or both. Despite his eyes being hidden behind long bangs, she could tell he was taking things in. She liked that; observant people were always interesting. She put her bucket down, ready to shake his hand, then remembered that people her age don't shake hands. With exaggerated movements she flexed her fingers, pretending the bucket had cramped them. "I'm Klara," she said. "Klara Tippins."

Corny's eyes grew wide. "A Tippins? Don't tell me you're related to Drake Tippins!"

"He is my brother."

"No way! You're his sister? Gosh, you're so lucky. He's like the greatest guy. I see him around school; everybody loves him. So you're his sister…" Corny's eyes filled with sympathy. "Sorry about your accident."

"I'm okay, thanks."

"Drake told us all about it. How you can never… I'm sorry, I'm sure you'd rather not talk about it."

"Talk about what?"

"Never mind." The tips of Corny's ears turned red.

"But I'm fine. Really, I am."

"I'm sorry, I assumed they'd told you. If I'd known you didn't know, I would never—"

"Look here, Corny," Pontus interrupted, "Drake sometimes makes things up. I can assure you there's nothing wrong with Klara. Mom works at the hospital, she—"

"Drake wouldn't make something like that up," Corny balked. "No one would. Perhaps your mom hasn't been told?"

Clenching his teeth, Pontus stomped off. "Bring the milk to the kitchen, Klara," he called over his shoulder. "We need it on ice. Now."

As Corny and Klara joined Pontus in the kitchen, it got crowded. All the same, they managed to fill his glass jars with steaming milk, place them in the sink, then dump enough ice to cover the entire lot without much spillage or animosity.

When done, Pontus handed them each a soda. "How about we go to the back porch and play Monopoly?"

The glassed-in porch was Klara's favorite spot at Otto's house. Winsome and peaceful, it was shaded by a large tree and had always been the one place Drake never visited.

While Pontus set up the game, Klara took out her phone and dialed. "Rani," she said to the mailbox. "Me again. No reason for calling, except trying not to, and failing." She hung up. "What!" she snapped, staring at Pontus.

"Nothing."

"I'm not worried about her."

Pontus popped his soda. "It's okay to worry."

"No, it's not. It shows a lack of trust."

"Maybe."

Klara's phone rang and she nearly dropped it. "Rani!"

"Klara, I got your message."

"Where were you?"

"On my rock not far from the cottage. I sit there and listen to the brook until everything disappears; all my troubles,

everything. I decided to visit there before burning the sage."

"I see."

"Can you imagine a world where everyone sits on rocks?"

"Not really."

"Formless in a world of forms, changeless in a world of change—is the Self. When the wise sees the Self as omnipresent and supreme, they leave behind all sorrow. Katha Upanishad."

"Uh-huh."

"If you ever go looking for me, the area is marked with Tibetan prayer flags."

Klara tapped her foot. "Are you coming?"

"To the Quaker meeting? Absolutely!"

"Thank you!" Klara hung up. "She's coming."

"Who's coming?" Corny knocked over the pewter tokens he'd been stacking.

"A friend. I… I worried she wasn't okay. There was an episode last night and I kept thinking something might have happened to her."

"What kind of episode?"

"It involves my brother so I'd rather not talk about it." Klara straightened Otto's beat-up gameboard, remembering the times she and Drake used to play with it. Had she ever played to win? For as long as she could remember, the aim had always been to ensure that Drake won. Drake losing was out of the question. Drake losing meant endless monologues of how he'd been cheated, how 'technically' he'd won, how it'd been a silly game for silly people and they needed to understand, ad nauseam, that he'd moved on. His ramblings would go on for months; some grievances never ended, ensuring that everyone got really, really bad at winning. Of all their games, Monopoly was his favorite. Probably because his oponents losing dragged on and on… Klara shuddered; she'd have to reprogram her brain. What if they mixed things up? She took a swig of soda. "How about we add new rules?" she suggested.

Pontus grabbed the pewter tokens from Corny. "Like what?"

"Like, when we end up in jail, we can get out in four ways instead of three? We can use a Get-Out-of-Jail-Free card, pay fifty dollars, roll a double, or… admit to something we don't ordinarily tell people."

"Oh…" Corny mused, grabbing the race car token. "I sense danger."

Taking the Scottish Terrier for himself Pontus handed Klara the elf shoe.

Klara, being the youngest, got to start, then Pontus, then Corny. On her second turn, she was sent to jail. "So…" Pontus teased, "what did you do, Klara?"

"Drat," she laughed nervously. "Maybe new rules weren't such a good idea."

"You don't have to admit to anything," Corny noted. "You can just roll or pay."

"I know, but I was the one to ask for it." She twirled a die.

"I... I'm from another planet."

"ERRRT!" Pontus bawled. "I already knew that. Besides, it can't be something obvious."

"Fine." She turned to face the pasture. "I sucked my thumb till I was nine."

"Nine?" Corny took a sip of his soda.

Pontus straightened his money. "Sure," he said, "That'll do."

She rolled the dice and moved her piece, the elf shoe clanking against the game board in the awkward silence.

Pontus tapped his can. "I believe they mentioned that on NPR, you know, how aliens begin to suck their extremities as soon as they land. They did some surveys."

She gave his shoulder a light punch. "Just you wait, you'll be in jail soon enough."

One turn later Pontus went to jail. "Not just thumb suckers, they're psychic too! Alright, I choose admission and I'm going to admit that... I pee in the shower."

"Oh, for God's sake," Corny pushed his chair away from the table.

"I do, too," Klara chipped in.

"But you're not in jail," Pontus gave the dice to Corny.

"You don't have to be in jail to pee in the shower."

"Oh, Klara..." Smiling broadly, Pontus ruffled her hair.

In the end, Corny went to jail more often than any of them and he always shared something. Turns out he had:

spilled milk on his sister's homework and blamed the cat, filled his sister's boots with live bait, and, most disturbingly, put a dead chicken in his parent's bed.

Pontus admitted to having had a crush on his first-grade teacher.

"Was she hot?" Corny asked.

"Mr. Gonzales?" Pontus blushed. "Not particularly. I just liked him."

Hands down, Pontus won.

He won with such a margin no counting was required.

38

Klara, Pontus and Corny were having peanut butter and jelly sandwiches on the glassed-in porch when Don Ricardo opened the porch door, causing a gush of cool freshness to rush in, mixed with musky scents.

"Hello there, young folks!" Scratching his forehead, his straw-covered hat slid back to form a prickly cone at the back of his head. "I could use some help setting up the fire."

"You guys are doing a fire?" Corny's face lit up. He did not seem surprised at seeing Don Ricardo. Perhaps hats like that were common in these parts.

"We're doing one for the Quaker meeting tonight." Don Ricardo explained. "A sacred fire." He scratched his forehead again and Klara felt sure the hat would slide off, yet it remained.

"Splendid." Corny took a swig of soda. "We are just the people you're looking for." Then he caught himself and looked at Pontus and Klara. "We are, aren't we?"

"When do you need us by?" Pontus asked.

"Well, I was sort of hoping right now, actually, so it gets

done before the sun starts setting."

Klara swallowed the last of her sandwich. This might be her chance to ask Don Ricardo her questions. She had so many questions. She looked out at the snow-covered ground. Some parts seemed slushy, others icy. Though the rocks, which made up the firepit, were clear of snow, the rest of the pasture was not, and the pit was a fair distance into the pasture. "I'm not wearing raingear. I'll wear boots if you have them, but no raingear."

"So, it's a deal." Grabbing hold of his hat, Don Ricardo forced it down on his head. Klara tried not to wince.

Turned out Pontus had an old pair of boots that almost fit and an extra jacket that smelled of barn. Klara buried her nose in the sleeve and inhaled. "I don't think I ever want to take it off," she sighed.

"Keep it," Pontus assured her.

"Really?"

"Why not. Mom is at work, but I know she wouldn't mind."

"The jacket brings out the brown in your... your hair." Corny blushed.

Klara looked at a strand of her hair. "...eh, thanks?"

The ground was not as 'groundy' as Klara had feared and a cluster of aspen trees, their trunks still wet from the previous rain, looked magnificent against the brilliant snow as they huddled together in the middle of the pasture, their blanched leaves trembling in the breeze.

"We are going to use the seasoned wood that Otto has stored in his woodshed but also add some of our own sticks, just to get a sense of the sacredness of wood. It would be great to use aspen, as the quivering leaves are said to converse with spirit and the joint root system to be a symbol of unity, but, alas, it does not burn well."

"Uh-hu…" Corny shook his hair, his long bangs slowly drifting away from his face.

"So, how do we find wood that wants to be burned in a sacred fire?" Don Ricardo asked.

It took a moment for Klara to realize he wasn't going to answer. On impulse she raised her hand.

"Yes, Klara."

"I'd probably think of the sacredness of the fire, as a reference point, then check who, or rather, which wood resonates with that. Is that how you do it?"

"Doesn't matter how I do it. Your way sounds good."

"I'm lost." In the light wind, Corny's hair drifted back to cover his face. "We're gonna talk to sticks?"

"Not 'talk' exactly," Don Ricardo scratched his chin, "but listen. There are subtleties in the world that can only be experienced, not explained. And to be sure, I'm not asking you to see the world as I do, I'm simply giving you options."

"What about bark?" Klara asked. "Burning bark to give up the idea of needing protection? Everyday I say and do so many things to protect myself, what if I thought I couldn't be harmed? What if I could burn the whole idea of being vulnerable—wouldn't that be an extraordinary way to live?"

Corny looked at Pontus. "Does she always talk like this?"

Pontus nodded. "Afraid so."

Don Ricardo reached over and ruffled Klara's hair. "You go ahead and add some bark, starseed, and don't you listen to them."

Klara watched Pontus and Corny stroll off into the woods. "Don Ricardo?"

"Yes, Klara."

"How did you figure out you were a starseed? Did someone tell you? How old were you?"

"When I was twelve I was hit by lightning for the first time and then again at age twenty-one. Amongst the Q'eros it's thought that surviving a lightning strike opens you up; it makes you more perceptive and a likely candidate for becoming a Paqo. Please, Klara, recognize that in the Q'ero nation, Paqos are well revered and starseeds are spoken of the way people here speak of musicians. Me, being seeded on this planet from another star system, did not seem strange to people, or to me. It was a different childhood than yours."

Klara quickly reached down for a stick. "Don Ricardo, do you ever have a sudden longing that takes your breath away and you have to sit down, like a homesickness, but it's for a space of acceptance more than memories of an actual place? Like you think you're about to burst and collapse, both at the same time, like you can't breathe?"

"Sure. It probably means you went through the Arcturian Gate before you incarnated, just like me."

"The Arcturian Gate… why does that sound familiar?"

"Because it is?"

"Don Ricardo, do you ever wish you didn't remember? I mean, would you rather fit in? Do you ever doubt who you are, like maybe it's all in your head?"

"I used to doubt. I used to feel all those things. But then, oh, I don't know, it's kind of like an hourglass; first you are the sand falling and everything feels uncertain, then more and more of you lands at the bottom and you find yourself surrounded by a life that breathes along with you, not against you."

Pontus and Corny came back from their escapades in the woods and, together, they stacked Otto's logs in the firepit. Once the stack was a good size, about three feet high, they laid their sticks, and bark, on the ground nearby.

Don Ricardo scratched his neck and the hat fell off. "Thanks a lot, you guys." He picked up his hat, looked at it and stuck it in his pocket. "See you after dinner."

Waving behind him, Don Ricardo's square form disappeared into the dusk as he strode towards the black jeep he'd parked in Otto's driveway.

"Mom said you can all stay for dinner if you want." Pontus offered. "She told me to heat a casserole."

39

The first person to arrive for the meeting was, by far, the most noble person Klara had ever met; dark skinned and quiet, he had lustrous dreads draping well past his elbows.

"Welcome," Otto greeted. "Always nice to see a new face." He took the boy's coat and signaled for Pontus to bring slippers. Gawking at the boy with his arms slack at his side, Pontus did not respond. "Pontus?"

"Here you go." Corny brushed past Pontus as he handed Noble the slippers.

At the sight of the large and frightfully pink foot-attire, Noble raised his eyebrows. "Beautiful, man, thanks." With slippers on, he walked to the coffee table, grabbed a handful of popcorn, then plopped down on the brownish leather couch—the toad one.

It was quiet for a moment, then hysterical shrieks and giggles broke out in the entryway. Corny covered his ears. "And then there is Rosalyn."

"Who?" Klara asked.

"My sister."

With bright purple hair and green lipstick, it was clear Rosalyn liked attention. At the sight of the large pink slippers, she erupted into a dizzying fit of laughter, which seemed odd considering her hair color, though not so odd considering her black clothing, which, in Klara's opinion, were at least two sizes too small, exposing pale skin with no jacket in sight. Had she walked from their house dressed like that—in *this* weather?

Arm in arm with Rosalyn was a red-faced, semi-mortified girl who seemed undecided on whether to distance herself from her friend or join her.

It couldn't be… but it was! … Or was it?

"Mia? Mia Rasmussen?"

Mia looked over and did a double take—"Klara?"

The hug that followed was bumbly. Bumbly, no doubt, because of Mia's bulky jacket but also because of the bumbly situation. Mia smiled awkwardly. "Whyever did we lose touch?"

Klara felt suddenly hot and hastily moved away from Mia's jacket. "Why did we lose touch? Oh, I don't know." She tried to contain her sarcasm though it was a slippery thing. "Was it, perchance, because you walked the other way as soon as you saw me?"

Mia blushed and nervously tucked tufts of hair behind her ears. Like Klara, she'd had it cut; hers a little longer and jutting out like a skirt held out to curtsy. "There was something your brother told me. I know I should have talked to you about it, but we were young. I didn't know how to handle it."

"My brother? When would you have talked to my brother?"

"At the dumpster, bringing trash."

"Drake brings trash! But he's got purgamentophobia. It's a fear of... a fear of..." Klara thought of his room. "It's supposedly a fear of trash, though I suppose he's cured. A miracle—Praise be to Him!"

Mia cocked her head quizzically, then took her jacket off and handed it to Otto. "Anyhow, seems silly now. Not sure why I let it bother me. I mean, they were just flies."

"Flies?" Of all the reasons Klara had braced for, 'flies' had not been one of them. "What about flies?"

"How you freeze them, pluck some of the wings, then watch them fumble as they thaw. That you think it's funny."

"Oh my gosh, that's what *he* does!"

"Can't be." Mia looked perplexed. "He said he worried about you; that you might have a brain injury."

"Oh, for snakes' sake, not the brain again!" Exasperated, Klara pounded her head with her fists. Realizing this hardly proved her point, she stuck her hands deep into her pockets.

"It might not be true, what he said," Mia suggested, "but I *do* know he was concerned."

"Listen to yourself, Mia. If it isn't true, then why be concerned? He told you about the flies to break up our friendship. Then he said he worried to throw you off."

Folding her arms over her chest, Klara gave Corny a stare. "Do you still think I'm lucky to be his sister?"

"I don't know. He's a great guy. You might be—"

"Too sensitive? Overreacting?" In her pockets, Klara clenched her fists, the denim pressing against her knuckles. "You, Corny, don't question him. In fact, none of you do, so he's all sweet to you. Me? I question everything so I have to be made rid of. Because, you see, when his world doesn't run according to him, it caves in and—POW!—he explodes. Living with him is like living with a ticking timebomb. I hush my feelings and contort myself, and I do it alone because—no one believes me!"

The room went quiet. It was one of those moments when, if you were in a movie, they'd cut the scene. But this was not a movie, so she stood there wondering if she ought to leave.

Otto rubbed her back. "Your uncle believes you," he said with a crooked smile.

Corny started to say something, then dropped his arms to his sides. Pontus put an arm around him, then around Klara. Before she knew it, they'd all ended up in a group hug.

A couple of car doors slammed. One of them was a Fiat.

40

Otto's living room transformed the instant Rani and Don Ricardo stepped through the door. To Klara, it was as if all the atoms kicked up their heels at the sight of them.

Don Ricardo carried a large basket and a bouquet of red and white carnations. He wore a simple black poncho and an intricate hat. Not the hat covered with straw that Klara had seen earlier. This hat was different and more like her pixie hat, but certainly not a pixie hat as pixie hats don't have trails of large colorful tassels hanging from their tops and earflaps, nor are they knitted with geometric patterns lined with white glass beads. This hat, Don Ricardo's hat, looked celestial, clearly turning him into something potent.

Otto took the bouquet while Pontus fetched a vase. The flowers were lovely even if the gesture was odd—did Peruvian men always bring flowers? When Pontus came back, Otto unceremoniously dropped the flowers in the vase and brought them to the coffee table, leaving them without water and drastically leaning to one side.

"One more person might be coming," Otto announced. "However, as it's ten after seven, I think we should begin. Please, everyone, have a seat."

Klara wanted to sit next to Rani, but Rani chose one of the kitchen chairs Otto set out for the adults. Deciding between a couch and a floor pillow, Klara picked the orange couch and felt confident about her choice... until she sank down to where her knees nearly touched her chin. When Corny sat down next to her, she sank even further. "Me and my brother used to jump on this couch."

"That explains a lot."

"If you haven't heard from me in a couple of hours, send a search party, will you?"

"I'll try," he chuckled. "Though I'm pretty gone myself."

His sister chose a floor pillow. Why any person in low-cut, skintight pants would do such a thing was beyond Klara. Yet, as Rosalyn arched her chest and puckered her lips, she became surprisingly well-posed.

Mia chose a floor pillow next to Rosalyn and positioned herself so not to look at Klara. She seemed a bit contorted and certainly uncomfortable, but no matter, Klara didn't need her attention, she could watch Pontus hand out sodas.

Pontus finished and headed for the orange couch. Klara's heart made a skip and she fumbled to make room, squeezing herself close to Corny. Awkward, but it's the thing you do to be accommodating. Then Pontus stopped, halfway across the room, and looked at Noble. Noble was the only one sitting on the toad couch. For a moment Pontus wavered, then he smiled at Noble, grabbed a handful of popcorn, and plopped down next to him. As best she could, and with her dignity whimpering, Klara scrabbled back to her old spot in the couch.

Then Don Ricardo took a seat and Otto closed the door to the entryway.

No Drake. Could it be that he changed his mind...

"Welcome, everyone, to the Pennington Friend's Youth Group," Otto began. "A safe place to explore Life's questions, big and small. I am Otto Hayes, a pastoral minister with the Pennington Friends, but call me Otto." He gestured towards Rani and Don Ricardo. "This evening we are honored to have two very special guests with us: Dr. Rani Ghaiwal and Don Ricardo Nunez. Rani is a scholar of Hindu texts and of Sanskrit. She has knowledge in both philosophy and metaphysics and ..." Otto made quick eye contact with Rani. "... would be happy to answer any questions on those subjects."

"Yes," Rani smiled courteously. "Though I am not so much of an authority as all that. We all think we walk around this planet learning things, when, actually, what we are doing is remembering. So, whatever I tell you, you already know."

"Like I said," Otto smiled, "a philosopher. Now, Don Ricardo and I go back many years and even though we didn't grow up together, we're like brothers. While I grew up to be a farmer, having been raised on this very farm, he grew up in the Q'ero Nations high in the mountains of Peru and became a paqo; someone who perceives the world beyond the mundane, who speaks to the mountains and listens to the wind—all with reverence. Someone who, in some cultures are called a shaman, and in others a mystic. Now, as he insists on doing everything by hunch, I have to admit I haven't the faintest idea as to what he's got planned for us this evening."

"Neither do I," Don Ricardo grinned, causing laughter.

"What about the flowers you bought? I doubt they're for me. Are we, perhaps, to do a despacho?"

"Perhaps considering," Don Ricardo smiled.

"And might you tell us what a despacho is?"

"A despacho is a hands-on expression of gratitude."

"That's it?"

"It's best understood by doing."

"Fair enough. Everyone, please help yourselves to popcorn and soda and, seeing as there are a few new faces, we'll begin by introducing ourselves. After the introductions there will be a moment of silence and then I'll hand the reins over to Don Ricardo."

Otto waited for everyone to get back to their seats, then pulled a golf ball out from his jeans pocket and held it up. "This here is a 'Truth Ball.' As you might suspect there's a story that goes with it. It has to do with me being a kid and breaking a neighbor's window and so on, and so forth. No need to go into details." He absently twirled the ball between his fingers. "This ball will be passed from person to person. As you receive it, I ask that you state your name and, using only two words, tell us why you came. Please choose your words carefully as well as truthfully. I'll start." Hypnotically, the ball moved round and round in his hands. "As mentioned, my name is Otto Hayes and the reason I'm here is for enrichment." He handed the ball to Klara.

"Klara Tippins." Awkward in the deep couch she fiddled the ball, dropping it twice. Both times Corny picked it up and handed it to her, probably assuming her clumsiness was due to her 'head injury.' She sighed. "Basically I've come looking for assistance in acclimating to Earth."

"That's a new one." Otto looked amused. "Not sure that was two words though."

"Like I said, I need help." She was about to pass the ball to Corny when, wanting to apologize for dropping it, she blew it a kiss. Realizing everyone was watching, she felt heat rise to her cheeks. "Just wished to clear out any impure thoughts, is all," she concocted, relieved to hear everyone laugh.

"Well thank you, Klara." Corny grabbed the golf ball like a microphone. "I am Cornelius Sullivan. Call me Corny—everyone does." They all chuckled. "I am here to meet girls." They laughed.

"I'm afraid you didn't blow hard enough there, Klara," Otto joked. Corny quickly looked down. Did he blush? After studying the ball he passed it to his sister.

"Here you go, Ping," he said.

"Name's not Ping," she chided.

"I know. It's the name of the golf ball, but it suits you."

"Whatever." Rosalyn rolled her eyes. "Name is Rosalyn Sullivan… that's plain Sullivan without the 'O'." She looked down at the ball. "Oh, it does say 'Ping'!" Gazing her eyes at the ceiling, she wheeled the ball up and down her slender neck. "Two words for being here? Hm… free snacks?" She looked around. "What! Honestly, isn't that why we're *all* here?"

Mia reached over and took the ball from Rosalyn. "Thank you, Ping." Closing her eyes, she held the ball with both hands. "I didn't plan on coming. I had other obligations, yet I felt I *had* to come and I listened. Now I met an old friend." She looked at Klara. "I think that's why I came, so 'old friend' would be my reason. Oh, and my name is Mia Rasmussen."

Noble was next. Swaying to-and-fro, he made his long hair waft. "Jacob Meyers," he said, his words but a whisper. In the formless couch Klara labored forward, wondering if he'd mind terribly if she squeezed him, just a bit, to hear him better. "You can call me Tech. I'm here 'cause my mom said I had to get out of the house." He handed the ball to Pontus. "So, 'meet people' would be my reason."

"My name is Pontus Hayward and… same reason as Tech except this *is* my house so, no, my mom didn't tell me to get out." They chuckled and he stood up and bowed, then walked over to Rani, giving her the golf ball.

"Thank you, Pontus," Rani said. "I am Rani Ghaiwal and I am both honored and delighted to be here." She winked at Klara, blew the ball a kiss and passed it to Don Ricardo.

"Yes, thank you, Rani," Don Ricardo winked. "I feel the purity." He was about to say something else when they heard the front door slam open.

41

Klara grabbed hold of the couch, the fabric soapy and coarse—Drake? She looked out the window, but it was too dark outside to see. Then the entryway door flew open.

Of course it was Drake. Drake, in all his glory, gleefully taking over the world like an exuberant ringmaster.

"Heelloo!" With legs in a wide stance and wearing aviator sunglasses (he wore them while driving?) he flexed his arms and popped his collar. "I have come in devotion to the Christ Jesus… or whatever you call him." He swung his glasses off, his eyes settling on Ping. "Heelloo there, cutie."

Otto moved to the edge of his chair. "You came?" he squawked.

"Yes, Uncle, you may say I had a 'calling.'" With a sweeping motion, Drake addressed the room. "Angels told me all things happen for a reason and, guess what—I'm the reason!" With arms raised towards the heavens, he swung around, giving Klara vertigo. Was he on drugs?

Abruptly the twirling stopped and, squinting his eyes, he looked at Pontus and Tech. "I knew it!" he exclaimed, pointing at the two of them with his glasses. "Ack, ack, ack, Pontus, you shouldn't be here, should you? You should be in hell somewhere playing with *Barbie* dolls, am I right? I bet the billy goats pray to see you go—Ba Dum Tsss!"

Drake's rimshot ripped through Klara and she dug her fingers deep into the couch. Perhaps she'd missed the gist of the joke, but she felt the menace and her stomach churned. She looked around. They were all dumbstruck. Pontus was white as a sheet. "Pontus is a trillion times the person you are!"

"A trillion times freakier," Drake countered, spewing his hatred into the room.

"You're the freak!" She stood up, the couch no longer holding her. "Destroying everything that's precious, that's what you do. You're a menace to this world!" With a humph she sat back down.

"Whoa, whoa, easy girl." He gave everyone but Klara a meaningful glance. "Don't go crazy on me now."

Rani stomped her foot. With cold eyes and nostrils flaring, she looked like a tigress ready to strike. "It was you!" She pointed an accusatory finger at Drake, her voice barely restrained. "You nearly killed me!"

Shoving his sunglasses in his pocket, Drake bared his teeth. "How dare you! I'm an American and would never—while YOU," He pointed *his* accusatory finger at Rani, "you're one of those migraines. Damn! I should have put TWO kettles up there! DAMN! DAMN! DAMN!" With a growl Drake stormed over to the coffee table, grabbed the edge and flung it, scattering popcorn and flowers everywhere, the table nearly hitting Mia. "YOU CALL YOURSELVES CHRISTIANS?" He roared. "YOU CAN GO TO HELL!" With his arms pressed to his sides he marched out, slamming the door behind him.

"Bloody hell!" Mia exhaled. "Are you okay, Pontus?"

Noble Tech reached out to Pontus, but Pontus pulled back. No one else spoke or moved. No one righted the table or picked up the popcorn. No one retrieved the vase or the flowers. It was as if they were all holding their breaths, waiting. Waiting to hear the motorcycle start and for him to be gone—why hadn't he left already? Testily, Klara inched her way to the edge of the couch.

Finally, the blessed coughing and hacking of a motorcycle. The hacking escalating to a noxious grating that bore into her bones. She thought she'd shatter, but then it drove off and vanished—taking her brother's fury with it.

Otto walked over to Pontus. "I am so sorry. Had I known, I would never…"

"I'm fine," Pontus snapped. "I'm friggin' fine." He pushed past his uncle and stormed up the stairs.

Klara went to follow, but her uncle stopped her. "Give him space."

"No," said Rani. "He does not need space. Let her go."

42

It was dark in Pontus' room and at first she could not see him, only hear his muffled cries. Then she noticed the hump, like a large snail, shaking and heaving in the middle of the floor. Next to the hump lay Pontus' model airplane, the Red Baron, all smashed to pieces. Other planes were broken as well, scattered all over.

Gingerly treading across the floor, she made her way to him and, with her arms around him, shushed into his ear the way she knew Rani would. After a moment his sobbing subsided, replaced by occasional hiccups.

"He shouldn't have done what he did," she comforted. "You didn't deserve that. No one does. I feel like I should apologize on his behalf, you know, so *someone* apologizes, but I can't even... right now I refuse to think he's part of me. I'm sorry." Klara shuddered. "It is a terrible thing, wanting your brother gone, like filling the cracks in your heart with tar. But I can't help it. Not for what he does to people."

"You want him dead?" The hiccups stopped.

"I want him gone. You're my best friend, Pontus. No one's

allowed to do that to you." She unwrapped herself and let him sit up.

"It wasn't just that he told everyone and now everyone knows, it's that he ripped open my soul and spit on it. It was the shock of it and how much he enjoyed it. It tears at you."

"I know, Pontus. I'm sorry."

"A part of me can't help but wonder if he's right."

"Right about you! How can you... Remember Otto said people talk about themselves when they lash out? Maybe, deep down, Drake thinks he deserves to go to hell. That certainly makes more sense than... Pontus, you can't possibly believe..."

Walking down the stairs, everyone stood waiting. Once at the bottom, there was a group hug.

Holding Pontus' head between his hands, Otto kissed his forehead. "Will you ever forgive me?"

"For what?"

"For inviting him in."

"You couldn't have known."

"I should have known."

"No." Pontus shook his head. "No, your job is to believe in people."

43

Someone, or some people, had righted the table. They had put the flowers back and added a fresh bowl of popcorn. A fire had been lit in the fireplace and the chill that Drake had dragged in was gone. All the same, Klara had a sense of unease.

Sitting in their seats, they waited. Otto looked around, then he leaned towards Don Ricardo. "Do you have the golf ball?"

"I do. And I suppose that means I should introduce myself." Don Ricardo stood up. "I am Don Ricardo Antonio Nunez Rodriguez. I'd love to tell you more, but I'm afraid that's already more than three words."

Otto slapped his thighs. "Nice try buddy, but I want more from you than that. Though, of course, if anyone objects to Don Ricardo taking over, let me know. He can be a bit long-winded."

No one objected and Otto waved him on.

"Thank you. I will try not to be so long in the wind." Don Ricardo smiled. "I agree with Otto that we should do a despacho. However, a lot of hucha needs to be cleared before we can begin. What is hucha you ask? Hucha is a Quechua word in the language of my people. It's the word we give to energies that are heavy. Not surprising, Drake left more than a little behind." Don Ricardo played with a tiny tassel that hung down from a trail of larger tassels, flipping it back and forth, looking straight at Klara. "Anyone with keen awareness may experience hucha. Perhaps as a metallic taste in their mouth; like wet gravel. 'Clean that up!' they'd shout. It'd be as obvious as that. As obvious as picking up the popcorn that spilled on the floor. Now, of course, you don't want to pick up hucha. What you want to do is to digest it; you want to transform it. Any questions?"

Ping raised a hand. "You're gonna eat that stuff, the gravel?"

"Yes," Don Ricardo shifted his weight. "Yes, I am going to eat it. And once it's digested, once it's transformed and sent on its way, it will be replaced with sami. Sami is light energy. According to Q'ero cosmology, the universe has two forms of energy: hucha and sami; heavy and light energy. To us Q'eros the world is not filled with good and evil, it's filled with different densities of energy. If you ask a Q'ero if the glass is half empty or half full, they will tell you it's always full; half with water and half with air."

"But if you eat the gravel," Ping protested, "then it's in *you*!"

"No, actually not. But thank you for your concern, Ping. The reason it won't stay in me is because it doesn't belong to me. To digest hucha is to swallow someone else's anger, not your own. It *could* stay in me if I thought it was mine. This is why it's crucial to know yourself fully before you do this work. So, you know—don't try this at home—that sort of thing. Also, you need to digest hucha in the spirit of ayni; of giving and receiving. Doing things in ayni lets us see that we are all in the 'same boat.' Ayni is important. In fact, you may say ayni is what anchors and fulfills us."

"I don't get it," Ping insisted. "Why would being in the same boat fulfill me?"

"Good question." Don Ricardo let go of his tassel. "To do things in ayni is to celebrate our connections, acknowledging that all our actions affect others. Since ayni is how creation works and who we are at our core, doing things in ayni is always fulfilling. Any more questions?" Don Ricardo looked around. "Then we shall open sacred space, though I believe we need more floorspace."

While Otto and Tech moved the coffee table out of the way, Don Ricardo pulled a cloth bag from his basket and placed it in the middle of the floor. "Pick a rattle everyone!"

Klara chose a gourd-shaped rattle with a carved image of a hummingbird. In fact, all the rattles were made of gourds and all of them had carvings. Some were round and mounted on sticks with ribbons. Others, like the one Klara picked, were altogether gourd shaped and made her think of a birthmark, which was absurd.

Holding it lightly, Klara fluttered it about trying to connect with the spirit of the hummingbird. She was the only one to do so.

Corny, true to form, shook his like a drink shaker, Pontus and Tech hit each other on the head with theirs, Ping stuck two of them up her shirt, jiggled them around, then laughed hysterically while Mia busily dug through the bag.

Then Don Ricardo rang his bell. It was a small bell, yet they all quieted. "Thank you," he said and held up a cloth bundle. The bundle was the size of a first aid kit and tied with a white-beaded ribbon. Though the cloth was not as colorful as his hat, it held many of the same geometric patterns and seemed to be every bit as potent, if not more. "This is my mesa," he began. "My medicine bundle. The items inside are things I found in the mountains that helped me become a paqo; special rocks that lent me their strength and clarity— sacred items. Also, in my mesa, are gifts from my mentors: crystals and brass trinkets, though mostly rocks. All these items, these sacred personal items are called khuyas. The cloth that holds them together, and thus holds my journey, is a mestana cloth. Here, let me pass it around." He gave the bundle a kiss, then handed it to Ping.

"Wow, it weighs a ton!" Her eyes widened. "And something buzzes... Do you have a pump in there, or something?"

Don Ricardo looked pleased. "No pump. What you feel are all the energies contained in the khuyas."

When Klara held it, she understood what Ping meant. Not only was the bundle heavy, it hummed with the most extraordinary power.

Once back in Don Ricardo's hands he kissed it again. "We are now going to call in the Kawsay Pacha. Kawsay Pacha is made of two Quechua words: Kawsay, which means existence, and Pacha, which means time and space. You may think of the Kawsay Pacha as the 'world of living energy' or the 'primordial energy that animates matter.' Kawsay Pacha surrounds all physical objects; everything from atoms to humans to planets, even coffee tables and popcorn. Now, you may think it's the objects that create the Kawsay Pacha. Not so, it's the Kawsay Pacha that creates the object, and it does so through a feedback loop—which means that nothing in our lives is by chance."

"Sounds 'loopy' to me," Ping giggled.

Don Ricardo smiled. "It does sound loopy, and I am certainly not saying that this is how it is. Life is strange and there are many ways in which to make sense of it. If my theory helps you, use it; if it does not, then discard it.

"The most important thing for me, regarding the Kawsay Pacha, is that it's a flow of living energy which works much like a matrix or an algorithm and, as such, is neither compassionate, nor has much regard for time. It may give me hardship when I ask for peace, because the hardship will *ultimately* give me the peace I asked for. It may also give me hardship because that's what I've surrendered to, it's how I see myself.

"Thoughts create emotions; emotions inform the Kawsay Pacha; the Kawsay Pacha creates reality." Don Ricardo paused and looked around. "That was a lot to take in. I appreciate you guys hanging in there. Know that it's taken me years to learn this… and I still don't fully comprehend. If nothing else, I hope you walk away with some sense of the connectedness of life. Be kind in how you see the world, but even more so, be kind in how you see yourself."

Don Ricardo clapped his hands. "Now it's time to open sacred space." He rang his bell. "When I call out 'hayaya,' you all repeat hayaya and rattle, okay? And don't worry, everyone will look just as silly as you do. We begin by facing the four cardinal directions, one at a time, starting in the east where the sun so graciously greets us." Again, Don Ricardo jingled his bell. On impulse they all rattled—they were ready.

"Greetings, Spirits of the East!" Don Ricardo called out. "Hampuy hampuy, come, be with us! Let our minds soar between heaven and earth with Hatun Kuntur, Great Condor, as we behold the splendor of creation. Mighty Spirits, we thank you for being here, urpichay sonqoy. Like a dove, our gratitude flies from our hearts to yours. Hayaya!"

"Hayaya," they called and rattled. Then they changed position to face the south. Don Ricardo sounded his bell.

"Spirits of the South, hampuy hampuy! Sachamama, Great Serpent, be with us and help us shed our past with courage as we walk towards new beginnings. We thank you for your presence. Urpichay sonqoy. As a dove, our gratitude soars from our hearts to yours. Hayaya!"

"Hayaya!" They rattled and turned to the west.

"Spirits of the West, hampuy hampuy! Mighty Puma, bring our gratitude to your heart as you help us walk our lands with grace. Urpichay sonqoy, like a flying dove, our gratitude flies from our heart to yours. Hayaya!"

They rattled more and more soundly. In fact, Corny shook his rattle so emphatically, it flew by Ping's head.

Don Ricardo grinned. "Better aim next time." Then he rang his bell. "Greetings Spirits of the North, Sacred Hummingbird, hampuy hampuy! Be with us! Share with us your joy so we may find the nectar in our lives. We thank you. We thank you for your presence here. Urpichay sonqoy. Hayaya!"

"Hayaya!" They rattled and looked at each other—Were they done?

"Not yet." Don Ricardo kneeled and placed his hands on the floor. They all followed suit. "Pachamama, hampuy hampuy, our dear Mother Earth, we greet you and honor you and pray that we shall find your blessings within us. Thank you for your sustenance, your patience, and your unending love. Thank you for being here with us and in our lives always. Urpichay sonqoy. Hayaya!"

"Hayaya!" Along with Don Ricardo they stood and raised their arms to the ceiling.

"Hanaqpacha, hampuy hampuy, we greet you Inti Tayta, Father Sun, Mama Qilla, Mother Moon, Mother stars and constellations, please illuminate us with your brilliant light. Wiraqocha, Lord of Creation, Great Spirit we thank you. Spirits of the Apus, the Mountains and the Mountain Spirits: Ausangate, Salcantay, Huaman Lipa Our Protector, Mount Washington, Mount Marcy, hampuy hampuy, bless us with your ancient powers. Hayaya!"

"Hayaya!" They rattled.

Thinking they were certainly done, they started to look for a place to sit, but Don Ricardo remained standing. He closed his eyes and brought his mesa bundle to his heart. "Sonqoykuna, hampuy hampuy, all our hearts. In this our space we open our minds to wisdom, our hearts to the world and our bellies to our being, that we may find that we are one and the same. We thank you, magnificent spirits, for being with us, urpichay sonqoy, as a dove, our gratitude flies from our hearts to yours. Hayaya!" Don Ricardo kissed his mesa and raised it to the ceiling. "Hayaya!"

The room buzzed: the colors, the lights, the air—it all buzzed... and they along with it.

"Hayaya!" They rattled. Then their hands fell to their sides; none of them quite the person they'd been when they started.

44

Don Ricardo clasped his hands over his heart. "Thank you for bringing in such wonderful sami everyone. Not an easy thing to do after what happened. Can you feel the difference?" They nodded. "Excellent! Let us put the rattles back... you too, Corny. Then, please sit down. Not on the couches and pillows, please, on the floor close to Pachamama." With unexpected grace he placed himself on the floor, cross legged, then righted his poncho to cover his legs. "I'd be most grateful if you all held space for me while I digest hucha. Otto, perhaps you can talk about the Quaker's way of holding space by sitting in silence?"

"I'd be happy to." Otto leaned forward in his chair. "Holding sacred space and sitting in Quaker-silence is very much the same thing in my opinion. It's about joining together in spirit as we open ourselves up to the energies around us. I know it may sound a bit eerie, however, as you stay with it, you'll find that it's very much your home. Any questions?"

"May I go to the bathroom?"

"Sure, Rosalyn. Anyone else?"

They all got up and before long there were lines to both the upstairs and the downstairs bathrooms, with random shrieks of amusement coming from upstairs.

Once they'd regrouped and were sitting on the floor, they fell into a solemn mood—hucha was to be eaten.

"Close your eyes," Don Ricardo instructed, "and open yourself to the Kawsay Pacha with gratitude. Love works too, but love is finicky and means different things to different people, some bad, some good. Gratitude is gratitude and we all know what it feels like. You could say it has a clearer tonal value. Words have tonation, you see, even when not spoken. That's important to know. As we use words and place emotions into them, we give them tone and tone is what the universe is made of, so you see how important that is." Closing his own eyes, he murmured softly to himself as his hands lightly danced across his stomach. He seemed calm. He seemed in control. Klara too closed her eyes.

At first there was nothing. Then she noticed a subtle energy circling the group; round and round the energy swirled; clockwise, but also counterclockwise. Stretching upward and out, it filled the space with buoyancy. Feeling expansive, Klara lost herself in its splendor. Time passed—and disappeared.

In an obscure distance, Don Ricardo's bell softly rang. Then it rang louder. "Welcome back," he said. "As you are ready, please stretch for a moment and, while you do, I will set up for the despacho."

"Did you eat it?" Ping prompted. "Is it gone?"

"Does it feel gone?" Don Ricardo asked.

Ping looked around, then closed her eyes. "Yes."

"Good. Then we are ready to make a despacho."

While the group stretched, Otto helped Don Ricardo set up. First Otto brought over a couple of egg cups, then red and white wine (making Corny's eyes light up), then a large bag with bay leaves, a placemat, and a jar of *Crisco*.

It looked quite witchy, in a suburban kind of way, and Klara could not wait to start. When Otto sat down on the floor next to Don Ricardo and handed him a large piece of folded paper, they all took this as a sign and stopped stretching.

"The despacho," Don Ricardo explained, "is a prayer mandala. Each item we place in the despacho will be infused with our intent. When it's finished, we'll fold it into a bundle and leave it to percolate. Tomorrow, I will burn it. As it burns, our intent—our gratitude and our honoring—will go out into the Kawsay Pacha."

"Percolate?" Corny asked.

"I have no better word for it."

"No bonfire?" Pontus looked at Otto.

"Sorry kid, it's too late. People need to get home." He stroked his beard. "Don Ricardo, is there any chance you might come back tomorrow so we could burn it together?"

"Our hearts think alike." Don Ricardo tapped his chest with his fist. "I wanted to suggest the same but didn't want to inconvenience you."

"It's settled then. Anyone who wants to take part in the burning of the despacho can come here tomorrow at… shall we say seven o'clock in the evening?"

"Sounds good." With his broad hand, Don Ricardo unfolded the large piece of paper and smoothed it out on the floor in front of him. Then Otto began handing him tiny packages from the basket. Opening the packages, Don Ricardo explained each content in turn. "Sugar brings sweetness, corn is for sustenance, and rice we offer the spirit world. We add raisins to honor our elders. Not sure how I feel about that one; it's nice to be honored and all, but—raisins? Anyhow, there's also tobacco, that's for the sky father. Ah, and confetti, confetti is for joy and will be sprinkled over the despacho at the end." He opened yet another package. "Also, we have animal crackers. Those are to honor the animal kingdom. Rather stale, but I hope Pachamama won't mind. Oh dear, we're missing garlic! Otto, do you have garlic?"

"*Crisco* and garlic? My friend, you are quite the connoisseur." Otto went to the kitchen. "Why garlic?"

"To absorb the negative."

Ping stopped twirling her eyeball ring. "I thought we did that."

"There might be more." Don Ricardo opened the bag with bay leaves. "Everyone, please grab a handful. They would be coca leaves if those were legal, but bay leaves work just as well. Join three together with *Crisco*, which, if we were in Peru, would be llama fat. Three leaves together is called a k'intu; one leaf for the world below, one for the middle, and one the upper world: respectively called the Ukhupacha, the Kaypacha, and the Hanaqpacha; the past, the present, and the future. Also include three petals from one of the white carnations and three from a red one. Red represents Pachamama and the feminine; white represents the mountain spirits and the masculine. Balance is everything.

"When you've blown your wishes and your gratitude into a k'intu, pass it to me and make another one. As I receive them, I will place them in the despacho together with all the items from the little packages." Don Ricardo reached into his cloth bag and handed Otto a rattle. "Background music, please."

Klara smiled. This was kindergarten. This was the kind of kindergarten she'd always dreamt of: one where you played together with leaves and gook and energy.

The despacho looked beautiful when it was done. Not only had Don Ricardo added their k'intus, along with the raisins and all the rest, he'd also added many of the carnations, making the despacho look like a celebratory flower wreath, especially with the confetti and the dappled wine. (Turns out that's what the egg cups were for; to hold wine so Don Ricardo could dip a carnation in them and dapple the despacho.)

Leaning in close, everyone watched as Don Ricardo folded

the despacho into a bundle (much like his mesa), tied it with a string, jingled his bell, then took a cloth that Otto handed him. "This is a mestana," he said, holding it up. "Same kind of cloth as used for my mesa, though this one has been woven by a child and is pristine. I will wrap our despacho in it to keep till tomorrow."

They nodded. The idea that their despacho needed to percolate, now made perfect sense.

Saying goodbye felt strange, though the evening had clearly ended.

"I assume we all meet for brunch at the ski lodge tomorrow?" Otto offered and they all looked relieved, even Don Ricardo.

"My wife Sarah invited her mother for Sunday tea," he chuckled. "I know they'll both be delighted when I tell them I can't make it."

45

PLANET EARTH
— Terra Firma —
44,2042°N, 73,9932°W
Sunday March 21, 10:23 a.m. EST
As Per: Klara Tippins

"Are you sure you want to sit outside on a rock?" Klara pressed. "You might catch a cold." She and Rani stood huddled under Rani's bony apple trees, the branches partially protecting them from the late morning drizzle and not at all from the chill.

"I have a dream that needs sorting. It will be a quick chat with my brook and then I will join you." She pulled Klara in. "Do not worry. No matter what happens, I will always be there for you."

"We're only going to the ski lodge."

"I know. Have fun with the others and tell them not to wait for me with the food."

"I believe it's a buffet." Like a scarf, Klara tossed one of the ties to her pixie hat over her shoulder. "Isn't it great—Having brunch with friends? I never thought… I always figured— oh, here they are!"

Bouncing on her toes, Klara patiently waited as Otto meticulously navigated his truck to the side of the road.

Rani chuckled. "You'd think the man is landing a jumbo jet."

Pontus, sitting up front, rolled down his window. "Hi there, Klara! Ready for some chow?" From the backseat Corny and Ping leaned over and waved. All of them smiling. Smiling because they were happy to see her—to see *her*.

Enamored by the lightness of her being, Klara walked over and—smack into Otto's truck.

"Oops, I guess you didn't see that there!" Clasping both hands over his mouth, Pontus shook with mirth. Before long he was in tears. "I'm sorry, Klara, it's just… you looked so surprised."

With gathered poise, Klara climbed into the backseat, which, regrettably, wasn't much of a backseat. Making herself as slim as possible, she squeezed in next to Corny. How far was it to the ski lodge? She could ask Pontus; except he was still laughing. She turned to wave to Rani, but Rani was gone.

Probably not long, she decided. Probably not a long trip. And the food will be good.

The road up the mountain was curvy and they all held on tight as they listened to Otto talk about his truck. Evidently it had a five-point-six-liter engine.

"Holy smokes!" said Klara.

"You know about trucks?" Her uncle gave her an appreciative glance in the rearview mirror.

"I know about being excited."

"That you do."

As rain began to fall, the rock wall outside Klara's window quickly turned a silvery black. On the other side of the truck, a chilling drop-off grew mercifully veiled behind a thick mist. She looked behind. No Drake.

Out of the blue, Corny did a drumroll, bumping into Klara repeatedly. "I spy, with my little sharp eye, something that begins with... 'O.'"

"For crying out!" Ping moaned. "No one plays that game anymore."

"Odometer?" Pontus called out. Corny shook his head.

"Ozone layer?" Klara suggested.

"Nope. Though I like your scientific bent there, Klara."

Pontus turned around. "Is that a clue?"

Corny grinned.

"Oh, pleeze," Ping groaned. "Don't tell me it's Ophiolites."

The teens all looked at each other while Ping stared out the window. Pontus cleared his throat. "Say what?"

"Ophiolites." Ping rolled her eyes. "They're pieces of oceanic crust that get hijacked when mountain ranges rise. They're all over the Appalachians."

Corny tapped his leg. "So actually, I was thinking of 'Owl.'"

"You saw an owl with your little sharp eye?" Pontus sounded incredulous. Leaning towards the windshield, he peered up at the sky. "In the middle of the day? In the rain?"

"It was there a minute ago, I swear. So, who's next?"

"Next!?" Ping banged her head against the window. "Nooooooooooo."

Crossing his arms, Corny grabbed his shoulders. "What games do you like, Klara?"

"Solitaire."

"Solitaire, eh?" He raised an eyebrow. "Not Monopoly or UNO, or any game like that?"

"I don't like going against others."

"She's a killer at solitaire," Pontus volunteered. "Goes out every time."

"Not every time."

"Often enough to be epic."

"Oh yeah?" Corny looked intrigued.

"You want to know how to go out in solitaire?" Klara asked.

They all nodded.

She thought for a moment. "I'll give you three guesses."

"Three guesses each, or three guesses total?" Corny leaned forward, rubbing his knees.

"Each. You can start, Pontus."

"Any hints?"

"You want hints? Okay, it's not a parlor trick. It's not anything you learn. It's something you realize. That's your first hint."

"That's not a hint!"

"Sure it is. To intentionally go out in solitaire you must realize that existence is nothing more and nothing less than a big group hug."

"Not helpful!"

"Want another clue?"

"Yes."

"If existence is a group hug, then everything is connected."

"C'mon, Klara, that didn't help either." Pontus turned back around to stare at the windshield wipers. "I think you're messing with me."

"What about luck?" Ping asked. "Maybe you're just very lucky?"

"It's not luck. Think of it this way: If everything is connected, and you want to go out in solitaire—what should you focus on?"

"It's about focus?" Corny asked.

"Yes. But what should you focus *on*? You have two guesses left."

"You should focus on winning?"

"Nope, not reliable. I tried that."

"Focus on how brilliant you are and see yourself winning?"

"That's not how I do it."

"Ah jeez!"

"Remember, everything belongs together," Klara prompted.

"Tell the cards to behave?" Ping chimed in.

"Getting closer, but no."

"Tell the cards to… *not* behave?"

"… eh… no."

"So how do you do it?" Corny rhythmically tapped his thighs. Unsuccessfully, Klara tried moving out of his way.

"How do I do what?"

"You're not telling us?" He stopped tapping.

"You were all offered three guesses."

"Oh, come on, you have to tell us."

"Do I?"

They all got quiet and Klara wished she'd said things differently. Perhaps Mother was right. Perhaps people were made uncomfortable around her.

For a long while, she tried to think of why Mother was wrong—she thought of nothing.

46

The only cars in the parking lot were parked far from the entrance and probably belonged to the staffers. Had they opened? Driving up to the door, Otto rolled down his foggy window and peered at a sign. "They open in twenty minutes." Getting wet, he quickly rolled up his window and drove the truck to face the grand view—or what would have been a grand view if it hadn't rained so hard.

Twenty more minutes of sitting next to Corny... Klara looked past the front seats and out the windshield, the rain so massive it seemed like fluctuating slates of water. She thought of Rani and shuddered.

"On a clear day, you can see all the way to Canada," Corny told them.

Klara tried to imagine. "How do you know it's Canada?" she asked. "Isn't there just woods, woods and more woods?"

"Canada is on the other side of the St. Lawrence River. It's a big river and you can see the water all the way from here."

Klara felt stupid. She should have realized this. Thankfully, no one sneered.

An old truck with bulging fenders parked next to them. Faded and rusty, it was anyone's guess what color it'd been, though maybe blue. A window cranked open and Tech's arm stuck out. Instantly, Pontus zoomed his window open and waved back. Mia, sitting next to Tech, leaned forward and smiled. The rain poured and both windows closed, Tech's window quickly fogging up.

"Mia got a lift," Klara said. "How nice."

Next, Don Ricardo showed up in his black jeep. He flashed his lights. No windows opened.

No sign of Drake. No sign of Rani either.

They waited some more, and then, on some unspoken cue, they all dashed out of their vehicles and ran for the lodge.

Warmth greeted them inside the lodge; a pushy in-your-face kind-of-warmth, but a warmth nonetheless. There were hooks for their wet jackets, but other than that... other than that, the place was surprisingly non-impressive. Shouldn't a place with splendid (or supposedly splendid) views be, in some ways, splendid? At least to the point of not reminding Klara of a school cafeteria with long bench-tables and dark paneling (from the same dubious era as Otto's couches, no doubt). The only thing *not* gloomy were the large windows; those were nice, even if they seemed drafty.

Pontus stood behind her, lost in thought.

She nudged him. "The walls don't like the paneling."

"Huh?"

"They want wallpaper and demand I tell someone."

"Yowza!" Corny nearly walked into a table. "That's freaky!"

"What?"

"I understood that."

Pontus jolted. "What did you say, Klara?"

"Nothing."

From a table in the center of the room, Otto waved them on. "How about this table? It's closest to the food with plenty of seating, even for when Rani gets here." He glanced out a window. "And speak of the Devi, here she is."

Klara grabbed Pontus' arm. "She's safe."

"Why wouldn't she be?"

"She told me she'd always be there for me."

"… Oh." Pontus scratched his head. "And that's a curse?"

"No, I mean, why would she say that?"

Rani's coat was dripping wet and Otto held it at arm's length as he helped her out of it.

"Otto," Rani said. "May I ask you a problem?"

"A problem? Sure."

"The brakes to my car concern me. It might be time for new… what do you call them… stop blocks."

"You mean brake pads?"

"… Yes."

"I'll be sure to check them before we leave."

"Here? You will check them here at the lodge?"

"Why not? With all of us here turning your car over should be easy. Heck, I could probably flip it myself."

"You are making fun of my car?"

"Yes. Yes, I am."

Rani put her hands on her hips. "My car may be small, but at least it does not make people wonder what I'm compensating for."

Otto laughed. "Not like my mastodon out there?"

Klara glanced at Pontus. "Past life, third century Europe?" she suggested. "She was a Roman empress and he the carpenter."

"What?"

"Never mind. Apparently, you, Pontus, were the sawhorse."

47

Having never been to a buffet, Klara could not have anticipated a spread where one could choose anything from green salads to fried chickens to sushi to scrambled eggs. Though it took some arranging, in the end she made herself a peanut butter sandwich with cottage cheese and sliced bananas.

"Looks like Rani's flair for the culinary arts has rubbed off on you," Pontus teased.

"I'm having scrambled eggs with bacon and apple sauce," Tech announced, a gleam in his eyes.

"Lame!" Pontus grabbed a heap of string beans and slapped them on his pancake. "Beat that!" Tech's eyes opened wide and the two of them lost themselves in a titter.

Mia, standing behind Tech, excused herself and walked over to Ping who was getting lasagna, a lot of lasagna. How could such a small thing eat so much? Klara shook her head and left to get a cup of hot cocoa at the beverage station. Hot cocoa and bananas were sure to go great together.

There was no hot water at the beverage station, but she

could wait. In fact, a moment to herself would be welcomed. "Won't be long," one of the cafeteria workers told her, a gangly college kid with a hairnet.

"Hi there!" Corny made her jump. "What did you wish for yesterday with Don Ricardo? I wished for better grades, though I probably shouldn't have told you that." He was at the soda fountain next to her, mixing all sorts of flavors into one cup: *Mountain Dew, Fanta, Dr. Pepper…* Klara tried not to stare.

"Grades are silly things for silly systems." Feeling suddenly impatient, Klara tapped her mug.

Then Ping was there, reaching in front of her, grabbing napkins. "Your brother, my gosh! Why did he get so mad?"

Klara shrugged. "What did you wish for, Ping?"

Ping blushed. "To fit in."

Barely stifling a snicker, Klara coughed. If Ping, with her strikingly purple hair and black lipstick, wanted to fit in, then she should hook up with *The Addams Family.* Klara meant to tell her as much when she caught the vulnerability in Ping's eyes. "Oh, Ping," she sighed, "we all do. We all want to fit in. Though not all of us are brave enough to admit it."

"So what about you, Klara?" Corny prompted. "You haven't told us what you wished for."

"You're going to think I'm corny. I mean, not Corny the way you're Corny, I mean… fatuous."

"Fatuous? Sure."

"Okay… so I was hoping for advice on how to help people

who are… you know… who are mean."

"Help them? Oh, Klara." Corny did a facepalm. "Serve *everybody*, that's so Buddha Buddha."

"There's nothing wrong with that," Ping chided. "Look at her face. It's such a Buddha face. All peaceful and shit."

"My face isn't peaceful." Klara turned her back to them, having finally gotten the attention of the guy with the hairnet. "How long for the hot water?"

"Sorry, miss. Just a moment."

"Don't get me wrong," Corny said, "I like your Buddha face, but why help your brother?"

"Yeah," Ping chimed in, "You want to strangle him, don't you?"

"Oh, Ping, you have no idea."

The college kid came back and flipped a switch. "Should be good to go in a minute or two."

Over at their table, Tech and Pontus were still at it: Tech tickling Pontus' neck with a dreadlock; Pontus feebly defending himself, grabbing Tech's head, rubbing his forehead. Mia, sitting next to them, looked like she wanted to sink through the bench. "Hi, Klara!" Pontus almost sounded drunk. "Me and Tech plan to fix Rani's bike. Wanna help?"

Her tray slammed the table. "You said it was a women's bike."

"Forgot." He gave Tech a quick smile. "We'll fix it up for you and Rani, then."

"We can fix our own bikes, thank you very much."

"… Klara?" Pontus let go of Tech.

"You know, I thought we were friends, but all you do is laugh. You laugh at me for getting wet in the rain and falling down stairs and walking into trucks, for wearing Frida's clothes and Otto's raingear, and now you laugh at my food. Laugh. Laugh. Laugh."

Pontus looked stunned. Rani too. A tiny voice told Klara to stop, but trolls had run up her spine. "You're not my friend!" She watched his face fall and did not care. If only she could sit far away from him, like Australia, but there was no seat other than the one opposite him. The entirety of her sandwich would have to be eaten with a fork lest she look at him—oh, bother.

Ping, sitting next to her, delicately removed a strand of hair from her face then raised her hand. "Reverend Hayes?"

"Please, call me Otto."

"Reverend Otto, there's something I've been wondering."

"Yes?"

"My mom reads this passage from the Bible before dinner. Like, if she doesn't read it, she'll get salmonella or something. It's weird. I mean, didn't God hear her the first time she read it? It's about death and shadows and stuff and, somehow, reading it will protect her." Ping removed a second strand, crossing her eyes in the process.

Corny raised a hand. "Can confirm."

"I see…" Pensively, Otto twirled his beard into a point. It

made him look significantly not like a minister. "Are you referring to the Shepherd's Prayer: 'Yea, though I walk through the valley of the shadow of death, I will fear no evil for thou art with me'—does that sound familiar?"

"That's it!"

"I don't think God is hard of hearing, Rosalyn, I think we are. Or, rather, we listen to our minds when we should be listening to our center, our heart. Our heart tells us to trust ourselves, to trust our ability to cope, but we ask our minds; the one organ whose entire purpose is to question." Otto chuckled. "Though it's not easy listening to the heart, I'll grant us that, it's so very quiet compared to the mind."

"That is why I sit on my rock," Rani piped in. "To feel safe. The mind likes to run around, but sitting on a rock quiets my mind and I can be present. And, you know, at the end of our time, the only moments that will count are the ones where we were present."

Though the rain had stopped, the air was raw and they shivered as they watched Otto jam coffee stirrers between the spokes of Rani's tires. Once a straw was in, he drew a line, pull it out, examined it, humphed, then repeated the process with the other tires.

"About six millimeters." Otto stood up, rubbing his back. "Time to change pads, but not so bad you can't drive a while longer. When it's time, I'd be happy to change them for you."

Rani gave the stirrers a skeptical look, "Thank you, I will take your offer under consideration."

Going back home, Klara didn't want to ride in Otto's truck with Pontus, nor did she want to go with Rani. Rani would ask questions and Klara wasn't ready to explain herself. Don Ricardo, bless his heart, didn't mind her fickle company.

Tech and Mia were first to leave, the bulbous truck saluting everyone with a cheerful *kapow!* as it exited the parking lot. Next to leave was Rani, then Klara and Don Ricardo, followed by Otto's truck close behind.

Though the Jeep's suspension was stiff, Don Ricardo's hand at the wheel was stable and Klara felt her nerves ease. "Don Ricardo, do you ever feel like you're on a mission?"

"You mean, like looking for a good place to eat, that kind of mission?"

"No, bigger than that. A life mission."

"Oh, I don't know." He tapped the steering wheel with his thumbs. "I'd like to think my soul goes to the stars when I die and I get to meet my cosmic family. I like to think they will pat me on my back when they see me, saying, 'Well done'— and I won't even know I did it."

"I have dreams where I'm told to love everyone."

"My goodness."

"I know. It pisses me off."

"Ah…" Chuckling softly, Don Ricardo stopped drumming.

"Don Ricardo, if someone is jealous of you from a distance,

like all the way from Malaysia, does that affect you, I mean, seeing as everything is connected?"

"Well, one's thoughts affect the Kawsay Pacha so it makes sense this would include the thoughts other's have of you and, very likely, would affect the energy-sphere in which you operate. However, and this is a big 'however,' no one is at the mercy of other's opinions as everyone's sphere is quite large and we all operate within it with our focus. In fact, the best defense against someone's jealousy is to send them love. Not only does this neutralize the heavy energy they're hurling at you, but it will undoubtedly amplify your understanding of yourself as a loving person. Seeing yourself as a loving person will raise your physical vibration within the sphere-continuum, perhaps to the point where their jealousy simply bounces off of you!"

"Uh-huh. So, like, love everyone?"

"Yeah… Including yourself."

"I am so screwed."

"Apart from yourself, Klara, it doesn't have to be a 'close-to-your-heart' kind of love. Broadening your understanding of love to where you care for them as a quirky, yet legit, part of the human species should be sufficient."

48

Ahead of them, Rani swerved. Then she swerved again, nearly missing a curve.

"Hold on, Klara, we need to keep up!" Clutching the steering wheel, Don Ricardo stepped on the gas. "She's got no brakes!"

Hurtling around turns, Klara braced herself against the dashboard, but no matter how fast they went, Rani went faster.

A delivery truck. White boxy and taking up the world. Rani going much too fast. Much too…

The Fiat tore into a guard rail—flipped—and continued. She continued…

Black smoke billowing from down a steep slope.

The Jeep skid to a halt and they were out and running.

Small car, compacted against a giant boulder… and smoke. Why so much smoke?

Scrambling to reach Rani, she was held back. She wrestled free and a bird flew at her face.

An explosion.

Flames so high. So high for such a small car. Like haughty dragon tongues, they licked the black smoke.

Furious, she glared at the sky. "HOW DARE YOU!" she screamed. "HOW DARE YOU TAKE HER FROM ME! YOU BRING ME HOME—YOU HEAR! YOU BRING ME HOME RIGHT NOW!"

She ran now. Away from the stinging black smoke and the burning air.

The ground let her. The ground let her run and she kept running until she ran no more, and the ground reached up and wrapped her into silence.

49

480 LIGHT YEARS FROM EARTH
— At Federation Headquarters —
Sunday March 21, 1:08 p.m. EST
As Per: Klara Tippins, aka Kalanna Boon

The being looks at her intently. Though she doesn't recognize the triangular face, it does not frighten her. "Where is my body?" she asks.

«What body?» The slim bipedal individual appears to be male, though the fluid movements seem female.

"My body!" Klara demands.

«Oh, you mean the physical one! It is resting in a wooden... give me a moment...»

"A coffin!?"

«I believe it is called... just a moment... a low-profile platform twin-size bed.» The being looks pleased. «This wooden structure is in a dwelling I believe you refer to as 'Otto's House.' The body of your inquiry is breathing. You had quite a shock.»

She examines her plasmic form. A powdery light emanates from it, like a mist or a memory. As she moves, the powder is left behind like footprints. She's wearing her nightgown. The one with ducks. The one Rani gave her.

Rani… something about Rani…

The chin on the triangular face is pointy to the brink of looking painful, the eyes small and set far apart. No nose, no ears.

The eyes again, watery (or very shiny) and full of concern. «Your grandfather has been notified. He will be with you shortly.»

What was it about Rani?

«My name is Exodun. Exodun Maeyenee the Third. I am here for calming and for observation. From your mind I detect you asking about your mother, the mother whom you refer to as Rani. It has been cleared that I may inform you that she has exited the Earth plane.»

"She died?"

«Yes, that would be accurate verbiage depending on what is implied. Presently your mother is in a balancing facility. She is confused, but beyond that she is in no pain.»

"Can I see her?"

«Visually yes, she can be seen, but visit her? No, you cannot visit her. She is in the process of refocusing the fractal energy of her electromagnetic structural field.» Klara senses him studying her. «Perhaps I am not doing well at the calming aspect of my services. I fear my words are inadequate. As previously stated, your grandfather should be here shortly.» The being crosses his long arms over his chest. His spindly fingers tap his forearms, two fingers on each hand.

"What happened?" Klara asks.

«Yes?»

"How did Rani come to exit Earth?"

«It has to do with the vehicle in which she traveled. I am here referring to the mechanical vehicle, not her corporeal one. A tubular structure that was to bring fluid to the braking mechanism had been punctured by the brother Drake. He did so in anger.»

"So that's what took him so long. We should have…"

«Yes.»

"Did he mean for me to… to be in the…" Klara feels suddenly cold.

«As previously stated, his person was angry. He does not have a stopping mechanism for his person.»

Klara feels her mind collapse.

«Oh dear,» she hears the being call out.

And all goes black.

She's flat on her back now, lying on a cot. It's dark and she can hear muted voices; Gompsie's and others. She senses the voices more than hears them and can feel their distress. Why distressed? Because of Rani? Keeping her eyes closed, she listens.

«There's a process to the grieving,» her grandfather sounds exasperated. «She can't just dash through this.»

Someone else says something she can't perceive.

«Understood,» agrees her grandpa. «I am well aware.»

More murmur. Then the voices fade and she feels her grandfather's loving presence. She opens her eyes and finds him coiled on the floor next to her.

«My child.» Tears well up in his eyes. He takes her face into his hands and light fills her—His light? Her light? Unexpectedly something sparks inside her, like a prism caught in a beam.

"Grandfather," she asks. "Why did Rani have to die?"

«The event-frequency was in alignment with our mission and I could not stop it. I'm sorry.»

"What happens now?"

«Depends on a great number of things.» He removes his hands and her cheeks become instantly cold. «Once the Council of Elders has assembled, we will meet with them. Hopefully they'll be able to give us some answers.»

"The Elders are coming to Buxtin?"

«We're not on Buxtin, Klara, we're in an inter-dimensional space on Antut. For your sake the organizers made it look like Buxtin.»

"And I am to meet with the Elders?"

«Absolutely.»

"In my pajamas?"

«Is that what that is? It looks splendid.»

50

The domed-shaped greeting hall is gray, smells of clay and has a liquid light that runs in a moat around its perimeter, giving it a cavelike appearance. Klara grabs tight to her grandfather's hand. As both hands are rather insubstantial, the handholding is more of a charged-like-suction than an actual hand-squeeze. It will do.

A wide desk sits at the opposite end from where they are. Behind the desk, six odd-looking beings stand, one of them a ten-foot-tall praying mantis.

"Do they have to be so intimidating?" she asks.

«You find them intimidating?» Her grandfather lets go of her hand and gingerly supports her elbow as they proceed forward; her wafting and him slithering. The arrangement is awkward, but sweet. «It's your projection you know; it's whatever you expect.»

"If I change my expectations, I can have them sitting on a beach?"

«Certainly.»

"And we can build sandcastles together?"

293

«Why not?»

She closes her eyes and imagines a beach. When she opens them, she finds the same huge dome with the same row of stern-looking Elders. "It's not working," she gripes.

«Oh, sorry, I forgot how strong Earthlings' emotions are. It's the emotions that inform creation, you see, not the thought. My apologies. Just know they are here to help you, not judge you.»

"Help me, really?" Klara looks at the beings again. A humanoid feline, about six feet tall, stands to the far left. She has green eyes, black luminescent fur, and large catlike ears. The woman tilts her head sideways and could possibly be more curious than grim. Klara can't tell if there's a tail.

Next to the catwoman is the praying mantis. With large triangular eyes and brown exoskeleton, he looks professorial, though perhaps in a learned way and not so very stern...

Even stranger than the praying mantis is the large bubble of water that hovers to the right of him. Inside the bubble is a manatee, or what resembles a manatee. Instead of gray skin, this creature has purple skin with rust-colored markings, each marking edged with bands of bioluminescence. And its eyes are to the front, not to the sides. They seem to look straight at her with... kindness?

Next to the bubble, at the center of the desk, stands a noble female with brilliant blue skin, a long slim neck, prominent deep eyes, and a large bald head with a slight depression, front to back, like a plum. All other features are small, the ears barely visible. She wears a flowing silvery robe with a golden sash and is about Klara's height. Not the tallest, yet she is clearly the spokesperson, and not only because she's in the center; there's something commanding about her.

As Klara continues looking down the wide desk, she sees, what can only be described as a blowfish lamp; round and illuminated from within, it floats in the air, incessantly scanning the room with its large yellow eyes, its spikes protruding in all directions. She tries to read its disposition, but it makes no eye contact; each eye independently staring at odd angles from the other.

Next to the blowfish is a woman so luminescent Klara can't see her facial features, nor what she's wearing. Except for the woman's hair being long and straight, she reminds Klara of her grandfather.

The last seat is empty except for a magnifying glass propped up on a stand. Even amongst the Elders, Klara reckons, people are late. She's about to share a snide remark with her grandfather when something moves behind the magnifying glass; something less than a few inches tall with wings on its back and antennae on its head, wearing baby blue spandex—A faerie!—She nudges her grandfather. "Grandpa, there's a faerie amongst the Elders!"

«Do you like faeries?» he asks cautiously.

"I do!"

«Good. Then there's a faerie.»

The blue lady in the center holds up both hands in a kind

of greeting. «Kalanna Boon, we are most delighted to meet with you.» The blowfish lamp gives the woman a prickly nudge in the side. Attentively, she leans towards it, listening. «By all means!» she exclaims. «We are most delighted to meet with you—Klara.» Lightly touching her heart, she bows cordially. «I am Ayvor Neteen, head of the Council of Elders, a delegate of the Galactic Federation. The reason we are meeting here today... that is applicable, yes? 'here today'?» Again the blowfish whispers to her. «Excellent! Here today we delight in your presence and feel confident we will reach many pivotal conclusions.»

All beings nod, even the blowfish lamp, who does more of a bob than an actual nod.

«Before we begin, let me introduce the Council members. As I do so, be advised that our names may not be easily digested by human ears. If they cause pain, please let us know.»

Ayvor gestures towards the black feline. «First let me introduce our honorable Zia Ferenit who bestows upon us the wonderful ability of bringing odd things together, creating harmony and cooperation in the most cumbersome of situations.» The catwoman waves. She has hands, not paws.

«Next, I would like to introduce our dear Ulmar Erknasoot. He holds the longest consecutive existence of all of us, and not looking a day past 4.8 billion.» Ayvor smiles broadly and Klara can't tell if she's being serious or not. «Thanks to his good memory, he has profound knowledge of time, space, and the altering of timelines.» The praying mantis slowly clasps his appendages together, indicating a small bow.

«Joining us from inside their marine sphere,» Ayvor continues, «is Paxin Plimm. Mx. Plimm is endowed with a high degree of intelligence and a deep understanding of subconscious emotions. Something that, unquestionably, is most desirable.» The manatee blinks jovially at Klara.

«To my left we have my close associate Ertnet Kvor.» The blowfish lamp bobs enthusiastically. «We go back quite a ways, me and Mq. Kvor. His main offering… here today, is to make use of his outstanding psychic abilities.» Without waiting for the blowfish to stop bobbing, Ayvor moves on.

«Standing on the other side of Mq. Kvor is a dear friend of mine from Otim Dorum, Lénah Merlekten, who has asked to be here to lend emotional support.» Studying the bright woman closely, Klara finds that not only does she resemble her grandfather physically, she seems to be just as mindful and true.

«Last, but not least, we have Bob Hilkentop, our friend behind the magnifier. His artistry of bringing dark matters to light is unsurpassed, something we are grateful for, especially here today.» The faerie leans towards the magnifying glass and Klara sees his face. With a large forehead and a pointy nose, he looks both young and old at the same time and seems to be wincing each time his wings hit the glass.

«So here we are, gathered and honored to serve.» In unison, they all bow, then Ayvor Neteen adjusts her commanding pose. «Klara, what do you think of your brother?» The question takes Klara by surprise. «You perceive him as a brother, do you not?» The plum-shaped head cocks to the side. The eyes glisten.

"I think…" Klara falters. "I think he should leave me alone."

The Elders exchange looks.

«Assuming that we still have a contract within RAMA,» Ayvor turns to the feline who nods, «what would you say, Klara, if we sent him far, far away to mine an asteroid?»

"Yes, thank you, I'd… I'm sure he'd love to explore space."

«Quite so,» Ayvor agrees. «What about karma? Do you, Klara, think Drake should be punished for what he's done to you?»

"You want to punish Drake on my behalf? But aren't you all-loving?"

«Did we ask you to tell us what you think it is that we are thinking?» Ayvor furrows her brow. «Or did we ask you to tell us what you think?»

All those wise faces. Klara sees no judgment in any of them.

"I assume punishment only makes heavy energies heavier, so… we should work out our karma for ourselves?"

Paxin, the manatee, blinks repeatedly. «What if I told you Drake's primal self is your son?»

Reflexively Klara bursts out laughing and the Elders recoil.

«My dear, you have very large emotions.» The manatee is

not laughing.

"Drake! My son? That's not possible!"

«You are correct.» Lénah mutes her light and Klara sees her pointy cheekbones and deep-set eyes. «Drake is your brother and thus cannot be your son. His primal self, however, is your son from Otim Dorum. Does the name Dwinndleton Mq. Boon ring a bell?»

"I had a toy dragon named Dwinn, but that's a name I made up."

«Or, dear Klara, perhaps you chose that name because it was close to your heart?» Lénah smiles gently. «You see, it was because of your son that you incarnated. Your primary order was to remain with Captain Writtum while the others went to Earth; first your parents, then Dwinn. Unfortunately, Thubans meddled with Dwinn's DNA causing him to have psychopathic tendencies. When you found out you decided to join him and, without hesitation, incarnated a mere three years later.»

"My son..."

«You hoped to mediate the situation. You see, if his quantum frequency is low when the one Earth becomes two Earths, you might not see him for... I believe the latest estimate is near eternity?» Lénah briefly looks over at the praying mantis, who gives a crisp nod.

"Drake... I have a son?... Then, who is the father?... Surely not Noburu!"

«Yes,» Lénah nods, «we can see it's a lot to take in.»

51

Fluttering intensely, Bob Hilkentop makes his way to Klara. As he hovers in front of her face, she notices he's put on a pair of aviator glasses, making him look quite adorable. «I wish to invite you to a time-point-repositioning and re-line-adjustment exercise to dissolve attachments,» he says in one breath, his eyes large behind the glasses. «I am delighted to see you have acquired a Pleiadian Comemeya necklace. This will undoubtedly come in handy.»

"A what?" Looking down at her powdery form, Klara sees blue orbs swirling around her heart. How long had they been there?

«The Comemeya has been noticed. Very good. Now hold out a hand and wait for Drake to appear in your palm. He will be in your mind's eye and hopefully not too large. Consciousness is a sticky thing so be cautious. Do not focus on grievances, focus on acceptance. And close your eyes, please.»

Closing her eyes, she sees her brother standing wide-legged in the palm of her hand with arms defiantly crossed over his chest. For some reason he's covered in soot.

Hopefully he's a good size.

«Your brother will not leave until you have released your anger towards him, that's the soot. When he no longer feels abrasive to you, bless him and let go.»

"My grandfather, Captain Gompsie, tells me the same thing, though in a different way."

«Of course. There are many ways to bake a pie.»

Trying not to think of coconut custard pie, Klara closes her eyes. Shoot, her brother grew bigger! With a sense of panic, she searches for memories of when he was nice, sometime before he turned everyone against her—even herself! All connections torn, all hope ripped, all sense of dignity and value clawed at. Always, everyday... Oh dear, this is not going well, now he's even bigger.

"Bless and let go. Bless and..." Klara feels hot from the effort. How on earth is she supposed to do this? There must have been a time when he was good. The time when... when... nothing? Really? Surely, he must have done something nice, even if by chance.

The old photo! In the hallway there's a photo of him holding her; she's an infant and he's smiling. That was nice, wasn't it? Except, he was three years old and who knows why he smiled, maybe she just farted... He gave her a barrette for her birthday! No, that can't possibly count, most likely he'd picked it up from the floor.

Is she to make amends without his help? No middle ground? No redeeming qualities? She looks down at the

Comemeya necklace. What would grandpa say? He'd say she is love; made from love into love. Focusing on the necklace, she thinks of being home on Otim Dorum and how it feels to be immersed in a love that is never sought and never lost... it fills her now and grows to be bigger than all her grievances. Her brother pulverizes and dissolves. Bless and let go.

She opens her eyes. The faerie has returned to his magnifier. Behind her, her grandfather stands waiting. The Elders look peaceful, even Mq. Kvor looks peaceful, his blowfish eyes half closed. How did she ever find these beings imposing? The manatee's kind eyes especially draw her attention.

«You have done well, Klara.» The bioluminescence around Paxin Plimm's markings scintillate. «So well indeed, that we've decided you may be the one to determine Drake's fate. There are two places to choose from: We can station him on Bertfer which, as the name implies, is a barren asteroid. In fact, 'the most godforsaken lump of rock this side of the Galaxy' according to commander Naarlet Ulkvadd.»

«Even the water they send there tastes terrible,» Gompsie chimes in.

«Quite so,» the manatee agrees. «Now, the other option is to send him to Havalay. Havalay is a dwarf planet with a temperate climate. Quite lovely. I hear they even have jet skis and music. So, what do you think Klara, where should we send your brother: Bertfer or Havalay?»

"Is this a trick question?"

«There is no trick to it at all.»

"No trick? No games…" She'd assumed she'd want revenge, that she'd want him to suffer like she'd suffered. Now she's not so sure. She will move forward, be empowered even. But what of him? Wherever he goes, he takes himself with him. With no appreciation or gratitude and no sense of connection to others, who could be lonelier?

"He can have sunshine and jet skis," she tells them. "I don't need to make him suffer. Once he's gone, I'll be free of him—he won't."

«Indeed, Klara,» Ayor Neteen clasps her hands. «As our ancient philosopher Ferlen Mq. Blunt tells us: 'Do not pity the rich, nor the poor; pity those who hold no gratitude in their hearts, for those are the ones who truly suffer.' You have done well, Klara. For this we would like to grant you your wish.»

"What wish?"

Lénah Merlekten smiles. «To visit Otim Dorum.»

"Really?! But I don't remember asking…"

«'How dare you! You bring me home right now!'»

"Oh, that."

«Your anger was well understood.» Lénah holds out her hands to Klara. «I will come with you, though I'm afraid it can only be a brief visit.»

"Brief would still be wonderful."

«We wish you good tidings,» the Elders tell her.

Her grandfather winks. «Don't eat too many marboons.»

She means to thank them, when—fully aware of every spin of every atom of her being—she blasts off into interdimensional space.

52

PLANET EARTH
— Terra Firma —
44,2042°N, 73,9932°W
Sunday March 21, 7:01 p.m. EST
As Per: Klara Tippins

Like a fleece that's been in the dryer too long, she feels fluffed up and staticky. Reluctantly, she admits she could have eaten too many marboons.

Then an oddity made her come around. Mainly it was a scent. An unsettling scent of burning fuel and rubber. She was not on Otim Dorum anymore. This was not her home; in fact, it was not even her room. As the realization settled, harsh memories began to invade her mind. Memories of fire and smoke. So much smoke. And screams. Her screams. She drew in a coarse breath. The throat burned. And the eyes.

Where was she?

Outside a window a darkening sky showed a few stars. They *were* stars, weren't they, not moving spacecrafts? And whose window was this? She tried to think. There'd been so many windows…

A model plane stood propped up on a windowsill. But not just any plane—the Red Baron; its broken pieces meticulously glued together. This was Pontus' room. Someone had carried her up the stairs, laid her on Pontus' bed and covered her with a blanket—Someone, most likely Uncle, with his own loss to carry.

… but there wasn't just *that* loss. Adding to that loss was the brother who had done the unthinkable. The brother that was *her* brother.

Drake. Except he wasn't a brother, was he? He was something else…

Did she love him? If she did, it had to be from when she was little, from when she looked up to him—a snapshot of untainted love placed in an airtight container in her heart. She would give him that and ask no more of herself and it would be enough. Freeze-dried love—not for him—but for herself. It was a relief to know she did not hate him.

Sitting up, Klara could feel her bladder. Such a merciless creation this was. Having sucked all life out of you, you'd think it'd take pity and suspend itself, wait for you to catch up. But no. Without a care in the world it trots along, forcing you to open doors and close them, go to bathrooms—all those meaningless things the world insists you do. No doubt, once she'd peed, she'd notice how thirsty she was. Then there'd be food she'd want to consume and there she'd be—all dreadfully absurd and improper—rummaging the kitchen.

Again she looked out the window. This time a bonfire

burned in the pasture. No, not a bonfire, a sacred fire. They must have lit it for the despacho. Exhausted, she closed her eyes. Coming together was good, she knew this intrinsically, though she did not feel it.

Now she really had to go.

The closest bathroom was Frida's; the magician's hat that had almost turned her into a rabbit, the whimsical whim-whams looking cluttered and no longer charming her.

Going down the carpeted stairs, she heard Otto in the kitchen talking to someone. Bracing herself, she listened.

"—as well as can be expected. Right now, she's sleeping. Funeral? That hasn't been arranged. The only arrangement has been for my friend Don Ricardo to do an on-site ceremony once the accident has been cleared… What?… By the police, they're doing a forensic investigation… Excuse me, what are you insinuating? Rani was a good driver! It was her brakes…"

Klara could hear her uncle bang into things, probably he was pacing. "Sis, I don't know if I can have this conversation. No, I'm not being testy, I just don't know why you're so interested in her accident… okay… okay… I think we're done here. Listen, I'm glad you heard from Drake. I'm glad he got a job with NASA… Absolutely… No, I am not going to your apartment ahead of the police… I'm not. Besides, they have the key… Why? Because I gave it to them!"

From all the way in Malaysia, and despite everything,

Mother managed to cuss in Otto's kitchen.

When Klara walked in, her uncle covered the phone. "Hi there, Klara!" Turning away from her, he resumed his conversation with his phone. "Sis. Klara is here." He held out the phone for her to take. The phone was sweaty and he quickly grabbed a napkin.

*"Klara?"*Mother twittered through the napkin. *"Oh Klara, how dreadful! Wish we were there."*Klara adjusted the phone. *"All the same, Otto has agreed to let you stay at his house. He's giving you the glassed-in porch, is insulating it and everything. Don't know why the fuss, but he's doing it so don't be a nuisance, okay?"*The phone began to slip and Klara squeezed tight. *"You and Frida will stay at the cottage while he tinkers with the porch. You know the cottage? The one Rainy had?"*

"Her name is Rani!" At the use of her voice, a pain tore through Klara's throat. Her eyes watered. She tried not to cough.

"Yes, of course, Runi. Did you hear about our dear Drake?" Mother's voice turned reverent. *"People from NASA want to recruit him for an important space program. Can you believe it?"*

"Barely."

"They knocked on his door. Actually knocked. I didn't know people from NASA knocked on doors. Though it wasn't NASA exactly. Some company he told me about. But they work for NASA. Had flown all the way from California."

"Was it RAMA?"

"Rani? No, not Rani."

Klara squeezed her eyes, bracing for the pain. "R-A-M-A."

"Oh yes, that was it. They're picking him up and everything."

"In a spacecraft?"

"What?"

"A joke."

"Well, I suppose they have to pick him up as he doesn't have a way to get around, other than a bike. Not sure why he bought one, but let Otto know he can have it."

"Uncle will be pleased."

"Whatever. I should let you go. Don't want to run up the phone bill. We're far away, you know."

"I know."

"Oh, and be a dear and water my plants, will you?"

Even with a napkin the phone had become difficult to hold. She handed it to Otto.

"It's me—Otto—no Klara was not rude. As a matter of fact—hello?" Otto looked at his cellphone, then at Klara. He crumpled up the napkin and threw it in the trash. "Hungry?" he asked. "How about I make you a grilled cheese sandwich?"

53

It was cold outside and she could see her breath. This was good. Seeing her breath felt safe, as did the hugs. So many hugs. They had all come.

Don Ricardo wore his beaded hat and black poncho. His hug was solid and rich and lasted forever—Literally. "You went home, didn't you? And you got your beautiful blue necklace charged? Good for you." Hugging him back, Klara did not ask for clarification.

Mia's hug was sweet. "I know she meant a lot to you, Klara, I'm so sorry."

Ping sobbed.

Tech's hug was willowy and sincere. "Wish I knew what to say. It just sucks."

Frida's mascara had run, though in the light of the fire it wasn't too horrifying. "Rani was like a sister. I'll never forget her."

Corny gave her an uncompromising hug, his well-worn barn coat infused with campfire. "I know how you do it," he whispered.

"Do what?"

"How you go out in solitaire."

"Oh, yeah?"

"You love the cards."

She pulled back, searching his face. How did he figure it out? Corny, of all people!

"—and I love you for it," he quietly added.

… and then there was Pontus.

"Pontus, I was rude to you at the lodge and I'm sorry. I thought I'd lost you and I freaked. It was selfish, I never meant to—"

"It's okay."

"I need to make it up to you."

"Sure." He pulled back his cap, a playful smile on his face. "Oh, I know, how about you milk my cow? She's a real sweetheart."

Laughing felt both so wrong and so right. The hug that followed was one where both parties lean in the same direction, bump heads, then switch sides and bump again. Smiling, they shook hands. Then Pontus pulled her in and held her.

After a moment, Don Ricardo chimed his bell and all eyes turned to him. "In times of sadness, it's not easy to come together," he said, his voice deep and steady, "but it is good." He picked up a dry stick and placed it on the fire. "As we make this fire, it does not matter how fine the wood is, or how well we stack it—nothing burns unless it gets air. This is a lesson to us. The fire teaches us we need air in our lives to bring fuel to our spirit. Sometimes, when it feels as if we cannot breathe, we need others to sustain us. We need friends who hold our better selves as we struggle. Always we need to be there for one another." Gently, his eyes rested on each of them as he looked around the fire. "It seems like a long time since we did the despacho, and yet it was only yesterday. In such a short time I have made many friends, one of them Rani, whose light shone so bright, it is as if I've always known her. And maybe I have."

Don Ricardo looked down and Klara felt sure he was done, but he continued. "When an individual dies in the Q'ero nation, family and friends come together and make an Aya Despacho; a unique despacho that creates a rainbow bridge to the afterlife. As nothing perishes, there are three parts to the afterlife: there is our bodies which return to the earthmother, our wisdom which goes to the mountains, and our soul which returns to the stars.

"We did not create an Aya Despacho for Rani, and the intentions and prayers we put into our despacho may feel out of place today. That's okay, the universe hears us, it does not hold us to the past, but always it walks with us in the present. As we call on the Kawsay Pacha, the world of living energy, it will hear whatever it is that our hearts speak." He sounded his bell and turned to the east. They all did. They all raised their hands to the sky and called out—*hayaya!* As before, Don

Ricardo offered his invocations and they turned in unison, calling out to the cardinal direction one at a time.

Once the space was made sacred, Don Ricardo explained the three energy centers while firmly pressing their bundled despacho to each of them; the belly, the Ukhupacha, which holds the past; the heart, the Kaypacha, which holds the present; and the forehead, the Hanaqpacha, where visions for the future are born. "The medicine in the bundle will clear out all hucha—not just my hucha, but everyone's hucha," he assured them. "Once that's done, I will fill our centers with munay. Munay is the Quechua word for love, but munay also means gift and it also means power. Munay is the force that sustains and creates the cosmos. And so it is with munay that I bring wisdom to our bellies, truth to our hearts, and clarity to our minds." With that, Don Ricardo kissed the bundle and, with steam rising from his breath, held it up to the heavens.

Their despacho… Only yesterday Klara had blown into k'intus, wanting to be free of her brother so she could be herself, and now… Was Rani's death the price she'd paid? Was she supposed to make that cost worthwhile? She could never do that! Or was she looking at it all wrong? Her brother made everything into negotiations and games. She'd laughed at that. She'd told him life was not a game, but a dance… Had she been wrong? She took a step to steady herself and felt something hard under her foot. Picking it up, she found it was the bark from the day before, the one that was to make her feel safe. She held it to her heart and closed her eyes. "I am an eternal being," she whispered, "traveling through a world of experiences to understand myself, all the while remaining indestructible." Giving it a kiss, she tossed it in the fire thinking it would burst into flames, however it was wet and for a long while it lay amongst the flames, fizzing and sputtering. And then she felt it. She felt all her protections melt away, not leaving her bare, no, but leaving her strong. And Rani… Rani too was an eternal being. She too seeked experience. Nothing had gone wrong.

Don Ricardo unwrapped the cloth from the despacho and laid it on the ground, then kissed the paper bundle and placed it on the fire. "In our tradition we turn our backs on the burning bundle so the spirits can eat in peace. So please, everyone, turn around."

With the crackling fire warming her back, Klara listened to Don Ricardo sing. Though she didn't understand the Quechua words, she felt the humble and deep gratitude they held. Death, too, was life; a door they would all walk through.

Pontus put his arm around her and, as she leaned against his shoulder, she could smell the end of winter in his scarf.

She would miss Rani. They would all miss Rani, but, in the end, they would be okay.

54

PLANET EARTH
— Terra Firma —
44,5956°N, 75,1691°W
Saturday April 10, 11:08 a.m. EST
As Per: Klara Tippins

Rani's keyring had a tiny silver elephant attached to it; an intricate little silver elephant showing off its blanket and all the jewelry around its face and legs. Standing outside Rani's door, Klara put the keyring around her finger and spun the key and elephant round and round in her hand. Lucky for Otto that he was patient, waiting, as he was, outside with his truck.

It'd been three weeks since Rani's passing. Three weeks since Mother asked Klara to water the plants. In the end it was the primrose in Otto's kitchen that'd jarred her memory. Wilting, as it was, it'd made her ponder the state of Mother's plants, and Rani's plants as well. This was how she came to stand outside of Rani's door, wondering how to walk inside.

She had the right key, it wasn't that; it was the falling into an abyss that made her hesitate. As long as she didn't go inside, she could pretend Rani still lived there. Once she opened the door… But this wasn't about her, was it? This was about Rani's plants and about Otto waiting.

Before she could change her mind, she turned the key, opened the door, and walked inside.

"Do not fear, oh ye houseplants!" she called out. "I have no intention of killing you—especially not all of you."

Had there always been an echo? She didn't think so, though clearly the silence felt pained. Even the dust balls seemed to miss their tenant. Nothing danced, nothing sang, and there was no smell of summer sandals. In the living room the mighty plants were wilting, some drastically so. In the kitchen a faucet dripped. She walked over and nearly turned turn it off when she noticed a pattern to the dripping. She listened and laughed in disbelief—the droplets fell to the beat of Ravel's Boléro!—*drip, drip, dripedippe dippe dip dippe dip…*

"Hi Rani! I've come to rescue your plants… which only need rescuing because I forgot them… but anyhow, I'll wrap them like Christmas trees and they'll be fine in the back of the truck… we hope. 'We,' that's me and Otto. Otto misses you too."

While humming along to Ravel's masterpiece, she fetched sheets and strings. Most sheets were a good size and a plain white color. Pillowcases worked well for the smaller plants and all plants cooperated. True, a few leaves dropped, but there were no broken branches.

Just as Klara stepped back to admire her mummy-like creations, a stray sunbeam poked in through the living room window, gallivanted about, then landed decisively on an issue of the Pennington Gazette; the daily paper folded to show the ad for the theatre camp.

Over in the kitchen, the faucet stopped dripping.

A theater camp? Klara picked up the paper, brought it to the kitchen table, and sat down.

No Drake…

No trying to predict the unpredictable. No penalty for being kind…

The thought made her lightheaded, almost woozy.

Without him she might well be the kind of person who joins theater camps. She might be someone who'd fix a bicycle named Sir Galahad and take said bike to the supposed camp. It was a hike, getting from Pinebrook to Pennington on bike, but perhaps she was the kind of person to do just that. It wouldn't even have to be a secret. No one would ridicule her for her initiative.

Tucking the paper under her arm she tied up the trash, then called Otto on her cellphone to let him know the plants were ready. Taking one last look around Rani's apartment, she waved goodbye to the altar, braced herself, and walked out to the stairwell and onward to the Tippins' apartment.

She could do this. She was only picking up plants.

The Tippins' entryway was tidy. In fact, the entire apartment was tidy. This was irksome. She had counted on it being messy and not at all as when Mother was there with smugness lingering behind every surface. Klara would look out a window and feel the warm sun on her face when Mother would show up and she'd have to guard herself, never knowing when a proclamation of negativity would come galloping out of the mouth, snagging her hair. And nothing was easy, and nothing flowed. Determinedly, Klara blew into her hand—*bless and let go, bless and let go, bless and let go.* This was a new thing she'd discovered, and it always turned her mind somehow.

Then she noticed Mr. Tippins' blanket tucked neatly into itself and realized Otto must have been there straightening up. Of course, he'd been searching for the motorcycle key. He'd even asked her about it.

So where would Drake put it? In his room? Probably not, or Otto would have found it. Besides, Drake would want to make things difficult; he'd put it somewhere he figured she'd never look.

—the blender!

Klara marched into the kitchen and there it was, at the bottom of the scratched-up pitcher, tucked under the blades. She turned the pitcher upside down and shook it—no luck. She tried getting it out with a bottle brush, but no. Fork? Nope.

Cussing her brother, she stuck her arm in and carefully

dislodging the key and keyring with her fingers. With a clang they fell to the counter.

Apart from the key, the keyring held a small pewter dragon with wings and a long tail. It reminded her of the little red dragon she used to own; the one named Dwinn.

Would this be the only thing she'd have from her brother? Though she was glad he was gone, she might not feel that way forever. Besides, it didn't fill her mouth with gravel.

On impulse she unhitched it from the keyring and stuck it in a separate pocket. Then she grabbed a trash bag and began collecting plants. *Dead* plants. Dead and full of fruit flies. Throwing them into the trash bag, she apologized to the plants for their demise, wishing the fruit flies a *bon voyage.* "You flies are gonna love it," she told them, tying up the bag. "Just you wait and see."

She considered taking her telescope but decided against it. The telescope had never really been hers and besides, Otto's telescope was much better.

On her way down the stairs, she ran into Otto.

"I found the key to the Harley; I'll give it to you later. Hands full." She raised her arms to show the trash bags.

"Roger that."

The dumpster had brick walls and double steel doors with a padlock. The owners of Mountain Manor took no chances with the bears. Luckily the combination was easy to remember. Five - ten - fifteen.

On well-oiled, well-balanced hinges, the doors swung open. Klara picked up her trash bags and was about to toss them when she noticed some dinglenut had closed both lids. Drats! If she wasn't such a 'Klara' she'd toss the trash anyway and leave them to rot… on the other hand, if she wasn't such a 'Klara' she'd be tall enough to open the lids.

Looking around, she felt sure there must be something to stand on. To the right of the dumpster was a wonky birdcage, several bags with baby clothes—much too unsteady. A stroller, a bike, an air conditioner—too unwieldy.

As she rummaged through the discarded stuff, she spotted some roundly bent metal-tubes in the back. Could it be? The color seemed awfully dark blue.

Making her way over, she carefully pulled up her chandelier between a tumbled pile of books and a down coat. Nothing bent. Just a few scratches and only one shade had a chip. Reverently, she placed it by the open doors. Imagine, she had her chandelier back! Who would have thought.

Turning back towards the dumpster, she spotted a tall stepladder on the left side where the dumpster nearly touched the wall. It was so perfect it made her laugh. With only minor trouble she managed to yank it out, fold it open, climb up, and flip one of the lids—Success!

While high on the ladder, her eyes caught something jammed between the dumpster and the left wall, some kind of book.

Once down from the ladder, she picked up a broken

broom and gingerly inched the book along the cement. The cover seemed familiar: A big tree with people sitting… Her knees wobbly, she grabbed hold of it and, clutching it to her heart, collapsed on the floor. Her Upanishads… Rani's Upanishads. Looking the book over, she found only minor dents and a few spider nests; no mouse nibbles, no mouse poop, and only slightly mildewed. She opened it to a random page and found a passage from the Taittiriya Upanishad: *It is the blessing of all blessings; the truth of all truths; the wisdom of all wisdoms to find Brahman dwelling in the lotus of one's heart. To know Brahman as both external and internal is to achieve the supreme goal; to know existence."*

Closing the book she polished it with her sleeve and gave it a kiss. Then she picked up her two trash bags and gave them a couple of snappy tosses over her back, right into the dumpster.

"By golly, is that your chandelier?" Otto stood waiting outside his truck. Without his beard he looked strange, though she respected his decision to cut it off.

"I think it's a bird feeder now," she told him. "I was hoping you'd let me hang it in the tree outside my windows."

"What about the owl, won't he feed on your lunch guests?"

"Owl? I think he left."

"Imagine that?" Otto softly tapped the roof of his truck, causing a ruckus to erupt inside the cabin.

Klara laughed. "I'm afraid there is no tapping soft enough

to evade Gilligan's fury." She glanced into the truck cabin where a border collie puppy spun around on the front seat, wagging its crooked tail. "Who let you out of your doggy-seat? Who let you out? Did the big man let you out?"

Slowly, she opened the door and, with the Upanishads as a shield, inched herself into her seat. Then, through a rumpus of kisses, she buckled Gilligan into his booster seat in the back.

With the puppy safely harnessed, Otto opened the backseat door, placed the chandelier on the floor, then closed the door and got into the driver's seat. He rested his hands on the steering wheel. "You okay?" He gave her a quick sideways glance. "Coming back here and all?"

"Oh, I don't know… yeah, I'm okay I guess. It's just… I feel rotten for not missing them. I don't mean Rani; I mean my family. How can I not miss my family? Am I a cold person?"

Otto let out a chortle. "Please forgive me, but if you are cold, then… oh, I don't know what. Your mother, she's my sister and I must admit, I don't miss her either. We can love people and not miss them. Not missing someone does not make us cold."

Klara looked at Gilligan, now sound asleep, his head flopped over the edge of his booster seat. "How can they look at the world and not notice its brilliance?"

Otto reached over and squeezed her shoulder. "The way I see it, it's part of their journey and all journeys have merit. If I can lessen someone's suffering, then it's my place to do so. If I can't, then at least I can be respectful." He took a deep breath.

The kind of breath you take before jumping off a cliff. "Klara, have you forgiven your brother?"

"Forgiven him?"

"I mean, it's understandable if you haven't. I was just wondering… I hope you don't mind me asking."

"I've accepted him for who he is but… forgiven him? That would be like forgiving a tornado, don't you think, or a hurricane; something that causes destruction without asking for forgiveness? Some people might feel the need to forgive God for a hurricane, but that's not me. I think you should try and forgive someone who asks for forgiveness, but my brother… forgive him? I think of him as a natural disaster so I can move on. For me, it's about setting my mind free—not setting him free. What about you Uncle, have you forgiven him?"

"I feel much the way you do Klara, it's just that I think of it as preemptive forgiveness; forgiveness that is so forgiving it doesn't have to be asked for. We don't forgive hurricanes and tornados because they ask for it but because no forgiveness is needed."

"You might be right."

"I know I am. Rani told me."

"Rani?"

"I sit on her rock sometimes, over by the brook, and talk to her. One morning she told me about deadheading primroses, that 'deadheading primroses' was the most important thing in getting blooms. Only much later did I realize she was talking about life, about grief—about letting things go to make room, you know, for…" His voice trailed off.

Klara reached over and placed her hand on his. "Room for new growth? I sit on her rock too. One time, I looked into the brook and something drew me in, perhaps it was the light dancing on the surface, I'm not sure, but I had the strange sensation of my third eye falling into my mind and exploding."

"What?"

"It was extraordinary. To fall into such vastness! I became the water. Not just the brook, or the St. Lawrence River, but the ocean. To be enormous, yet stable and rich. There was an incredible balance in that moment. Everything was perfection. Of course, it didn't last. It couldn't last—only the memory."

"Ah, a field of consciousness state."

"A what?"

"It's what one of the Apollo astronauts called it after he had a profound experience of being one with the universe. I believe it was Edgar Mitchell."

"Perhaps I went to say hi to Brahman?" Klara suggested. "I found the Upanishads at the side of the dumpster and there's a passage there that talks about that exact thing; about finding Braham within."

"You found *both* your chandelier *and* your Upanishads? That dumpster is a treasure trove!"

"I know it!"

Otto reached over and ruffled her hair. "Sounds like we

have a lot to celebrate. How about you and I stop by the bakery on our way home and pick up some pastries.”

“Or coconut custard pie?”

“Or coconut custard pie.”

325

55

22,236 MILES FROM EARTH
— In a Geosynchronous Orbit —
Friday, October 22, 01:13 a.m. EST
As Per: Captain G. Writtum

The holographer bleeps as Naarlet's bioluminescent hair blazes into view. «Captain Writtum, I may have a word with you?» A bone chilling rasp numbs Gompsie's left ear and he tilts his head, tapping his head lightly. «It's in regards to the Dwinn debacle.»

«So, it's a debacle now, is it?»

«Headquarters has informed me of Mz. Boon's, of Klara's...»

«Go on...»

«Apparently... apparently she's to receive some award or other. Anyhow, I thought I should check in on the mission status.»

«Of course!» Gompsie chuckles as his hover chair does a little skip.

«Captain Writtum, you are alright?»

«Sorry, just a click of the heels is all. We are perfectly fine,

thank you.»

«Your heels?»

«Yes. Regarding the mission status, I am happy to report that Frida, the aunt of Klara, recently joined the Alcoholics-Not-Quite-Anonymous ten-step program run by Don Ricardo. I'm sure you've heard of Don Ricardo. Not only that, but Frida's brother, Otto, has decided he is not too old for a pilot's license after all. In fact, he and his nephew Pontus take flight lessons together. When he's not in the sky with Pontus, he and Klara look at the sky through his telescope. First rate, by the way. Very, very good quality. Then we have Mia Rasmussen and Tech Meyers, friends of Klara, who've started a grassroots organization to bring awareness to the Earth's climate change. All this together I believe accounts for one percent of the population at 1.2 Hz.»

Naarlet's image zooms in and out. Is she fiddling with the instrumentation? «And the parents? Agnes and Bruce Tippins?»

«Mr. and Mrs. Tippins are still in Malaysia and have made no immediate plans to return to Pennington, nor, as far as I am aware, is Mrs. Tippins planning on eating squid. This, however, should in no way deduct from our numbers.»

«And Klara?»

«Klara is doing well. She took a metallic dragon from her brother's keychain and placed it in a glass jar. This was to mentally keep him separate from herself. The jar was tossed into Rani's brook where it cleanses and cleanses. Quite

ingenious really, with the jar. Being freed, she joined a theater camp this past summer. She and her friend Corny Sullivan biked to the camp when the weather was nice. At other times Klara's aunt Frida drove them. Aunt Frida also helped sew costumes, both for the theater group and to teach Ping Sullivan. Ping is planning to launch her own line of clothing called Gothic Me. *Which, by the way, is estimated to add an additional 0.6 Hz to the EEP, the Energy Expansion Program.»*

«I know what EEP is!» Naarlet's image stops zooming.

«Of course you do.» Taking his glasses off, Gompsie folds them, smiles, then unfolds them and puts them back on. «Also, Klara has finally started painting.»

«And what of Drake… Drake is well?»

«To be frank, Drake is a bit miffed. Apparently, you cannot play your music loudly on Havalay. The Elders try to provide him with harmless mischief, but mostly he's bored.»

«Well I… I commend you, Captain Writtum. I do. Work well done. Perhaps we can—»

EPILOGUE

Together with her new friends, Klara has come to understand her mission. It's a simple one: Be kind and do no harm. A sentiment simple enough to print on a T-shirt yet challenging to live up to. She's decided to begin with the T-shirt.

As of this writing the crew of Captain Gompsie Writtum* are still working to fill their quota of raising ten percent of the human population to the frequency of 8 Hz.

If they succeed is up to us.
It's up to you and me.

I wish you munay.

*or 'Buxtin's crew,' as one sentient spacecraft likes to call them.

Linn Aspen's Tidings

My inspirational Tidings are published regularly and may be
viewed on my website: linnaspen.com
or on my Facebook author page: Dreamtidings

On my website you will also find questions for Book Club
Discussions along with my blog and other tidbits.

And, as always, remember to leave a review. It's such a gift,
both to us authors and to your fellow readers.

Last, but not least, thank you for your willingness to take
this journey with me. Urpichay sonqoy!

— Linn

According to intel at our inter-dimensional office space on Artut, Ms. Aspen appears to be an INFJ. This is per the Myers-Briggs personality typology, of which we are familiar. INFJs are the rarest of personality types and suspected to be represented by as few as 2% of the human population. (Which may, or may not, be a good thing, depending on one's perspective.)

Quite sensitive, the INFJs are deep thinkers and have a profound fondness of others, while at the same time being secretive as a way to protect themselves.

This creates a conundrum then, when writing Ms. Aspen's bio, for though she learns much from others, she shares little about herself. What we have gleaned so far is that she lives in Vermont in the United States and has a wonderful husband who, by no fault of his own, married a writer. Despite his predicament he is quite accepting of her oddities, sources tell us, such as her proclivity to grab her industrial-grade, noise-canceling headphones whenever her muse comes visiting (no matter if it's in the middle of his sentence).

Ms. Aspen also has two dogs, small, hardly visible from our satellites. She appears to be happy, loving and, as mentioned, very, very private.

— The Elders